CW00496022

SAY YOU DO

WESTON PARKER

BRIXBAXTER PUBLISHING

Say You Do

Copyright © 2020 by Weston Parker

All rights reserved. This book or any portion thereof may not be reproduced or used in any manner whatsoever without the express written permission of the publisher except for the use of brief quotations in a book review.

The novel is a work of fiction. Names, characters, places and plot are all either products of the author's imagination or used fictitiously. Any resemblance to actual events, locales, or persons – living or dead – is purely coincidental.

First Edition.

Editor: Eric Martinez
Cover Designer: Ryn Katryn Digital Art

FIND WESTON PARKER

www.westonparkerbooks.com

DEDICATION

To all of the readers who've enjoyed my books, thank you for your support and your love. It's a weird time in the world right now, and it sure feels like there is no better time for a book. I hope you enjoy the heck out of this one.

-Weston

CHAPTER 1

LUNA

2 Years Before

A lot of people believed Christmas was the most wonderful time of the year.

I disagreed.

As a florist and a New Yorker, the most wonderful time of the year had to be springtime. A light breeze drifted into my shop, the windows now open after the long winter months.

The bride-to-be who had an appointment with me flitted from bucket to bucket, examining the colorful offerings in each intently before moving on. I stood off to the side, watching her do her thing while advising her when necessary.

"Spring is my favorite season," she gushed, her cheeks flushed and her eyes wide and bright. "That's why we decided to get married this month. We've been engaged since last winter and I just can't wait to finally walk down the aisle."

"Spring is a beautiful time for a wedding in the city," I agreed, my heart speeding up as I conjured up mental images of what I was hoping my own wedding was going to look like. "I'm thinking of waiting for next spring to get married myself."

"The wait will become nearly intolerable, but I think it's worth it." She gave me a radiant grin, her skin practically glowing with excitement and her dark curls bouncing as she clapped her hands together. But then her brown eyes darted to my bare left ring finger and a crease appeared between her eyebrows. "Are you having your ring cleaned?"

"No." I absently linked my hands together behind my back and rubbed the spot where there would soon be a ring—if all went according to plan, which it would. "We're not engaged yet, but we've been talking about it a lot and the time is right."

Her eyes softened with understanding as another smile spread on her lips. "It's such an exciting time, isn't it? The anticipation? I loved every minute of it, but I'm loving every minute of wedding planning as well."

"Yeah, it's great. I can't wait to get into the planning and the nitty-gritty details myself." I breathed in the sweet, floral scent of the fresh blooms lining every wall in my shop and almost got all dreamy about it before I remembered I was in the middle of a consultation. "But for now, it's your turn. Do you have a better idea of what you might want now that you've seen what's available?"

We spent the next hour picking out the flowers she wanted. Then I played around with several ideas for arrangements for the main table. She snapped some pictures to show to her fiancé and promised she'd be back with her final decision but placed the order for the basics for the other arrangements.

"Okay, so you can send the invoice to my father. I've left his details on the form. When Joe and I decide on our table, I'll be back." Her voice was several octaves higher than it had been when she'd first come into the shop, and her eyes were so shiny, I thought she might cry. "Thank you so much. These were just what we needed to make our day perfect. Thank you, Luna. I'll see you soon."

She pressed a kiss to my cheek, even though I'd only met her little over an hour ago, squeezed my hand, and then flicked her hand up in a wave as she practically skipped out of the shop.

On her way out, she nearly bumped into April. My best friend rolled her green eyes at the sight of the overly excited bride, shaking her head as she let the door swing shut behind her.

"Another sucker whose heart is going to be broken soon enough, I presume?" She shrugged out of her light jacket and set it down on the counter with her purse.

I sighed as I moved behind my computer to finish the invoice so I could send it out before I had to close up for the afternoon. "Why do you have to be so down on marriage? Maybe this guy is perfect for her and they live happily ever after."

"Or maybe he's just using her to pay his way while he finishes his studies, and then when he's finally done and starting to earn the big bucks he was supposed to use to help her achieve her dreams, he leaves her with a toddler and goes off to travel instead." She raised both her brows and pursed her lips before tapping them with a pink-tipped finger. "Oh no, wait. That's not her story. It's mine."

Lifting my hands with my palms turned toward her in surrender, I nodded. "Okay, fine. You may have a point. Some people do really shimmy things to others, but that doesn't mean we can't hold out hope."

"Shimmy? You mean shitty, don't you? Why don't you just say it? What Craig did to me was shitty. Shitty, Luna. Not shimmy."

"You know I don't like to curse."

"Yeah, I know. It's my pet peeve about you. Some situations desperately need curse words to express just how truly *shitty* they are." She emphasized the word, shooting me a pointed look. "Your turn. Say shitty for me, Luna."

"Nope." I turned my attention to the ancient box of a computer screen standing on the counter and entered the order information from the form the customer had filled in. "Speaking of the toddler you got left behind with, where is Adi?"

"She's at school. I have to pick her up soon, but I thought I'd come swing by here first. I haven't spoken to you since Tuesday."

3

"It's only Friday." A beautiful Friday afternoon since my windows were finally cracked open and the breeze blew out the mustiness left behind by winter.

Sure, scents from the hot dog cart outside and the Chinese laundry across the street wafted in as well, but it also circulated the sweetness from the flowers inside and the fresh dampness of the dirt from the flower boxes on the windowsills.

Soon, those babies would be filled with colorful buds and bulbs, which would hopefully serve to make the shop look more attractive to passersby. New Yorkers were starting to hit the streets again as they shed their winter clothes and came out of hibernation from their tiny apartments. It was my favorite time of the year for many reasons, but one of the most important reasons was my bottom line.

People weren't looking to buy flowers during winter, so every spring, I had to try to make up for it. Things were looking good so far, though, and not even the thundercloud that brewed above April's head whenever anyone mentioned weddings or love was going to ruin my day.

"So what you really mean is that you're waiting until the last possible second to pick Adi up, and coming to me was a good excuse?" I teased, a smile curving my lips when I saw her narrowing her eyes. "Don't even try to deny it."

"I wasn't going to, but it's good for her to stay longer. Social interaction outside of classroom situations is the best teacher, you know? Also, a bit of waiting builds character and teaches patience. As long as she's waiting in a safe space, I owe it to her to provide her with those opportunities."

Despite my best efforts, I couldn't hold in my laughter. "Keep telling yourself that."

"I will." She gave me a mock pout with her arms crossed loosely over her chest. Then she let out a sigh and leaned over to rest her forearms on the counter. Crinkles disappeared from the corners of her eyes and the light in them dimmed as she grew serious. "Thanks for never judging me for trying to carve out some me-time in the midst of the insanity that is my life."

4

"You work the front desk in a hospital and you're a single mother of a four-year-old. You can come hide out for five minutes anytime you like. This is a judgment-free zone."

"Thank you," she said, her eyes following me as I slipped out from behind the counter to flip the sign on my door to *closed*. Her nostrils flared in alarm and her eyes widened before they dropped to her watch. Lifting her arm in my direction to show me its face, her brow furrowed. "For a second there, I thought I was really late to pick her up. Why are you closing so early?"

"I'm meeting Landon for dinner." My heartrate kicked up a notch, baby butterflies hatching and stretching their wings in my belly. "We're finally going to start planning the wedding tonight."

April's eyes clouded over, the air between us thickening as she shoved a hand through her fiery red hair. "You're seriously still thinking about marrying him?"

"Of course, I am. We've been dating for two years. It's time." At the distressed look on her face, the butterflies hit my stomach lining one by one and knocked themselves out. "Look, I know you're down on marriage, and I understand why, but I'm going to need you to put all that aside and just be happy for me. I'm getting engaged soon and I want you to be my maid of honor."

"You know I'd do just about anything for you, babe, but I can't do that." She straightened up and lifted her chin. "I don't want to bad mouth Landon, but I don't trust him. Just because he made this huge success of himself and has money of his own doesn't mean he can't be a dick. He's a piece of shit, Luna. I might not know why yet, but I can smell it from a mile away."

My heart dropped to join the useless butterflies passed out at the pit of my stomach. "He's not a piece of crap. He's going to be my fiancé and I'm happy about it. Why can't you be happy for me?"

"Because I'm not and I refuse to fake it, even for you." She winked. "I refuse to fake orgasms too, which used to piss Joe right off. But I mean really, if you're married and you have every opportunity, why wouldn't you want to learn what brings your wife real pleasure?"

I waited her joke out, used to her attempts at comedy to lighten up the mood. Then I raised my eyebrows.

April huffed out a breath. "Fine. It's been two years, right? It's the logical next step, correct?"

I nodded but didn't need to say anything. She cocked her head and narrowed her eyes on mine. "Wouldn't the first logical next step be for you to go to his house? Because last I checked, in the entire two years you've been dating, you've never been there."

She had me there. I couldn't even argue. Landon had never invited me to come over, and whenever I asked, he made up some excuse.

Hell, I didn't even have his address to surprise him. His home address wasn't listed anymore. Apparently, he was that kind of big deal now.

When I'd looked it up at some point to try to plan a Valentine's Day rendezvous to make up for him having to work late, I'd only found an address for an old apartment he'd told me about that he had lived in when he first moved to the city.

"I'm sure it's nothing sinister." I filled my lungs with air and ignored the dull ache in my gut that I got whenever I thought too much about all this. "He's just been busy."

"For two years?" She scoffed, then came around the counter to give me a hug. "I love you. You're my sweetest, quirkiest friend, but you're not dumb. Something's going on with him. Just find out what it is before you let him slip a ring onto that finger, okay?"

"Okay." I nodded into her hair, letting the soft strands and familiar scent of vanilla soothe my sudden nerves about dinner. "I'll let you know how it goes."

April left when I locked up my shop, grabbing a cab to fetch Adi from school. I opted to walk the few blocks to the restaurant where I was meeting up with Landon, joining the army of people choosing to enjoy the warm breeze and the crunch of the last leaves left behind by winter beneath my ankle boots.

He was already there when I arrived, waiting at a table in the far corner of the stylish yet low-key bistro he'd chosen for dinner.

6

Landon liked to choose where we went and he always grabbed the seats with the lowest possibility of him being spotted.

After launching a popular social-dating site, he had become rather popular with certain people. He preferred privacy though, which was why he always tried to avoid being seen out and about.

I got it, even though it was another thing about him April didn't trust. As I sidestepped past tables and dodged rushing waiters, I took a good look at the man I was planning on saying *I do* to next spring.

With his dark blond hair, angular features, and deep brown eyes, he was classically handsome. He stood about half a foot taller than my five foot four, which made it easy for us to kiss without either of us having to strain.

A clean-shaven jaw and preppy sense of style made him seem approachable, like the "typical millionaire next door," as he'd been called by the media once. He wore a salmon-colored button-up shirt tonight, cream slacks, and a matching vest.

I smiled as I approached him, but he didn't look up from his phone until I pulled my chair out and took a seat across from him. Even then, it was only a perfunctory glance to make sure it was me before his eyes were back on his screen. "Hey, Luna."

"Hi, love," I said, reaching across the table for his hand. He moved it to his phone well before I could touch him, all still without looking at me. "Having a busy day, huh?"

"They're all busy these days." He scowled at the phone, tightening his grip on it until his knuckles were white, then tossed it down and finally met my eyes properly. For a second.

Then he picked up his menu and studied it instead. "You look good. Shop doing all right?"

"It's fine. I got an order in today for a wedding in about a month, so that's exciting."

"That's great," he mumbled, but it was easy to see he was distracted and not just by the menu. He glared at the pages, his eyes slightly unfocused.

I cleared my throat and sucked in a breath, pushing forward. Eventually, I'd get his attention. It was like this with him sometimes. He got so lost in his own world at work that it took some time for him to relax.

"Speaking about weddings, I thought we could talk about ours," I said as I pulled my phone out of my purse. "I've saved some ideas I wanted to run by you."

"Oh yeah?" he asked.

I frowned, ninety-nine percent sure he was only throwing out random phrases to make it sound like he was listening.

"That's great, baby," he said. "I'm so proud of you."

My eyes closed and I shot up a quick prayer for patience. Making a scene in a restaurant was not my style, nor was it Landon's. It could take him time to come out of his shell after a long day at work, but I'd honestly thought the prospect of our wedding would snap him right out of it. Apparently, I'd been wrong.

"You're proud of me for coming up with some ideas for my own wedding? Or are you proud of me for wanting to run them by you?"

Whether it was the forced sweetness in my voice or the words themselves that made him do it, he finally wrenched his gaze toward mine. His Adam's apple rose and fell as he swallowed. "Wedding planning, huh? You really want to get into that right now? We're not even engaged, Luna."

"Yet," I tacked on, but Landon's eyebrows pulled together like he didn't understand. I sat up straighter and looked him right in the eyes as I tried to tamp down the suspicion brewing in my stomach.

"We're not engaged *yet*," I said. "We've been talking about this for months, Landon. Have you forgotten about that? Or is something going on with you that I should know about?"

Conflicting emotions suddenly warred behind his eyes, his jaw clenching and relaxing before he licked his lips, nodding to himself. "I know we've been talking about it, but I've been thinking, and I can't get engaged to you, Luna."

Blood roared in my ears and my heart stuttered. *What the fudge?* "What? Why not?"

His tongue swiped along his bottom lip again, a nervous tell I hardly ever saw and it had made an appearance twice now. My palms grew slick with sweat and my hands were unsteady as I fumbled to fold them in my lap.

"I can't get engaged to you because I'm already married." The words came rushing out of him, each one of them a separate yet devastating blow to my plans, our future. "I've been married for a few months now. I didn't know how to tell you. I thought about leaving her, but I can't."

My heart pounded wildly in my chest as thoughts spiraled through my head. *Landon never letting me near his house. Landon always working late. Landon making excuses for every Valentine's Day, birthday...*

"Leave," I demanded, my voice barely above a whisper and my entire body recoiling but refusing to move.

He reached for me. "She's the kind of woman I'm expected to—"

"I said leave, Landon. Now. Don't you dare try to rationalize it to me." My gaze zeroed in on my water glass, even though I felt Landon's drilling a hole in the top of my head as he tried to get me to look back at him.

When he didn't make a move for the door, I threw out an arm and jabbed a finger at it. "Get the fiddling duck out of here, Landon. I never want to see you again. Lose my number and send my regards to your wife."

I was practically spitting at that point, spots dancing across my vision and my lungs burning with the need for air even as I panted.

The slide of his chair against the wooden floor let me know he was pushing it out. Then I caught his shiny brown loafers in my periphery as he walked away. Salty tears burned my eyes as they begged to fall free, but I wouldn't let them. *Not here, not now.*

Then a shadow fell over the table and I did my best to blink the mistiness away before looking up. The waiter stood there, holding a bill folder. "I didn't get all of that, but I thought you might want this right around now."

A bottle of wine Landon must have ordered sat in a bucket of ice next to the table. I hadn't paid any attention to it before, but my eyes nearly bulged out of my head when I saw the price.

My throat tightened as I handed over my card, knowing that the

9

wine was going to make a huge dent in my meager bank account. For someone who'd been adamant nothing was going to be able to ruin her day, karma had sure decided to teach me a lesson. Tramp that she was, she'd even decided to leave me with Landon's check.

Maybe April had the right idea about men. Maybe marriage really was a sham made for losers, liars, and codependents. Or maybe it just wasn't meant for me.

CHAPTER 2

CYRUS

2 Years Later

"Welcome to the Disrupt Entrepreneurial Retreat, Mr. Coning," this year's host said, holding out his hand for me to shake. "May I just say that it's a real honor to meet you. Thank you for agreeing to address our millionaires in the making."

"I had some time available in my schedule." I gripped his hand in a firm clasp and released it after a brief moment. I'd learned a long time ago that there was power in a firm handshake—no pump—and how to harness that power without crushing anyone's bones like some wannabe.

It had the desired effect on the host, who dipped his graying head in respect and gestured me to the stage where a solid wood podium was waiting. "We have you slotted in for twenty minutes, but feel free to take more time if you need it."

I only just managed to hold back a snort. "Twenty minutes is plenty."

No way was I hanging around there longer than that. They were paying me a pittance and I'd already achieved the only goal I'd had when agreeing to do this: to assess the supposed cream of the crop in emerging businesses so I could come in at ground level if I saw anything that caught my eye.

Nothing had, which meant I was pretty much done there.

"Ladies and gentlemen, it gives me great pleasure to introduce Mr. Cyrus Coning," the host boomed into the microphone. "Please put your hands together for the man who revolutionized security, disrupted the market with his products, and has agreed to tell you a little bit about how he managed to do it."

How I managed to do it was pure, dumb luck and good timing, but I doubted any of the supposedly brilliant entrepreneurs gathered in the ostentatious ballroom wanted to hear that. After all, they'd paid over a thousand dollars a ticket to hear assholes like me make insightful, inspirational speeches all weekend long about how to make their dreams come true.

Nose to the grindstone, bitches. Companies don't grow out of retreats. If I had a heart, I would have felt sorry for all these fuckers who'd wasted money on tickets when they could have made more by working through the weekend instead.

Crossing the stage to the podium in three long strides, I didn't bother to thank the host. I slid the microphone out of the stand with one hand and hooked the thumb of my other into the pocket of my jeans.

Letting the mic dangle from my fingers, I leaned against the side of the podium casually instead of standing behind it like I was supposed to. I didn't care if I looked like an entitled douchebag who was disrespecting the stiffness and formality of this *prestigious* retreat. I was what I was, which just so happened to be an entitled douchebag.

Now, anyway.

One side of my lips curled upward as I waited for the raucous applause to die down. It took a minute before the crowd quieted enough for me to start speaking.

"Five years ago, I was nothing. I didn't have two pennies to rub together. I was living with my brother, busting my ass to cover my share of the rent each month."

Lights blinded me, making it impossible to see past the first few rows. The people I could see, though, were riveted. Lips parted and sitting forward, like I was about to impart some great secret or wisdom. "I was a low-level coder stuck in a company with no opportunities for growth."

The years I'd spent there had been dark times for me, but no one knew that. Other than Peter, my brother, the world thought I'd had it easy and had become an overnight success from nowhere. People didn't have to know exactly how dark it had gotten over there at times, so I skipped that part.

"The security system you all know me for now was my side project, something I spent years developing. When I sold it, it made me a billionaire, a poster child for success."

A smattering of applause and several catcalls from the audience made me pause, a smirk dragging the corners of my lips up once again. "Yeah, I know. Lucky me, huh?"

I raised a hand and felt like a fucking superstar or a president when they settled down again almost instantly. It gave my ego that insane boost I got in every high-powered meeting these days, my heart soaring like I'd injected a shot of adrenaline right into it.

This was why I was an entitled douchebag now. I'd earned the fucking right to be because I was entitled to some goddamned respect after all the work I'd done and how shitty I'd been treated before everything had changed.

"An investment by a single man who believed in my vision set me on the course I'm on today. His investment allowed me to finish a product I could take to market and to build the prototypes I needed to be able to demonstrate it."

Darius had been a millionaire when he'd met me, but he'd died a billionaire a few years ago. *All thanks to that belief he'd had in me.*

"They say everyone has a million-dollar idea at least a couple of times in their lifetime, but very few people actually put it into action. I'm not interested in those. I'm interested in the billion-dollar ideas, the ones that only come around once in a lifetime for most. After I sold my system, I started investing in businesses I believed in. They're few and far between, but if you have a new business idea that you think I should know about, one that will take whichever industry you're in to the next level like mine did, get in touch with me."

I gave a curt nod and set the mic down on the podium, about to walk offstage when the host appeared again. He hurried to grab the microphone, then turned his sights on me.

"You still have some time left in your slot, Mr. Coning. Maybe you'd like to stay to talk to some people in the crowd, see if they have any ideas you might be interested in investing in."

"No, thanks." I dragged a hand through my hair and flicked the other toward the crowd as I shook my head. "It's a waste of time I don't have. If they're real entrepreneurs, they shouldn't have time to come to a retreat. There's a reason why I said they should contact me if they have *new* ideas because there's nothing here I'm interested in."

I knew I was being a dick. The host tried to cover for me by shouting my name into the mic he was still holding and asking them to put their hands together for me again, but he shouldn't have bothered.

Although I hadn't been holding the microphone, I knew it had caught enough of what I'd said that a decent chunk of the audience would have heard me. Those who hadn't would hear about it later, I was sure.

It might have been a dick move on my part to say it out loud, but that didn't mean those people hadn't needed to hear it. Maybe some of them would find investors for what they were peddling now, but it sure as shit wasn't going to be me.

Peter was already waiting for me when I got back to the city. The retreat had been held at a lodge only a couple of hours away, so I managed to make it back in time for dinner.

"How'd it go?" he asked when I sat down at the table he'd grabbed in our favorite bar. The food there was cheap, good, and unhealthy, and the beer was cold. *In short, it's perfect.*

"It was a quick buck," I said, signaling to the bartender to bring me a round.

Peter and I had been coming there for years. Charlie knew what we wanted and never failed to deliver.

This was the one place I could cut loose, the only place where they didn't give a shit about the size of my bank account. I wasn't even sure they knew how much things had changed in the last few years.

Peter was the only person I'd ever looked up to and, as such, was the only person I generally wasn't a dick to. His green eyes were several shades lighter than my own, and his hair was a deeper shade of brown, but we had the same height and build.

Some of the tabloid vultures who kept an eye on everyone they deemed rich enough for the society pages had mistaken him for me a few times. I thought it was hilarious. I thought he was going to murder me one day for thinking it was hilarious.

"A quick buck?" He sat back in his seat and lifted a brow at me. "Like you need a quick buck. Find anyone worth investing in there? I know you, bro. Which means I know why you really went. I bet you probably fucked up your speech, too."

"I didn't fuck it up. I just chose a different method to inspire than some of the other speakers might have." I pretended to buff my nails against the breast pocket of my black shirt. "I'm known to be a game-changing, trend-setting badass. Why would I go there to tell them how clever they all are for wasting a thousand bucks on a retreat in the middle of fucking nowhere? They're idiots and they should know it. If they worked harder, maybe I would have found someone to invest in. I gave them all a kick in the ass. They needed it."

His deep sigh didn't hide the twitching at the corners of his mouth. "A game-changing, trend-setting bad ass? Did you come up with that yourself?"

"I was paraphrasing." I dipped my head in thanks when Charlie dropped off my beer, then took a long swig of the dark liquid. After swallowing the creamy Irish froth I loved, I wiped my mouth with the back of my hand. "Anyway, what did we need to talk about so urgently? You nearly gave me a heart attack when you said you needed to see me *at my earliest convenience.* Since when do you say shit like that?"

"I was with Jenny's aunt and uncle." He sighed and rested his hand on top of his glass, turning it slowly between his fingers. "I was trying to make a good impression, if you must know. They still think I'm an uncultured blue-collar worker from the wrong side of town."

"Dude. You're a plumber from the other side of the tracks. Therefore, you *are* a blue-collar worker from the wrong side of town. She grew up a couple of blocks away from us, so she's from the same wrong side of those damn tracks. Since when do you give a fuck about what anyone thinks about you anyway?"

"Since we picked a wedding date and she'd like her uncle to walk her down the aisle." He kept his eyes on mine, and when I opened my mouth to protest, he shut me down. "I don't want to hear it, Cyrus. I asked Jenny to marry me and I'm marrying her."

My cheeks cooled as blood drained from them. "Please don't, bro. Don't marry her. I know you love her, but that's no reason to rush into anything. You've just gotten promoted. Now isn't the time to—"

"Save it, Cyrus." His tone had an edge to it that brooked no argument, but I argued anyway.

"I can't just sit here and shut up. You know how I feel about weddings and marriage and you know why. Why would you willingly open yourself up to that?"

"I love her. I want to spend the rest of my life with her. Jenny isn't after my money, Cy. She's not going to leave me because I don't have any and she's not interested in what I do have."

"That's what I thought once, too." Bitterness crept into my voice, lacing itself into every word I said. "I'm not saying Jenny is after your money, or after mine for that matter, but marriage only leads to pain. There's no reason for you to subject yourself to it."

Peter's lips thinned as he pressed them together. Then he lifted both shoulders and dragged his hands through his hair. "I don't care. If she hurts me eventually, I'll deal with it. It would still have been worth all the good times. We can't *not* live just because we're afraid we're going to get cut up some day in the future. We have to try, bro.

16

Even if it means we end up getting hurt. I think it would hurt even more not to try at all."

His words hit the iron shield I had up around the hole where my heart used to be. "There's no talking you out of it?"

"There's no talking me out of it," he confirmed with a grim smile. "How about this? If she hurts me, you get to say I told you so as many times as you want. In the meantime, you're on board."

"Fine." I crossed my arms and cocked my head. "I'm on board. By, like, half a foot. What did you need from me so urgently?"

He shifted in his seat, his gaze sliding to the side. "I need you to help us plan the wedding."

"Fuck no." I slammed my elbows down on the table and shook my head. "I thought you were going to say you needed me to plan your bachelor party or something, but your wedding?"

"You get to plan that too, but we really need help with the wedding, man." Darkness saturated his eyes, his lips turning down at the corners. "Neither of us have parents that can help us. Jenny's aunt and uncle will turn it into a spectacle and expect you to foot the bill. You're all we've got. Neither of us can do what needs to be done during the day, but you can."

He pleaded with me, both his voice and the look in his eyes nothing short of desperate. "Please, Cyrus? I know what I'm asking, but there's no other way. We really want to get married on the date we chose. It means a lot to us, and we need help."

My eyes screwed shut to block out the glint in his. I couldn't say no to my brother under the best of circumstances, but seeing that desperation, that grief over neither of them having anyone else left to ask, broke me.

"I can hire a wedding planner," I said suddenly, the idea jumping into my head out of nowhere. "That's what those people do for a living, right? I'll get you the best in the business. They'll do a much better job of it than I can."

"We've already looked into it. They charge a fortune, and even the affordable ones will eat into our budget, but they're not available on short notice anyway."

"I said *I'll* hire one, which means I'll pay for it. Problem solved."

"No, you're not." He narrowed his eyes in a meaningful glare. "Before you say it, you're not getting us a wedding planner as a gift, either."

"But I have to get you a wedding gift. I'm your only brother, your only family even. I have to get you something and it has to be something big and special."

"If you want to get us an extravagant gift, get us the fancy toaster from the registry," he said. "You're not forking out thousands of dollars for someone who's only going to push us over budget with their suggestions anyway."

"But—"

"No. You've got the time to do a few things for us. It won't keep you busy for the next few months until the wedding and it would mean the world if you'd just help us out. Like you said, you're my only family. I don't want to pay someone to do me a few favors my best man could just do."

I heaved out a sigh, but I knew I didn't have much of a choice. My brother was the one person in the world I had trouble saying no to.

"Fine."

How hard could it really be? I'd designed one of the best security systems in the world. Surely, the intricacies of wedding planning wouldn't thwart me.

Besides, the grin that broke out on Peter's face when I agreed was worth it. "Good. That's settled then. I'm going to go hit the bathroom. Then we'll order food."

"Yeah, okay." I watched him walk away, a cold pit forming in my stomach as I thought about what I'd just agreed to. Getting roped into planning my brother's wedding was not how I'd expected this day to pan out. "Fuck."

CHAPTER 3

LUNA

I*'ve been paying off nothing but interest for a year. How is that possible?* Blinking at the numbers in front of me, I pulled the books closer and squeezed my eyes shut before opening them again. *Surely, I couldn't have read that right.*

Unfortunately, the numbers in front of me remained the same. The capital amount on the debt I owed had hardly shrunk despite the extra money I'd been paying into the loan whenever I had it.

It was ridiculous. At this rate, with the way the interest kept piling on, it would take me years to pay the bank back.

Disbelief and shock coursed through me, making my legs numb and my mouth dry. I licked my lips, half surprised they didn't feel cracked.

The bell above the door tinkled, but the sound didn't fill me with hope the way it once had. It was spring again, but the last two had given me none of the same reasons I used to have to feel optimistic.

Landon had walked out on me when all the blossoms were just about to show their color, and last year, I hadn't been able to stay in the black either. People didn't buy flowers just because anymore, and most who did ordered them off the internet. Since I didn't have the resources to deliver and couldn't afford to close the shop while I made the deliveries myself, people could order my flowers online but had to pick them up themselves.

A knock at my office door reminded me of the bell ringing. I turned around, about to apologize to the customer, when my gaze landed on Adi's pretty face. "Hey, sweetheart. What are you doing here? Where's your mom?"

"Right here," April's voice called just before she appeared behind her daughter. "How are you?"

"I've been better, but it's always good to see you guys." I opened my arms and Adi bounded right into them, her backpack from school bouncing on her shoulders just before it whacked me in the chest when she turned on my lap. "Whoa there, baby girl. What's got you so excited?"

"I have a new teacher," she said, turning to look at me over her shoulder. Her soft brown eyes shone and she flashed me a gap-toothed smile. "She's so great, but I'm happy it's the weekend. We should eat ice cream on Sunday."

"That's a good idea." God knew I could use some ice cream myself. "Let's see if you still feel like it on Sunday. Then we can talk. Tell me about this new teacher of yours."

Adi went on and on about her. April sat down in the threadbare chair I kept in my office for the odd occasion when I actually had someone in here, animatedly adding to her daughter's tales.

"She's a real old-school teacher," April said. "She said she's working on a book filled with phrases she says on a daily basis that most people won't even say once in their lives."

"Such as?" I asked.

"Don't lick the playground," she replied, her eyes crinkling with silent laughter. "There are more. I'm totally buying that book if it ever comes out."

"It sounds like a winner." I could have used a book like that to go with my ice-cream binge this weekend. Just thinking about the loan repayments was threatening to tip me over the edge, right into Sulksville.

Adi managed to cheer me up a bit, which I was grateful for. At least, she did until she asked her next question. "What are you going to do this weekend?"

"Me?" I did my very best not to grimace. "I need to work. I'm thinking about extending my store hours. Might as well give it a try this weekend to see what happens."

April pulled a face before sitting up straighter, flashing me a smile. "I have a better idea. Why don't you come have dinner with us tonight? You can try the extended shop hours tomorrow."

"I..." I trailed off when I noticed the look in her eyes, practically begging for my help with Adi. At six years old now, she was a handful. A sweet, adorable but ridiculously busy handful.

April hardly ever asked for my help, so the fact she was looking at me like that meant she really needed me. "I'd love to."

Saying no to her would have been too cruel, even if that was what I had been about to say.

Besides, it wasn't like people had been tripping over themselves to get into the shop today. Maybe as the days kept growing longer and the season came into full swing, people would be more inclined to spend money on flowers as opposed to warm drinks on their way home.

April brightened, mouthing "thank you" before holding a hand out to Adi. "Come on, baby. Let's let Luna lock up and wait for her outside."

"I'll be there in a minute," I said. "I just need to put the books away before I can go anywhere."

I slammed them shut as April and Adi made their way out of my office, burying them under a stack of papers in my bottom drawer. If I hid them from view, maybe I'd be able to forget about the potentially devastating consequences the numbers in them hinted at.

There was no more of the winter chill in the air when I stepped onto the sidewalk to join my friend. A breeze ruffled my hair, carrying on it whiffs of meat grilling from trucks parked nearby and the sharp stench of garbage.

Spring was the season of new beginnings, of fresh buds blooming, and both people and animals coming alive again. As we walked to their apartment, I couldn't help but feel a pang of nostalgia for the days when I still believed in the magic of springtime, in what the new beginning would hold for me. These days, even springtime felt more like the smell of garbage suited it and not the sweet scent of flowers.

No. Snap out of it. You're not this person.

Darn straight, I wasn't this person. I'd be darned if I was going to spend the entire weekend sulking. I straightened my spine instead and pulled back my shoulders. *Everything* will *work out in the end. It* has *to.*

It didn't matter that I didn't know how it would work out. It only mattered that I had to believe it would.

"I saw Landon on the cover of some or other business magazine earlier this week," April said as we walked into their kitchen, making me wonder if she had read my mind. At least I knew the situation with Landon had worked out right in the end. *Dodged a bullet with that one.*

"I'm going to say hi to my dollies," Adi announced, seemingly oblivious to her mother's statement or how sick I felt just from hearing his name. She didn't wait for an answer before she dumped her backpack by the door and took off down the short corridor to her room. The sound of her greeting her dolls in a quiet voice filtered back to us a minute later.

Settling on a chair in the breakfast nook, I propped my elbow on the table and rested my chin in my open palm. "I don't understand why they're still doing so many features on him. Surely, his site has to be old news by now."

April shrugged as she walked to the fridge and pulled out a bottle of cheap wine. She twisted the lid off, then reached for two glasses from the cabinet above her head and filled them.

"I think it's his way of trying to stay relevant," she said, taking a seat across from me and handing over my glass. "He was such a dick. I wish they would just stop paying attention to him."

I took a long sip of my crisp white wine, my taste buds shrinking back as the acidity hit my tongue. The spots beneath my ears ached for a moment. Then I swallowed and figured the next sip would be better.

"That relationship was, hands down, the biggest mistake of my life." Taking another swig, I was happy to find I'd been right. This one went down better, even if it did still burn my throat. I kept the glass in my hand, leaning my cheek against it. "But I will find someone eventually. I know I will."

"You still planning on getting married?" She arched an eyebrow as she tossed half her glass down in one go. "I really thought you'd have learned your lesson on that one."

I shook my head. "I won't let Landon take that away from me. I might not have any idea when it's going to happen or to whom, but I do want to get married. I just need to find the *one*, you know?"

"That *one* can be pretty elusive." She refilled both of our glasses, then carried hers with her to the fridge to start getting ingredients for dinner out. "Better idea. Just marry me. We already know we get along well. All we'll need to get ourselves are a couple of super-strength vibrators and we'll be good to go. Who needs a man? You can take care of Adi and we'll change your name to Leo."

I laughed. "Thanks for the offer, but I enjoy a good man. I'll keep it in mind, though. If I can't find a good husband, maybe I'll change my mind and we can grow old together."

"You'll find a good husband," Adi said as she drifted into the kitchen, hopping up on the seat beside me before turning to look at her mother. "What are we having for dinner? Can I help?"

"Thanks for your support, sweetheart," I said and ruffled her hair. "At least someone has faith."

April chuckled, spreading out fresh ingredients on the counter. "Well then, maybe while we're waiting for this great husband of yours to show up, you and Adi can make a salad while I cook the chicken."

I stood up and carried my wine over to her. "I'm sure he'll be right here."

Ha. I wish. I peeked at the door, but there was no knock from a handsome, mysterious new neighbor who needed to borrow a cup of sugar. *Too bad. It would have been a pretty decent story if my future husband had knocked on the door right then.*

In real life, the man of your dreams didn't just appear out of the blue like some knight in shining armor. *Still, how cool would it have been if he had?*

CHAPTER 4

CYRUS

"Good to see you again, Cyrus," Billy said, standing up as I walked into the conference room. He was a fellow investor in an educational technology company and we'd been called to their headquarters downtown. "Do you know what Mike wants to discuss with us?"

I shrugged after shaking his hand, taking a seat across from him at the polished boardroom table. "All the email I got said was to come in to talk about the upcoming year."

"I got the same one," Daniel said.

The three of us had bought into EduTech around the same time, and while I didn't see them very often, Daniel and Billy had invested in a couple of other companies together. They were friendly with one another, which suited me just fine since it usually meant they entertained each other and I could just sit back.

Billy glanced down at the gold watch on his wrist. "Mike's assistant said he'll be here on time. He's just finishing up a conference call down the hall."

I nodded and pulled out my phone to reply to a few emails while we waited. Daniel and Billy speculated about what Mike had asked us down here for before moving on to discussing some of their other investments.

Mike, the owner of EduTech and the man who had convinced all three of us that he was worth investing in, came through the door a few minutes later. He was big and boisterous, his meaty hand coming out to shake all of ours as he flashed us a white-toothed grin.

"Gentlemen, thank you for coming in today," he said as he clasped my hand first, then moved on to Billy's. "Did Barb offer you something to drink? I've arranged for snacks and—"

"That won't be necessary," I said. We weren't here for a party or a mixer. "What did you want to talk to us about?

His grin faltered, his shoulders coming down a notch. I narrowed my eyes as I watched him take the seat at the head of the table, the steely fingers of suspicion tightening around my gut.

"I wanted to speak to you about the new fiscal year. I have some figures to present to you. Then we can have a discussion." He lifted the old brown leather briefcase he'd had for as long as I'd known him onto the table and snapped it open.

Extracting four identical folders, he handed one to each of us and kept the final one for himself. After setting the briefcase back on the floor, he opened his folder and cleared his throat.

"As you'll see from the summary on the first page, our numbers are down from last year," he started. "It's been a struggle with the economy being what it is and so many educational institutions making cuts instead of acquiring new technology. In fact—"

"How are you going to fix it?" I interrupted his little speech to get to the only part that really mattered. "I'm not interested in hearing about the economy and cuts. All I need to know is what your plans are to boost the numbers in the coming year."

Mike's cheeks became mottled with red blotches, a heavy sigh parting his lips before he licked them. His brown eyes flicked from mine, to Daniel's, to Billy's, and then came back to mine. "I think it's important to understand the context of—"

"I think we all understand the context. Competition is tough, the economy isn't booming the way we might want it to, and a lot of companies are being forced to make budget cuts." I glanced toward the other two. "Do you guys need this explained or can we move on?"

"Move on," Billy said in a low voice. He'd crossed his arms over his chest and was leaning back in his chair, steely blue gaze locked on Mike.

He cleared his throat again, a tremor in his hand making the paper ripple as he turned a page. "We have a new product in mind that should boost our sales going into the next financial year, but we're going to need additional investment to develop it."

Daniel clenched his jaw but didn't say anything. Billy simply raised a brow, obviously waiting to be told how much they needed.

I sat forward and braced my forearms on the table, leveling Mike with a no-bullshit look. "Do you have a plan for any of this? Because it seems like you should have come in here prepared and you're not."

I rifled through my folder, pushing it away from me as I snapped it closed. "All I see in here are excuses and statements proving the knock you already told us you took this year."

He opened his mouth but closed it again without saying anything. The column of his throat moved up and down as he swallowed. "Yes, well, we need more money to be able to develop a prototype of the new product. Then we can plan for it."

My brows rose slowly as I glanced at both of the other investors in the room. Neither of them said anything.

I released a short puff of air. "Fine, it's obvious the others aren't going to speak up, so I will. If you're expecting me to give you another dime without being able to present me with a solid plan for it, then you've lost it. Why would you even ask for more money without having the proper presentations with you to back it up?"

"I just thought…" He trailed off, tiny droplets of sweat appearing on the brow. "If we can't get our numbers up, you'll lose everything you've invested so far."

"So you thought you had us by the balls, that we wouldn't have a choice but to give you more money?" A humorless smile kicked up the corners of my lips as I shook my head. "Here's the thing, Mike. I know you've been having issues with the software on your devices. I know you've lost big clients because of it, so perhaps the economy and budget cuts have contributed to your losses, but they're not the reason for the significant drop in profits."

His face paled, but he didn't deny it. Daniel and Billy's gazes both snapped to me, shock evident in their tight postures and furrowed brows.

"If we were to throw good money after bad returns and invest in this new product of yours, are you planning on using different software?"

"Our software is what you invested in to begin with," he muttered, his eyes wide. "Of course, we're not going to use different software."

"Then what are you going to do to fix the problems it's been having?" I cocked my head as I waited for his answer.

"We don't know yet," he admitted after pausing for a minute. "We're banking on the new development division to pull us through while we try to sort it out."

I pushed my chair back, having heard enough. "Until you can present me with a plan about how you're going to fix the issues with the software, you're not getting another cent from me. Next time you call me in, you'd better be prepared, Mike. I don't appreciate having my time wasted and I don't appreciate being lied to. I'll expect a plan for the software in my inbox soon."

Giving each of the men in the room a curt nod, I stood up and walked out of the meeting early. I didn't mind having to be a hard ass in meetings, but it was fucking annoying that Mike had called us down here while knowing he wasn't prepared for it.

I was also livid about the fact he hadn't been upfront with us about the problems before trying to wheedle more money out of us. One of my contacts in the tech world had given me the heads-up about EduTech's software malfunction, and it had been obvious Mike hadn't been planning on admitting it to us.

I didn't want to cash out just yet because the company had some real potential, but I'd have to watch him closer in the future. There were other companies like his I could invest in if he tried to pull this shit again.

Scratching the back of my neck as I waited for the elevator, I pulled my phone out again and discovered a message from Peter waiting for me. A string of curses left my lips when I read it and remembered what I had promised him.

Peter: Hey bro. Call me when you can. Jenny has a place she'd like you to check out for flowers for the wedding.

I rolled my eyes and stepped onto the elevator when it arrived, scowling at my phone all the way down. When I walked into the lobby, I hit the dial button and pressed my phone to my ear. *Best to get this over with.*

"What's up, Cy?" Peter greeted me. "Thanks for calling me back so soon."

"Yeah, sure." I moved my hand to the back of my neck and squeezed, weaving my way through the crowd of people in the lobby of the skyscraper. "I just got out of a meeting. What do you need?"

"Like I said on the text, Jenny found a floral company online she might want to use. A place called The Watering Can. I'll text you the address. Do you think you'll be able to check it out for us sometime this week?"

"Yeah." I sighed and pushed my way through the double doors leading out onto the street. The humidity level was starting to rise, and soon, the city would be stuffy and sweltering once more. "I'll go tomorrow. Anything else?"

"That's it for now."

Thank God. "I'll let you know what I find out."

"Thank you again for doing this for us. We really do appreciate it."

And that right there, the genuine thank you and appreciation in his tone, was why I couldn't back out of our agreement. No matter how much doing all this wedding shit was going to suck, my brother needed me to do this properly and there was no way I could let him down. Not after everything he'd done for me.

CHAPTER 5

LUNA

"Before I had Adi, I had all these fantastic ideas about how to raise children," April said as she pushed her sunglasses up into her hair and collapsed into the chair across from mine. "It's amazing how much those ideas have changed over the years."

We were meeting for lunch at an outdoor cafe near both our apartments and I'd managed to snag us a table underneath a large umbrella. Whiffs of melting butter, bitter coffee and the occasional hint of garlic drifted out from inside, drawing more and more people in like moths to a flame.

Maybe I should do something like this with my shop, start frying bacon in the office or making toasted sandwiches at the counter.

April's voice broke into my thoughts as she slumped back in her chair, letting her purse drop to the ground next to her feet.

"I mean, I swore to anyone who would listen that my kid would never eat fries for breakfast. Guess what Adi had for breakfast this morning, Luna? Fucking fries."

"At least she ate," I said, offering my friend a smile as I pushed a menu over to her. "Now it's your turn to do the same. In case you don't feel it today, let me remind you that you are an amazing mother and you're doing your best."

"Thanks," she said, her voice calmer now. "I guess being a mother is just nothing like how I thought it was going to be. For starters, I never thought I'd be doing it alone."

"Your ex is an ape. As far as I'm concerned, you're both better off without him."

"Don't insult apes that way." Her eyes sparkled with laughter despite the seriousness of the topic. It was one of the things I loved most about April, her ability to smile through anything life threw at her and to make others laugh about it too. "At least when they fling shit at you, they're letting you know honestly that they want you to fuck off. They don't keep lying about it until they finish their studies."

"True. He's a real class act to follow. I'm sorry to say this, but it's a good thing your marriage to him didn't work out. I shudder to think about the damage he would have caused you both if he was still in your lives."

"Don't be sorry. You're right. Divorcing him was the best damn thing I've ever done. I should have thrown myself a fucking party." She snapped her fingers before waving one at me. "You should look into that, flower arrangements for divorce parties instead of for weddings. Doing flowers for weddings only fuels the idea of marriage. You should do re-bachelorette parties, divorce-iversaries. All those kinds of parties instead. It's a way more realistic industry to be supporting."

"That's actually not a bad idea. I know all those things are, well, a thing, but I've never really thought about catering to that market." The romantic inside me kicked and screamed against the idea, but at this point, I had to take whatever I could get.

Hope flickered in April's eyes. "So you're going to stop doing weddings?"

I snorted out a laugh. "No way. Weddings are still the best way for me to make money. The other functions and day-to-day sales help, but weddings are what keeps the doors open and the lights on."

"Damn right," she said. "It's a well-known fact that anyone who works in the wedding industry charges at least double what they normally do when they're doing it for a wedding. If I had the ten thousand dollars back I spent on my wedding, I'd go on vacation for a month."

"I don't charge more," I protested, but then I remembered that I had done it once or twice. "I've only ever charged more when it's taken me forever to source something special the bride insisted on or something like that. But then I've put in a lot of time to track it down and I've used my own phone to make all those calls."

"Fair enough, but I wasn't talking about you anyway. You have to be the only honest person in the entire industry, I swear. If you look at my pictures and I tell you what I was charged for things, you'd faint."

"If it's for your wedding, though, I figure it's worth it. Didn't you feel that way at the time?" I couldn't help it. That romantic who lived deep down in the depths of my soul just wouldn't quit.

As much as I hadn't been in a serious relationship since Landon and wasn't looking for one, I still desperately believed in love. I figured I'd get back on the proverbial horse eventually and start looking for my own Prince Charming, but I wasn't ready yet.

April rolled her eyes so hard, I thought they'd get stuck in the back of her head. "It doesn't matter if I felt that way at the time. I was wrong. I learned my lesson. Now I just have to pass it onto you so you don't have to learn it for yourself."

I propped my elbows on the table and rested my chin in my palm, noticing that despite the laughter still in her eyes, she was also deadly serious. "Do you honestly believe there's no one else out there for you? You're such a loving, radiant person. There has to be someone out there you were meant to be with."

"If there is, he's going to be alone for the rest of his life." Her tone was resolute, her chin tilting up in determination. "I mean it, Luna. I don't care if I meet the hottest guy on the planet when I get back to work this very afternoon. I don't care if he's every dream I've ever had come true and I don't even care if he's desperate to be the father of a six-year-old. All I'd do is fuck him. I'm never getting married again."

My heart felt like it'd been whacked by a skillet at her words and the absoluteness of them. April deserved only the very best in life, and yet she'd been dealt a pretty crappy hand in love. I wondered if that was how it worked, though. If someone got burned that badly once, was it impossible for them to ever really move on?

I wanted to believe it was, but I just didn't know. Landon hadn't burned me that badly. He'd stung me enough to leave a scar, and I definitely wasn't the same happy-go-lucky, trusting girl I was before, but he also definitely hadn't taken me out of the game for good. I was merely recovering.

"We'll see," I said. "I'm not trying to be contrary and I'm not saying it because I'm trying to convince you that you're wrong. All I mean is that we will eventually see if there isn't maybe a man out there who can convince you that you are, in fact, wrong."

She flipped me off, then picked up her menu. "Sorry to crush your hopes, my little romantic, but there isn't a man alive who would be able to do that. We'd better order or we're both going to be late getting back."

It turned out that we were a few minutes late getting back anyway. When I got to the shop, I heard the *beep-beep-beep* of a delivery truck from the bay around back and rushed over to check if it was one for me.

It was.

The driver hopped out with a clipboard in his hands once he'd parked. His eyes darted from side to side until they met mine. The smile he gave me as his gaze raked down the length of my body was nothing short of lecherous.

For a moment, I thought back to what April had said about meeting the hottest guy in the world when we got back to work. It seemed I was out of luck because with bald patches on his head, a beer gut that seemed to have grown from an entire case of the stuff, and red, blotchy skin with sweat running in rivulets down his cheeks, the driver was definitely not hot.

Nor was he the man of my dreams if the lascivious way he looked at me was any indication of his personality. *Well good, because I'm not looking for my dream guy right now anyway.*

"You Luna from the Watering Can?" he asked after lifting the clipboard to check my name. "I've got a delivery from the Fresh Market I need you to sign for."

"I'm her," I confirmed, taking the clipboard from his sweaty hands and trying to hold back a shudder. I ignored his watery blue eyes on me and dropped my own to check the delivery note instead. "Do you have another note for me to sign? This one doesn't have everything on it that I ordered."

He shrugged and produced a toothpick from his pocket, shoving it between his lips. "If it's not on there, it's not in my truck. I loaded this up myself."

I scanned the clipboard again and frowned. "But this isn't even half of what I ordered."

"What do you want me to do about it? I loaded up everything on that form. If it's not on there, the system must have made a mistake, or you didn't order what you think you did. I'll check when I get back to the office, but you'll have to wait the normal amount of time between deliveries. My schedule is full."

"I need those other flowers." I batted my eyelashes at him, not above a little low-level flirting if it would help, but I quickly saw the man wasn't going to budge. He was in defense mode with his arms crossed and his widened stance.

It was a strong hint that a mistake had, in fact, been made. "I have orders to fill, and if I don't have them, I can't do that. There has to be something you can do. I know I placed the order correctly. Could you please call in and check your system?"

Arguing with him wouldn't make the flowers miraculously appear, nor would throwing blame around. I was hoping that if he called in and confirmed some kind of mistake or miscommunication, he would be able to fit another delivery in for me sooner than the week it had taken for this one to arrive.

"Even if there has been a problem with our system, I still can't clear my schedule for you." He lifted one shoulder in that what-you-gonna-do way. "I don't have any other deliveries around here this week and my truck's filled up with what I got anyway. No space for more."

I scrubbed my hands over my face, a scream of frustration bubbling up in my throat. Swallowing hard, I pushed it back. He was only the delivery guy. Maybe I could reason with someone at his office instead. "It's fine. I'll—"

"It's not fine," a commanding voice said from behind me. The fine hairs at the back of my neck lifted at the sound of it, like a rasp of gravel wrapped in the smoothest silk. "If an order has been placed and paid for, the responsibility is on you to ensure delivery."

I spun around to face my mysterious defender with the words to tell him to butt out already on my tongue. Despite how sexy his voice was and how much I appreciated his willingness to jump to the aid of a total stranger, I didn't need his help. I fought my own battles.

Whatever I was about to say flew right out of my mind when my eyes landed on him. *Because holy wow.*

Once again, my brain flickered back to that *meeting the hottest guy in the world this afternoon* conversation, and strangely, that might be exactly what had just happened.

But it didn't take more than one look at him to conclude that this man was no Prince Charming. He definitely didn't look like the type who was going to give anyone a leg-up onto the back of his white horse and ride off into the sunset.

He was more of a *pretty to look at, lovely to hold, but he will break you so don't consider yourself sold* kind of guy. Easily a foot taller than I was, I had to tip my head back slightly to take in the whole package, even when he stood a short distance away from me.

Sandy, light brown hair shone in the mottled sunlight filtering in through patches of clouds. He might not have been standing that close to me, but the green of his eyes was so bright and brilliant that the color was obvious even across the space separating us.

A white button-up shirt with the sleeves rolled up to his elbows stretched ever so slightly over his chest and biceps, the fabric just a touch tighter there than in other places. Not so tight as to make it look uncomfortable, but more like the shirt fit so well it had to have been made for him but it couldn't quite hide the toned physique it covered.

Broad in the shoulders and narrower at the hips, he had that swimmer's build I had always found attractive. But that was the pretty part.

The part that made me convinced he wasn't the type to sweep women off their feet and romance the heck out of them was all in the attitude. His eyes might have been bright and brilliant, but the green orbs were also ice cold.

His angular features were set in an expression so sharp it could cut diamonds and he radiated a certain dominance, the very air itself crackling with the almost aggressive vibe he was throwing off.

Feet spread apart with his hands in the pockets of the black slacks he wore, he had this haughty mask of entitlement as he jutted his chin up and glared at the delivery man. "So, what are we going to do about this?"

The gravel and the silk were still there in his voice, but there was also an edge to his tone that made me curious to see what was about to happen if I *didn't* intervene after all. I really did need those flowers and this guy might be my best chance at getting them.

Besides, he was really lovely to look at. I'd never get to hold him, and I couldn't have him, but looking couldn't hurt. So I let my protests go and simply watched him, reminding myself all along that I wasn't in the market for that dream guy right now.

Even if I had been, this particular guy was too cruel and confident to be him.

CHAPTER 6

CYRUS

The delivery guy was clearly very bad at reading people. He took a step toward me and narrowed his eyes, his head dipping to the side. "Who are you and why are you in this conversation?"

If he thought I was intimidated by him or that I was about to just back away because of the unspoken threat in his tone, he was very, very wrong. The malice seeping out of him rolled right off me as I curved my lips into a smirk. "I'm the new bookkeeper for the Watering Can and this delivery is only half of what we wanted."

"Yeah, well. Nothing we can do about it. Like I said. My schedule is full for the rest of the week. You can sort it out with my office and I'll be back next week."

"I'm afraid that's not good enough." I cracked my neck and moved closer to the man, my smirk growing when he took a step back and paled a little. "We're going to need you to sort things out with your own office and fix your own mistakes. We're also going to need those flowers to be delivered tomorrow at the latest."

He started to protest, but I held up a finger and locked my gaze on his. "I don't give a fuck about your schedule. Move things around, go into work early, or stay late tomorrow to get it done. Ask another driver if you have to. I really don't care what it takes, only that it gets done. If it doesn't, not only will we be moving our business elsewhere, but I'll also make a few calls that I guarantee will be detrimental to your job security and to your employer's bottom line."

He sputtered with indignation, but when he looked at me for long enough to realize I wasn't joking and the threat was very real, he reared back and nodded. "I'll have double what you ordered tomorrow."

The beautiful woman next to me sucked in a sharp breath. "It's really not necessary to double it. Just what I ordered will be fine."

"We'll expect double the order by this time tomorrow, not a minute later," I said. "And without any extra charge. You fucked this up, so you're going to fix it and make up for it all at the same time."

The driver kept nodding and raced back to his truck as fast as his bulky body could move when I inclined my head toward the vehicle.

I shook my head at the coward who'd given in a hell of a lot easier and faster than I'd expected, and a chuckle escaped me. That had been fun.

A pair of cerulean, Caribbean-sea blue eyes latched onto mine the next second.

Right. The woman. The owner or manager or whatever.

She really was beautiful. As I'd rounded the corner to see if I could find another entrance to the locked shop Peter had sent me to, it had been her that had caught my eye.

Coming closer to ask if she knew about another entrance or when the shop would reopen, because I sure as fuck wasn't coming back here if I could help it, I'd heard her pleading with the driver.

I raised an eyebrow at her now, shifting on my feet so I was facing her fully. "You have to learn to stand up for your company. I'm assuming you own the flower shop?"

She nodded, those eyes never leaving mine. They were wide and clear, open and honest.

Tendrils of pitch-black hair that had escaped the messy, wind-blown bun on top of her head framed her heart-shaped face, her skin pale and porcelain smooth. Her lips were bare but deliciously red.

If fact, she was like the living embodiment of that princess from the kids' movie, the stupid one who ate the apple her stepmother gave her. I couldn't remember the name of it since I didn't make a habit of reading or watching fucking fairy tales, but it was one of those ones everyone knew about. *Snow White maybe?*

Giving myself a mental shake because it didn't fucking matter anyway, I snapped back to reality just as she opened her mouth. "I do own the Watering Can, yes. Thank you for your help, but it really wasn't necessary."

"It wasn't?" I very nearly started laughing. The only reason why I didn't was that I could respect that she wanted to take care of business herself. "Look, there are a lot of bad businesses out there that will take advantage of you. That guy caved in less than three minutes and now you'll have your delivery tomorrow instead of next week. Surely, that's worth accepting just a little bit of help."

She blew out a heavy breath, searching my eyes for something she must have found because she nodded after a few seconds. "I guess so. Anyway, assuming you're not just some businessman on the prowl for spontaneous threats and negotiations, how can I help you?"

Her witty comeback surprised me and I chuckled as I pulled my phone out of my pocket. "The shop was locked and I need your help with a wedding."

"Now that, I can do," she said, dipping her head in the direction of the building. "Come in through the back with me. You'll have to excuse the mess there, but making you walk all the way around to the front door seems unnecessary since you just helped me."

"It was no big deal." I fell into step beside her and watched her unlock the door with an ancient-looking brass key. "I deal with people like that all the time. You'd be surprised what people would do if you threaten to take your business away from them."

"You also threatened to 'make a few calls.'" She put air quotes around the last part of the sentence and rolled her eyes, but a smile played at the edges of her mouth. "I can't do that. The only calls I'd be able to make would have been to complain to customer service, if they even have that, which I doubt. It wouldn't have done them any real damage."

"But he didn't know that," I pointed out as the door swung open and she led the way inside.

Black plastic buckets in a variety of sizes littered the floor of the back room, along with random leaves and stems lying around a table I assumed she used for making arrangements.

The walls were lined with rickety wooden shelving holding different-shaped vases, green sponges, and a whole host of other things. It smelled vaguely musty beneath the sweet floral scent drifting in from the main area, like it had been damp for years and nothing could clear the smell out completely.

It wasn't altogether unpleasant. It was earthy and familiar, just not something I'd caught a whiff of in a long-ass time.

"So," she said as we made our way into the shop. "What kind of help do you need for this wedding?"

I lifted my phone and tapped my passcode into it, drawing up the pictures Jenny had sent as I joined the woman at her counter. She set down the purse that had been slung over her shoulder beneath it and then leaned over to peer at my screen.

Her nose wrinkled. "Darn. I don't have any of that in stock right now. I've ordered it, but it was part of the shipment that wasn't delivered today. Speaking of which, I'd better go grab the plants that were delivered. Give me a minute."

She dashed away before I could offer to help, but I figured she'd turn me down anyway. The last thing I needed was to piss off the florist Jenny and Peter wanted to use and I was ninety percent certain that if I interfered with her business again today, that was exactly what would happen.

Besides, I'd seen carts back there. With the small amount of plants that had been delivered, it would take her two trips with one of those at most to get everything into the shop.

Deciding to use the time to get caught up on some business of my own, I scrolled through my emails and had only replied to three when she came back inside. Her cheeks were slightly rosier, but she hadn't so much as broken a sweat.

Clearly, she really hadn't needed my help. I put my phone down on her counter and leaned my hip against it. "I'm Cyrus, by the way."

She smiled and it transformed her entire face, animating her and softening her in a way that made me wish I had offered to help her again, even if it would have meant risking her wrath. It had to have been some previously dormant protective instinct that made the caveman within me want to roar as I rolled boulders out of her way.

"Luna," she said. "Luna Willet."

"It's nice to meet you, Luna Willet." I gave her a smile of my own as I ignored my suddenly fucked-up instincts, watching as she looked down at my phone with interest instead. "So, do you think you're going to be able to help me out?"

"Of course. Everything we need for mock-up arrangements will be in the delivery tomorrow." She frowned. "I hope it will be anyway."

Fuck. I'd really hoped to get this done today, but it wasn't her fault she didn't have what I needed. "Okay, I'll just have to come back tomorrow then."

Curiosity darkened her eyes as she lifted them to mine. "Sure, but it's usually the bride I deal with when it comes to weddings. Will you be bringing your future wife with you tomorrow so we can iron everything out and finalize your order while you're here?"

My brows shot up even as laughter burst out of me. I waved a hand at her. "No. Absolutely not. It's not my wedding."

"Um, okay." She cocked her head. "Why are you laughing like that?"

"Because it's fucking hilarious that you thought I was here for my own wedding." I shook my head and offered her a smirk. "I think weddings are bullshit, and if I ever come in here wanting flowers for my own wedding, I hope you'll slap me and remind me that it's the worst possible idea a person can ever have."

An eyebrow arched, she sighed, and something flashed in her eyes as she shook her head. "I knew you weren't the type, but just so you know, it's not always the worst idea a person can have. Some people really do it for the right reasons."

I laughed again, letting my head fall back while I waited for it to subside. "I don't think so because there are no right reasons. For one or the other, it's always for the wrong reason."

The corners of her full lips pressed in and she just stared at me for a beat before giving me a small smile. "Sure. I believe that you believe that. I also believe you'll change your mind one day, and I hope you do end up coming back here to get your flowers. I'll slap you and remind you of this conversation. I'm sure your fiancée will think we're both insane, but at least she'll know how serious you are about her to have asked her to marry you anyway."

Oh, if only she knew. "Yeah, that's not going to happen. Anyway, I need to get going. I'll see you tomorrow, Luna Willet. Let's hope that delivery guy is on time. Otherwise, I'm going to be making those calls anyway."

She rolled her eyes at me again, amusement lighting them up as she gave me a knowing look. "You really do enjoy being ruthless, don't you?"

"I do." I laughed again and winked at her. "And that's the only time I'm ever going to say those words."

Her laughter was soft and melodic, the sound of it following me as I gave her a wave and left her shop. I wondered if she'd still have laughed if she'd known I'd said those words once before and I was hellbent on never, ever saying them again.

CHAPTER 7

LUNA

"Adi had to be at school early this morning," April said as she let me into their apartment. She shut the door behind me and walked to their kitchen, talking to me over her shoulder. "Her class is going on a field trip, so she won't be here for our girls' breakfast this month."

I set my purse down on the coffee table in the living room before following her. "I'm sure she'll have a lot more fun on a field trip with her friends than hanging out with us. Where are they going?"

"A museum. They had to go in early to get organized and go through all the rules before they head off. You know how it goes." Without asking if I wanted any, she filled a cup of tea for me and passed it over. "What's new with you?"

I raised my shoulder on a nonchalant shrug, but I couldn't hold back a coy smile as I wiped imaginary dust off the kitchen island when I sat down. "Oh, you know. Not much. We did only have lunch yesterday. Whatever could have possibly happened in less than twenty-four hours?"

April froze in the middle of fixing her coffee and spun around to face me with her eyes wide, her expression demanding. "Spill, Luna.

What happened? Don't you dare say nothing or I'll give you floppy bacon instead of crispy."

An actual shudder traveled through me. "There's no need to threaten the food of the gods. I'll tell you, but I need you to promise you will not disrespect the pig that way."

"Fine." Her body relaxed and she finally finished fixing her some coffee, then smirked at me as she sat down. "Now, spill."

"Remember yesterday when we hypothesized about meeting the hottest man on the planet when we got back to work?"

She frowned but nodded. "What about it?"

"I did."

"You did what?" Her eyes narrowed before they reversed course, opening wider than before as her lips parted. "You met the hottest man on the planet when you got back to work? How? Where? Who? Oh my god, did you take a picture?"

Laughing at the rapid-fire barrage of questions, I held up my hand and counted down on my fingers as I answered them one by one. "Yeah, I'm pretty sure I did. He's definitely one of the most attractive men I've ever seen in person, though I don't know about him empirically being the hottest man on the whole planet."

She rolled her eyes at me. "Let's not get caught up in technicalities. What does he look like, and most importantly, you still haven't told me if you took a picture."

"I also still have to answer the rest of your questions." I quickly gave her the cliff notes version of how it had happened, then shot her a look. "Of course, I didn't take a picture. How would I even have done that? Just asked him to keep still so I could take a few selfies with a potential new client?"

"Well, yeah." Her brow furrowed like she really didn't understand why I hadn't done it. "If people can take selfies with their regular morning coffee, why couldn't you take one with him?"

"Maybe because he's not a coffee?" I deadpanned.

April chuckled. "Maybe not, but it sounds like he ended up being your knight in shining armor."

"I wasn't some damsel in distress, though. I didn't really need his help." I was glad I'd gotten it, provided that my delivery was actually made later in the day. But until then, I'd reserved judgment on the issue. "Besides, he's not a knight. Trust me. He just gets his kicks that way, you know?"

"No, I don't know. Why don't you tell me?" She glanced down at her watch and cursed. "You're going to have to talk while I cook, though. Otherwise, we'll be late. Again."

"Our meals do tend to run over often, don't they?" I got up to help her. "I don't really know how to explain it. Yes, he did help me, but it wasn't like he was really doing it for me. It was more like he couldn't resist going toe to toe with the driver."

"He's probably a businessman then. So what?" Oil snapped in the pan as it heated up, and the kitchen soon filled with the smells of breakfast cooking.

"So I'm pretty sure he's not the type to go around playing a white knight to others. A dark knight, maybe, but that's the last thing I need in my life. He admitted to enjoying being ruthless, April. You should have seen how easily he threatened the driver and how serious he was about it."

"The driver who was trying to fuck you over?" Her brows pulled together. "I don't see how threatening that guy is somehow a con for the hot guy's column. What's his name, by the way? I don't want to keep referring to him as hot guy."

"Cyrus," I said, the slightest little tingle tickling my palm as the memory of having his hand against it brushed up against my subconscious. I shoved it down because there was no way I should have been feeling any tingles whatsoever when I thought of him. "It's not a con for him because of who it was against. It's about how naturally it came to him."

"In other words, he's a dick." April tossed me a glance as she turned the bacon, letting it simmer to crisp it up properly for me.

God, I love her.

But she wasn't wrong about Cyrus. "Yes, he is. He wasn't so bad once the driver left, but he's just got this air about him, you know?

Definitely not white-knight material and it's a good thing too, since I'm really not looking for that at the moment."

"Why'd you bring him up then?" She shifted slightly to look at me while still keeping an eye on the stove, her spatula resting on the side of one pan.

"Because I thought it was ironic that I met a hot guy after that conversation we had. Anyway, like I said, there's nothing there. I just thought I should tell you about it."

"Are you going to see him again?" she asked, turning down the heat as she removed the pan containing the bacon from the stove. She transferred the pieces to a plate covered by a paper towel to absorb some of the fat. "You did mention he was a potential client, so you're going to see him again, right?"

I sighed. "Yeah, I am. He insisted on being there when the delivery arrives."

"He can't be *all* bad if he wants to make sure it actually gets delivered this time," she argued as she reached for the toast that had just popped up. "Grab the butter, will you? The tomatoes are almost done. Then it's just the eggs left to do."

"That sounds so good. I'm thinking we should do girls' breakfast every morning before work, not just once a month." I opened the fridge and grabbed two bottles of water, along with the butter. "But to get back to the point, I didn't say he was *all* bad. I just said he was hot and not really my type. Why are we still talking about him?"

"Because I'm thinking you should fuck him and I needed you to admit that he had some kind of redeeming quality before I could do it," she said so offhandedly that I turned to stare at her with the fridge still hanging open.

She waved her hand through the air with a smirk tugging at her lips. "What? Don't look at me like that. Just because you don't curse doesn't mean you're an angel. I know you're not some naïve virgin who hasn't ever even considered hooking up with someone just to hook up with them."

I rolled my eyes and nudged the door closed with my shoulder, then carried my loot back to the island. "Don't be ridiculous. I'm not propositioning a man I've only met once, who has an edge of danger to him even if he does also have a nice smile, and who also just so happens to be a client."

"If he's as hot as you say he is, I'd bet he's got enough experience to be dangerous to your poor deprived body with his cock." She waggled her brows at me and rocked her pelvis in an obscene motion.

I groaned and buried my flaming cheeks in my hands when I sat down. "Why do you insist on saying things like that?"

"Because you react like that." She burst into a fit of giggles as she cracked eggs into the pan. "Besides, just because you don't like the way I said it doesn't mean I don't have a point. It's been over a year for you, Luna. In all that time, I've never even heard about you looking at a guy. Why not hook up with one who has caught your eye?"

I couldn't even deny how long it'd been, but it wasn't as simple as all that. "For starters, because it's kind of a team sport. Both parties have to be into it for a hookup to happen and I'm pretty sure he gets his rocks off only in high-powered business meetings where he gets to fight with people or with supermodels."

"And?" She cocked her head as she dished up the eggs. "You'll never know if he's interested if you don't try."

"Why would I try with someone I just told you wasn't my type?" I helped her bring the food to the counter, snagging a piece of bacon from my plate and popping it into my mouth.

So good. So unhealthy, but so good.

April sat down across from me and shook her head. "He's not your type for a relationship. That's a completely different type than for a hookup. Just let the soulmate idea go and sleep with this guy. I'm sure if you bring up the idea of no-strings-attached sex with him, he'll jump at it."

My teeth sank into my lip as I thought. It had been a long time since I'd been with anyone, and I couldn't deny that the thought of breaking that dry spell with him was tempting, but I just didn't know.

Eventually, I nodded at April and swallowed my next bite. "I'll think about it."

She grinned and pumped her fist in the air, still clutching her fork.

"In that case, my work here is done. Now let's stop talking about your hot guy. Sheesh. Have a heart, woman. It's not like I'm getting it on the regular."

I laughed and didn't point out that she was the one who'd kept talking about him. Instead, we talked about some arrogant jerk of a new doctor who'd started at the hospital where she worked, Adi, and our plans for the rest of the week.

When I got to the shop five minutes before it was due to open, I was surprised to find the delivery van already waiting for me. The red-faced driver was the same guy we had dealt with the day before and he was already offloading the plants right in front of the back door.

He wiped sweat from his brow with the back of his chunky forearm and noticed me approaching. "It's all here, Ms. Willet. Double what you ordered, as promised. I'm really sorry about the mix up and my superiors have told me to assure you it won't happen again."

A strange little thrill of vindication ran through me. "Thank you. I appreciate you coming in early. I'll be sure to convey my thanks to your company as well."

A relieved sound slipped from his throat, but then his eyes narrowed as they peered over my shoulder. "Where's that other guy today?"

"He's, uh, checking out other options for the business." The lie slid from my tongue too easily. Less than an hour in Cyrus's presence and he'd already corrupted me somewhat, but I couldn't help keeping up with the story he'd spun before. "I'll call him and tell him about you being early and delivering what you promised today."

"Please do." He heaved the last pallet of flowers out of his van and tipped his head at me. "Can I help you carry these in before I go?"

My brows wanted to climb into my hair, but I hid my surprise. "That would be lovely. Thank you."

As I was watching him drive away about fifteen minutes later, a smile formed at the side of my mouth. I couldn't believe he'd even carried the delivery into the shop for me. In all the years I'd been ordering from that company, it had never happened.

The entire encounter had been empowering actually. A sense of victory hummed in my veins, the smile staying on my face as I went inside. While I didn't condone his threats, there seemed to be a method to Cyrus's madness.

I might actually just owe him for jumping in like he had. *Whoever would have thunk it?* I knew I certainly hadn't.

CHAPTER 8

CYRUS

As I pushed down on the rusted metal doorjamb to enter the flower shop, I noticed Luna's fingers flying over the keyboard in front of her ancient computer. The pink tip of her tongue was only just visible between her plump lips, her brow creased in thought.

Her eyes slid away from the screen even as she continued typing, skipping along the buckets on the walls before her mouth spread into a brilliant smile and her expression of intent concentration eased.

It dawned on me that I probably looked like a creep, my hand on the doorjamb without actually opening it as I peeked at her through the window. It was a very good thing I didn't give a fuck what other people thought, though, because I just couldn't quite force my gaze to leave her yet.

She really was fucking gorgeous in a wholesome, whimsical kind of way that—

Did I really just think the word whimsical?

I was so shocked that I finally pushed down on the handle and the bell above the door jingled to alert her of my presence, making it so I couldn't stare at her anymore anyway.

"Hi," I said. *Thank fuck I'm an expert at hiding my thoughts.* "How's it going? You hear anything from our mutual friend yet?"

"Yeah, I did actually." The smile hadn't completely left her lips when she looked up, her warm blue eyes twinkling like precious fucking gems as they met mine. "He came early. Told me to let you know. I think he was rather relieved when he found out you weren't here."

"Did he ask where I was?"

She shrugged, the loose black curtain of her hair shifting around her shoulders as she did. "I said you were off exploring other options for us."

"You did, huh?" I was honestly a bit surprised to hear it. *Pleasantly so.*

This woman had that butter-couldn't-melt-in-her-mouth thing going and knowing that she'd played along with my little white lie was kind of hot. I offered her a smirk, but it was closer to a smile than it usually was. "It was a pleasure doing business with you, Luna."

"Likewise." The corners of her lips were still turned up as she rounded the concrete slab of the counter. "Speaking of business, should we get down to yours? What's the color palette for the wedding? I've checked and I think I have all the major types of flowers in that arrangement you showed me, but I'll obviously need to know what else you had in mind if you want it exactly like that or if that's just a point of departure and we'll need to get the colors right, obviously."

"Obviously," I said, but I felt the smile-smirk slipping. "Right. Let's get on that."

Luna rubbed her palms together like an evil genius getting ready for a plan to take over the world, then spread her arms wide. "Okay, well, think of the shop as your playground. I've already set the stars of the show out in the back room so I can mock something up for you, but we need to pick fillers. We're probably also going to need a variety of different arrangements. The pictures you showed me yesterday were of what the bride wanted on the tables, I'm assuming? So we're also going to need to think of the church, any outside areas, the main table, the bathrooms."

It was then that I realized I had no idea what the fuck I was doing. *A rare moment for me.*

I drew in a deep breath, my eyes narrowing as I surveyed the walls of flowers. "Yeah. I'm going to need your help."

"No problem." She smiled brightly. "That's what I'm here for. Let's start with the colors you need. That'll narrow it down a bit."

"The color palette?" I cocked my head and tried to remember if Peter had said anything about that, but nothing came to mind. "I'm not sure."

Luna's eyes flared and brows lifted. "Um, okay. Those pictures you showed me then. Let's start with those. Are those arrangements set in stone or are they just an idea of the style the bride wants?"

Again, I drew a blank. "I don't know."

She paused for a second, her gaze sliding across my features like she was trying to decide if I was serious. When she must have seen that I was, she released a slow breath. "Okay. Do you have any information at all that we can use?"

"No." I had the pictures, which she knew about, and Peter had told me Jenny wanted to use the Watering Can. That's it. "I can speak to the bride, but as of right now, I don't have anything else."

"Do you want to give her a call?" she asked, moving back to her counter.

I shook my head. "She's a shift worker. She won't be able to speak to me right now."

Luna's eyes softened as she nodded. "I think you'll need to speak to her before we can really do anything here then. I'm going to need at least a little bit of information before I can help you. Just a question though. How are you planning a wedding you know nothing about?"

Fuck. This was already day two of having to deal with this wedding bullshit. I didn't mind spending my time helping Peter like I'd promised, but evidently, it was going to take a lot more time than I'd bargained for.

"I'm doing it as a favor. The bride and groom can't really get away during the day, so they asked me to step in for them with vendors who need to be consulted during working hours."

"As in, all the vendors?" Her chin lowered and her head dipped slightly to one side. "Do you have any idea how much work that's going to be? Just about everyone involved in any wedding, except for the venues and their people, pretty much stick to office hours. Especially during the week."

"I'm just starting to realize that, yeah." My hands found my hips as I tilted my head back and glared at the ceiling. "Fuck."

In my peripheral vision, I saw her chewing the inside of her cheek. "I can help you, if you want. I'm sure you have lots of friends who would be willing to help as well, but I know this industry. You did me a solid favor and I owe you."

"You don't owe me anything." I scoffed, bringing my head forward again to meet her eyes. "I stepped in because what that guy was doing was bullshit. I can't stand it when people just shrug their shoulders in business, is all. That's not how it works. If you've got a job to do, you fucking do it or you move over so someone else can."

My breathing was a touch heavier now. I couldn't help it. One of my pet peeves had always been people who shrugged things off at work.

Before I'd sold my system, before I'd been able to convince someone to give me a shitty, entry-level job, I used to wonder if those people just coasting through had any clue how lucky they were. I had skills, sure, but they'd been self-taught, and with no formal experience or qualifications, it had taken me a long time to find someone willing to give me a job.

I'd gotten to where I was by clawing my way up, fighting tooth and nail against the world when it kept shooting me down. It used to make my blood boil when I saw people who had been given chances just fucking wasting them, and that had never changed.

Luna's gaze was on mine, questions in the slight wrinkle between her brows, but she didn't ask them. Instead, she took a small step toward me and nodded. "I get it. Let's say I don't owe you. Will you let me help you anyway? Again, I'm sure you have friends who—"

"I don't have many of those actually." My breathing was no longer irregular, but my fists clenched as I shoved my hands in the pockets of my slacks. "Especially not ones who know a single fucking thing about wedding planning."

Frustration blew through me again. This shit would have been so much easier if Peter just would have caved and let me hire a goddamn wedding planner. *Why does he have to be the only person on the fucking planet who doesn't want my damn money?*

Maybe I should find a wedding-planning agency to invest in. That way he couldn't get pissy about it if they did it for him.

On the other hand, I'd given him my word and I couldn't go back on that. Plus, I didn't particularly want to sit with a wedding-planning agency in my portfolio once Peter and Jenny were hitched. I wanted to be able to go back to that happy plane of existence where I never had to think about weddings at all.

My fingers uncurled as I dragged one hand out and ran it through my hair. "I would appreciate your help very much."

Luna's mouth split into a smile and her eyes lit up. "Great. I'm glad. We're going to have fun with this."

"We are?" I frowned. "I very much doubt that."

Thankfully, Luna didn't take offense to my statement. She rolled her eyes and waved a hand. "Come on, Cyrus the Wedding Grinch. Have a little faith, would you?"

Despite my annoyance and frustration, I smiled a little. "Never. I can have faith in a lot of things but not weddings and certainly not marriages."

"You really are Grinch-like." Her eyes rolled again, the corners of her mouth still turned up. But then she inclined her head at the counter. "Let me print out a list for you of information we'll need for a start and then we'll jump in tomorrow. Does that work for you?"

Does it work for me to dedicate time on a third fucking day in a row to wedding planning? Hell no. "Sure. Let's just get it over with."

"Oh, goody." She clapped her hands with mock excitement, her tone dry but her eyes sparkling. "It's going to be such a pleasure to be working with someone who's got such a passion for what we have to do."

"Hey, you offered to help, remember?" I smirked as she moved to the space behind her computer and wiggled the mouse to wake it up. "I didn't force you into working with me."

She laughed. "True but you're stuck with me now, I'm afraid. If you can get all the information on here before we meet tomorrow, we should be able to make a decent headway. I'll have to bring in one of the temporary employees I use sometimes to watch the shop for me so we can head out, but I'll have to talk them through a few changes I've made recently first. Could you be here by about ten?"

"I'll be here."

It honestly hadn't even occurred to me when she'd first offered to help that she'd have to get someone in to watch the shop for her. Probably because it hadn't occurred to me we'd have to leave. I was surprised by how helpful she was willing to be, to the extent she was willing to spend money on a temporary employee.

"Thank you," I said, and I couldn't remember a time when I'd meant it more.

Luna just smiled and waved me off with a roll of her shoulders. "It's not a problem at all. I'll see you tomorrow, Grinch. Do try to find some joy in all of this, would you? It's not a death sentence."

I chuckled, already turning to leave. "Well, it's not mine. Marriage is just that for the groom, though."

CHAPTER 9

LUNA

Excitement rippled through me as I waited for Cyrus to arrive. Despite the fact that love hadn't quite worked out for me, despite his cynicism about it and April's, I really did love weddings.

Planning my wedding to Landon had actually been what I'd been looking forward to most about getting engaged, which probably should have clued me in to the fact that something wasn't right between us.

I'd long since come to the conclusion that at that time of my life, I'd been more in love with the idea of marriage than I'd been with the man I'd wanted to enter into one with.

It had been a rough blow to take when I'd realized it, but ultimately, it had helped convince me that Landon hadn't been the one for me anyway—married or not. Having realized that really sped the healing process along.

So even though I wasn't ready for relationship, it certainly wasn't because I was pining for my ex. I was well and truly over Landon. I'd also just learned a few lessons in the process and I wasn't eager for a repeat of them.

Now finally, two years after the opportunity to plan a wedding had been yanked away from me, I was finally going to get to do it. All thanks to Cyrus.

It was an added bonus that in doing so, I'd get to help him just like he'd helped me. He might not have felt like I owed him, but I sure felt like I did.

Plus, wedding planning? *Swoon.*

I was bouncing on the balls of my feet when a fancy, sleek black sports car pulled up at the curb.

A quick glance at the driver was all I needed to confirm my suspicion that the car belonged to Cyrus. No one else around here drove a car like that. I rushed over to him before he'd even gotten out, eager to get started.

He saw me coming and reached for something on the inside of his door as he gave me a curious frown, his head tipped to one side. I didn't hear the lock clicking, but I assumed that was what he'd done since the door handle gave way easily when I pulled on the warm metal.

I hopped onto the buttery leather seat, barely sparing a glimpse at the ridiculously fancy interior of the cab before I buckled up and turned to face Cyrus. "Did you speak to the bride? What did she say?"

"Good morning to you, too." A grin spread on his lips as he shook his head at me. "You're really enthusiastic about sorting all this wedding stuff out, aren't you?"

"Shamelessly so," I said with absolutely no hesitation. "I can't wait to get started. How about we go grab coffee somewhere so you can share what you've learned with the class? Then we plan our day from there?"

"I think I'm going to need something stronger than coffee," he muttered but drove us to a small cafe nearby anyway.

When we took our seats at the cocktail-type table on the sidewalk, he ordered an extra-large coffee for himself, while I got a tea. "Okay, let's get this over with."

I rolled my eyes at him again, just like I had the previous day when he'd said the same thing. "Are you really going to be like this all the time?"

Chest rising as he took in a deep breath through his nostrils, he held it for a second before shaking his head. "No, but not because I've suddenly changed my mind. You're helping me, so I probably shouldn't be a dick about it."

"Imagine that, you not being a d-word about something," I teased, even though he'd never really been that way to me. I had seen him in action with that driver, so I knew he definitely had it in him, but all our interactions had been pleasant enough.

Cyrus wrinkled his nose, his eyes narrowed, and his brow rose in confused disbelief. "A d-word?"

It wasn't the first time I'd gotten a reaction like that when people realized I honestly never cursed. "I don't like cursing, so I don't do it."

"A dick is a body part, not just a curse word," he said, his expression remaining unchanged. "And also, you don't curse?"

He said it in a way that made me think he couldn't quite bring himself to believe it.

I caught his gaze and held it firmly. "No, I don't. A few words have slipped through once or twice, but as a rule, I don't use any cuss words."

He grunted. "How the fuck does that work? And why?"

"I'm off-beat and quirky," I said as if that explained everything. When Cyrus didn't look away and gave his eyebrows another quick lift, I sighed. "I just don't like it. I don't feel like I need to curse to express myself, so I don't."

"Never?" he asked like he really couldn't believe it.

I shook my head. "Like I said, I've had some slips here and there, but it's been a long time."

"Not even when you're so pissed off that you can't see straight?" A wicked gleam flashed in his eyes as his lips curved into a smirk. "Or when you need someone to fuck you harder so badly that you feel like you might die if they don't?"

A flush crept onto my cheeks, but contrary to what most people assumed when they either found out or realized I didn't curse, I wasn't a complete innocent. "No, not even then. I don't get that angry very often, and when I have, I've found there are other ways to express what I'm feeling. As for the other thing, harder is a word all by itself. It doesn't need to be accompanied by the other one to get the point across."

His eyes widened momentarily while I spoke, making it obvious he hadn't been expecting me to address that last part. His smirk grew when I did. "If no one's been able to make you say fuck in the heat of the moment, they haven't been doing it right."

"Heat of the moment as in an argument or sex?"

"Both." He leaned back in his chair, but his gaze stayed glued to mine. "When done right, both have the capacity to make you lose your damn mind."

I swore I saw a hint of heat breaking through the amusement dancing in his green eyes, but when I blinked, it was gone.

Even if I had imagined it, it took my mind to a place it definitely shouldn't have been at just past ten in the morning. In public. Surrounded by throngs of people in the cafe or dashing past us on the sidewalk.

I cleared my throat and shoved the dirty thoughts from my mind. The cool yet confident way he talked about sex made it clear he thought he was good at it, and wondering about whether he was right was only going to reduce me to a puddle of lust right there on the oil-stained concrete beneath my feet.

"Okay, so now you know something about me." I licked my lips and tried to distract myself from the dull ache building between my legs, even as I fought to keep the lid on that box of dirty thoughts. "Tell me something about you."

"What do you want to know?" He spread his arms to his sides, seemingly not at all as affected by just talking about sex as I was. *Then again, it probably hasn't been anywhere near over a year for him.*

"Why are you so against weddings?" I asked, giving voice to the first question that popped into my head. It was something I'd been curious about since he'd first let on that he shared April's view of the institution of marriage.

His entire demeanor changed in the space of a heartbeat. Something shuttered in his eyes and he tensed, stilling almost completely before he blew out a breath and offered me a watered-down version of his smirk from before.

"Wow. I wasn't expecting you to go right for the balls, but okay." He paused when the waiter came back to our table to deliver the drinks. Then he reached for the sugar and stirred it in before looking back at me. "I've been married before."

Whatever I'd been expecting him to say, it wasn't that. My jaw nearly hit the ground, and for the first time in forever, I was just this side of speechless. "What?"

He chuckled at my reaction, but the sound was humorless. "I know, right? But yeah, I was. I met a girl, fell in love, and did what I thought I had to do."

"And then?" My ears were ringing a little. "I honestly can't picture this really happening, or you doing anything you didn't absolutely want to be doing."

"Firstly, we're sitting here because we have to plan something I absolutely do not want to be planning, but secondly, I wanted to do it."

"What happened?"

Cyrus snorted. "We got divorced. It turned out it wasn't really me she wanted. It was the money she thought I was going to make. Within a week of us separating, she met someone else. Another guy doing stuff in the tech world that she thought might pay off, and that time, it did. The dude was an up-and-coming entrepreneur when she met him, and on the day he reached the top, she married him. Literally the same day he sold his website. Marched him right down to city hall and put a ring on it, so to speak."

I knew I had to look like an idiot, but I just couldn't stop gaping at him. "Are you serious?"

He nodded. "As a fucking billion-dollar deal to a broke kid. Which I was at the time, by the way. I had no money, and when it started looking like it was going to stay that way, she ditched me."

"That sucks." I whistled under my breath. "No wonder you're not exactly a supporter of the institution. Your ex-wife is a prime example of someone who did it for the wrong reasons instead of the right ones."

"Like I said, there are no right reasons. What about you? I'm guessing you've never made the walk down the aisle if you're still so optimistic about it."

"I never made it that far, no. I was about to get married once, or so I thought. Unfortunately, the guy I was seeing turned out to be married already."

He arched a brow, lowering his chin closer to his chest. "And yet you still believe in marriage and people doing it for the right reasons?"

"Yeah, I do." I knew I was going to look insane, but I smiled. "My parents were very much in love right up until the death part of 'til death do us part. Their example of what a marriage should be like is one I would very much like to follow someday."

For a long beat, his deep green eyes stayed on mine but he didn't say anything. When he'd looked at me for long enough that it was becoming awkward, I was about to break the silence when he finally talked.

"Fair enough. I can respect that. How about I stop being so overtly against it and you don't rub it in my face too often that you want it?"

"Deal," I said and stuck my hand across the table. He shook it, and the tingles from before instantly reappeared. Instead of dwelling on it, I released him and dropped both hands to my lap. I'd have to remember to keep them firmly off him from now on. "So, do you want to tell me what you learned from the bride?"

He pulled a face, but before I could remind him of the deal we had just made, he held up his hands and turned his palms out. "That wasn't about the wedding thing. It was about the color scheme. She wants teal. Cream and teal."

I nodded slowly, trying to hold back laughter when Cyrus grimaced as he said the words. "I can work with that."

Another hour passed as we sipped our drinks and talked about the bride's wishes. Before we left the cafe, Cyrus leaned over the table and smiled. "How do you feel about going out to dinner tonight? My treat.

I would have gone crazy trying to get all this done myself. The least I can do is buy you a steak."

"A steak? Well, I can't say no to that, can I?"

"Great." He stood up then, paid the bill, and gestured for me to walk ahead of him on our way to the car. He groaned when we got there and scrubbed a hand over his face. "Fuck, I never thought I'd say this again, but let's go talk to a man about a ceremony."

CHAPTER 10

CYRUS

L una and I spent the day lining up some appointments for wedding shit—at least in my own head, I could still refer to it as that—and scrolling through links and pictures Jenny sent over. After dropping her back off at her shop a couple of hours ago, I'd gone home to shower and get dressed for dinner.

A critical glance at my appearance later, I grabbed my keys, wallet, and phone and stuffed them in my pockets. I'd reserved a table at a nice restaurant on the rooftop of a five-star hotel and had dressed the part.

Black button-down shirt with the sleeves rolled up to my elbows because it was way too fucking hot already to keep them down, charcoal-gray slacks, matte-black Oxfords with a slightly rounded toe.

I knew I looked good.

What I didn't know was why I'd made the effort. All I knew was that I'd pre-gamed like this was a date, even though it wasn't.

On the other hand, I supposed people acted the way they did on dates because it was the polite, decent way to act. As for my clothes, well, they weren't really that much different from what I wore normally anyway.

I shrugged off the weird feeling that I was about to go on a date and headed out to pick up Luna. She'd offered to meet me at the restaurant, but I'd insisted on picking her up, and eventually, she conceded.

Once I was settled in my car, I pulled out my phone and plugged in the address she'd texted me into the navigation app. Picking her up from her house and not the shop still didn't mean it was a date, though.

Traffic wasn't as bad as it could have been and I made it to her place with five minutes to spare, but Luna was already waiting for me. A simple emerald-green dress wrapped around her curves, the neckline dipping low enough to cut a V into her cleavage.

The skirt hit just above her knees, but despite the length, it didn't look too conservative. She looked gorgeous, classic.

A smile lit her eyes as she saw me pulling up. Then just like she had done earlier in the day, she darted toward the street. I was ready for her this time, getting out and rounding the hood to open the door for her.

"Hey," she said as she came to a standstill next to the open door. "Thanks again for picking me up. If you would have told me where we were going, I really could have met you there."

"But then it wouldn't have been a surprise." *Wait a second, am I flirting with her?*

"It didn't have to be one, but I do like surprises," she said before sliding into the seat.

I shut the door, shaking my head at myself.

Sure, she was attractive, and if she had been anyone else, I might have taken a shot at getting in her pants. Unfortunately for me, she wasn't anyone else. She was the woman who was helping me with Peter's wedding and, more importantly, one who believed in marriage and relationships.

Despite my own preference for casual, I would never lead any woman on and I didn't intend on starting now. I knew where she stood as well as she knew where I did. Which meant my dick had to stay in my pants and the flirting needed to stop.

"How was the rest of your afternoon?" she asked as I started the engine and flicked on the blinker to move back into the traffic.

I glanced at her as I checked the road, shifting the car into gear when I spotted an opening in the traffic and pressing down on the gas. "It's only been a few hours, so it wasn't anything special. Yours?"

"Same." She reached up to adjust the sleek ponytail holding her long locks out of her face. "Are you going to tell me where we're going yet?"

"Nope. You've come this far. I'm sure you can wait a few more minutes."

With the way she had shifted to be half facing me while I drove us, her thigh was enticingly close to the hand I had on the gear shift. Her pale skin looked soft and smooth, the milky white in stark contrast to the deep green hem of her dress.

For a second, my mind conjured up images of sliding my hands over that soft skin, of hitching up her dress and bundling it around her waist. I wondered what kind of panties she wore and immediately put her in something lacy and French cut.

My dick twitched and I caught my groan in my throat just before I was yanked out of the fantasy by the tinkling, melodic sound of her laugh.

"Yeah, I guess I can wait a few more minutes. Have you spoken to the bride yet about what we managed to get done today? I'm dying to know what she thinks of it all."

I'm thinking about fucking Luna until she can't walk while she's thinking about a wedding. Fuck my life.

"No, she's probably only getting off shift sometime around now. I'll speak to her about it in the morning."

"Will you let me know what she thinks once you've spoken to her? We should probably run all the details by her as we go along. She is the bride, after all."

"Yeah, sure." I shrugged, but I was still distracted by the lingering images I'd conjured up that were now torturing me. At least talking wedding stuff was keeping those images from running rampant and taking over my brain. "Everything we've done has been according to the information I got from her, though. We should be fine."

Luna nodded and made small talk all the way to the restaurant while I banished the remainder of my dirty thoughts. By the time we pulled into the hotel parking lot, I had them well under control.

As I parked, she craned her neck to catch a glimpse of the name of the hotel displayed above the bank of elevators. Her brows rose. "The Maslow? Really?"

The tone of her voice made me frown. "What? You don't like it here?"

Humor flashed in her eyes as she grinned. "I wouldn't know. I've never been here. I thought they would perform checks on your bank balance before letting you in the doors."

I chuckled under my breath. "Nah, but they did warn me that they'll be keeping an eye on the silverware since they decided to forgo our credit checks."

Her head tipped back as she laughed and reached for the door handle. Acting fast, I climbed out of the car and strode purposefully around it, offering her my hand once I'd opened the door.

Her brows pulled together in confusion. Then she arched one as she accepted the offer. Her touch was feather light in my hand, her fingers delicate but strong.

The humor still hadn't left her eyes as she looked up at me. "You know, you claim not to want a relationship yet you're treating this a heck of a lot like a date."

"It's called being a gentleman," I retorted and released her hand to take a step back from her once both her feet were planted firmly on the concrete.

I couldn't argue her point too hard though, considering how I'd had the same thought earlier. Surprise crossed her features again when I offered her my elbow. "I thought chivalry was dead."

"Only to the dude-bros and hipsters who think they're too cool for it," I replied, surprised again by how naturally it came to banter with her.

The only other person I ever bantered with was Peter. To the rest of the world, I was a total and utter dick. With all except Luna, it seemed.

I refused to think too much about why it came so easily with her. It didn't really matter. We each still knew where we stood, and in the meantime, why not enjoy each other's company?

She used her hand in the crook of my elbow to tug me to a stop as we were walking past the ramp that led to street level. Her eyes darted to the elevators, to the ramp, and then to mine.

"What would you say to bailing on the fancy dinner and hitting up a taco truck instead?" she asked, her head cocked and her lower lip sinking between her teeth. "No offense. I'm sure the food here is good, but this isn't a date, right?"

"Right."

One of her shoulders lifted as a mischievous gleam entered her eyes. "In that case, we don't have to do a fancy dinner where we both try to impress each other with put-on wit or charm. Let's just go have fun."

"There's nothing put-on about my wit or charm, I'll have you know." I dragged my gaze from hers to look at the rapidly fading sunlight creating a glow at the top of the ramp. "But you're right. Let's go have some fun."

"Excellent." Her fingers tightened on the inside of my elbow and she started walking again. "Thanks for not taking offense, by the way. I'm just not a fancy restaurant kind of gal if I've got a choice."

"What if this was a date?" I asked, genuinely curious. It fucking intrigued me that she'd choose a food truck over the Maslow, and I was curious about her reasoning. "Would you still want to go to a street truck?"

She snorted. "I'd always want to go to a street truck instead, but I would have gone to the fancy restaurant and beguiled you with my charms."

"You're not planning on beguiling me with your charms, then?" I tilted my head to watch her expression as we made our way up the ramp.

With humor still dancing behind her eyes, she shook her head. "Nope, no charms. Just plain old me."

"There's nothing *plain* about you." It was unlike me to blurt anything out, and yet the words had come without any active command from my brain to say them out loud.

Luna blinked several times in surprise, lifting her chin and angling her head so she was looking at me now, too. "Thanks, I guess."

We reached the top of the ramp and hooked a right, merging with throngs of people out on the sidewalk but walking at a much slower pace than most. Luna was still holding on to my arm. I was sure it looked like we were a couple out on an evening stroll.

Unease clenched my gut. My free hand came out of my pocket and went to the back of my neck.

Blowing out a breath while we waited for the red man on the traffic light to turn green, I tightened my grip on my skin. "Here's a random question for you. What are you looking for out of all this? You agreed to help me with the wedding, we're going out for dinner, and from the looks of things, we're going to be spending quite a lot of time together. I—"

A smile tipped the corners of her mouth upward as she bumped her hip into mine. She tutted her tongue. "Why, Cyrus, are you asking me if I'm doing all this with the ulterior motive of luring you into a relationship?"

The teasing lightness of her voice made the grip of tension on my gut release. "Yeah, I was."

"Don't you think that's a bit presumptuous? I offered to help you before I even really started getting to know you. I might believe in relationships, but I don't believe in love at first sight, and I definitely don't believe in tricking someone into falling for me."

"Falling for you? Now who's being presumptuous?" I joked.

She pursed her lips and shot me an unamused look, but I could see the smile she was trying to hide. "Well, they say it always happens to those who aren't looking for it, so who knows?"

"Me. I know. Absolutely no offense meant, but I'm not going to fall for you."

"We should be okay then because I'm not going to fall for you either." There was so much certainty in her voice that I actually almost ended up taking offense anyway, until I reminded myself of the realities of what we were talking about.

Her mouth moved to the side as she chewed the inside of her cheek, obviously less certain about whatever it was she wanted to say next. I didn't get to find out what it was, though.

With a sudden sniff of the air, she dispelled whatever thoughts had been brewing in her head and shot me a grin instead. "We're right around the corner. I can smell the awesomeness that is Ben's Tacos already."

Ben's Tacos turned out to be a food truck that appeared to be reasonably established and well known. It was parked beside a small green space in the center of the upmarket district we were in.

Tall elm trees burst over the park surrounding them, in the process of creating a canopy that would be lush by mid-summer. Benches were placed in their shadows, though I could only just make them out in the fading light as we approached the truck.

Large plastic containers had been placed on the counter, partially obscuring the body of the server inside. "What can I get you?"

Luna stepped up and glanced at the menu before turning to look at me over her shoulder. "Are you okay if I order for us?"

"Go ahead." I made a sweeping gesture toward the truck but moved so I was standing behind her. I was curious to see what was on offer and what she'd choose.

As it turned out, she ordered one of everything—although they only offered four different kinds of tacos, so it really wasn't too much. After ordering drinks, she pulled her wallet out of her purse.

Before she could try to pay, I handed some bills to the server over the top of her shoulder and was ready for the narrow-eyed glare she sent me when she spun around. I smirked as I raised a shoulder. "Chivalry isn't dead, remember? I'm allowed to pay for our dinner without getting any shit about it."

"You already paid for lunch, so this is my treat."

"I invited you out for dinner, so it's mine," I replied, watching as her eyes became slits before she shrugged it off.

"Fine, but the only way I'll eat is if you promise it will be my treat next time." She held my gaze. "I mean it. We're going to end up eating together again sometime, and when that time comes, it's on me."

"Deal." I didn't like it, but I could see from the determination in her rigid stance that she wasn't going to back off. I understood that— feeling like you needed to pay your own way.

Money wasn't a problem for me at all anymore, but that didn't mean I'd forgotten how it sometimes felt like your independence was tied in with it from back when I hadn't had any.

Also, it wasn't even really about the money here. Luna was doing me a huge favor and I didn't want her incurring any expenses she might not have otherwise. As it was, she'd paid that employee today to stand in for her.

If she had been a wedding planner, she would have been earning good money for the work she was helping me do right now. It wasn't right, but somehow, I didn't think she'd like it if I offered to pay her for her services, even though it would have been more than fair for me to do it.

Piping-hot tacos were passed down from the counter and Luna covered them in a variety of sauces without asking if I wanted any. She stuffed two of the tacos into my hands when she turned and jerked her head in the direction of the park.

"Try those. If you don't like them like that, I don't think we can be friends. Let's go grab a bench. I'm glad we got here early. You won't believe how busy this truck gets."

When I took my first bite, I understood why the truck was so busy. Speaking around the bite I'd just taken, I let my eyes go wide. "This is amazing."

"Isn't it?" She smiled almost serenely down at her food. "It's like a religion."

"Seconded." I inhaled the rest of my taco and dabbed the side of my mouth with a napkin before starting on the next one. "What made you decide to bring me here instead of just having dinner at the restaurant?"

Something flickered in her eyes as her chewing slowed. When she swallowed, it seemed like she was doing it for more than just to swallow the last bite of her taco. Almost like she was nervous about something.

"I wanted to talk to you about something, but I'm not sure how to say it."

"The easiest way is usually just to say it." My curiosity was piqued. I'd give her that much. "You haven't seemed to have any trouble saying anything to me before."

"Yeah, but this is…" She closed her eyes and sucked in a breath, releasing it slowly. "You don't want a relationship and I'm ready for some freedom. Earlier when you asked me what I was looking for in this, I had to make sure you knew that I'm not looking to turn this into a relationship. There really are no ulterior motives to me helping you. I really do want some freedom, even if one day in a long, long time from now I do hope to settle down."

"Okay?" I frowned. "I get what you're saying, but why are you telling me this?"

"Because I think we could use each other," she blurted out after a brief pause. The words came tumbling out of her mouth so fast, I almost didn't understand them.

But then I put the near unintelligible sounds together and my brows rose as my tongue flicked across the inner seam of my lips. "Use each other how?"

"How do you think?" she muttered, her eyes seemingly stuck to her taco. "I'm sure you know this, but you're a good-looking guy. I'm attracted to you, and unless I've read the way you look at me sometimes very wrong, you're attracted to me too."

"So you want us to use each other for sex?" I said the words slowly, carefully enunciating each one. "Is that right?"

"Yes. No strings attached. Would that be something you'd be interested in?"

Could I believe what I was hearing? No.

Would I be interested in it? "Fuck, yes. When and where?"

A flush crept to the apples of her cheeks as she stood up. "My place. Right now?"

"I can definitely go for that."

We practically jogged back to my car and I pushed the speed limit all the way to Luna's place. Neither of us said a word, but I was turned on as fuck, and if the heat in her eyes was any indication, she felt the same way.

She let her apartment door swing shut behind us, her hands moving to the thin sash around her waist but her gaze on mine. "No strings attached, right?"

"No strings attached," I confirmed.

Luna didn't waste any time after that. Her fingers tugged at the loose knot on the sash and then she reached up to her shoulders to push a strap off each of them.

Before I could fully comprehend that this was really happening and that the hot, sweet florist with the innocent mouth and never-ending energy was actually stripping for me, her dress fell to the floor to pool around her feet.

And she was stark. Fucking. Naked.

CHAPTER 11

LUNA

R isky wasn't really my business, but I'd decided to throw all caution to the wind tonight. I was glad I had, though. Deciding to live a little was definitely paying off big time.

Cyrus cycled through a montage of facial expressions when I dropped my dress, but the one that stuck was lust. Raw, primal lust that darkened his eyes as his pupils grew until there was only a hint of emerald around the rims. It made him look downright carnal, hungry even.

Both of us just stood there for a moment, me with my hands on my hips and my heart hammering. Cyrus with shock, awe, and finally that mouthwatering expression of absolute lust.

In the entirety of my twenty-eight years on the planet, I'd never felt as crazy or as vulnerable as when I'd propositioned him earlier. It would have been worth it even if he turned and walked out right now, just to have seen that look on his face. It was making me feel more desirable than I ever had before, which was a nice boost for my self-esteem even if nothing else happened.

Cyrus curled his long fingers into fists at his sides, then cocked his head and narrowed his eyes. It would have been intimidating if it wasn't so damn hot, but it was.

"I guess you're sure about this then?" His voice was as rough as a growl. "Because I'm not asking you again."

"I'm sure." Not at all sure what I was getting myself into by trying to be with a guy like him, but sure that I wanted to find out. Gun to my head, I'd guess I was in for a pretty wild but spectacular night—if his body could cash the checks his expression was writing.

I swallowed hard under his heated gaze but nodded. "I was the one who brought this up, wasn't I? I brought you here, so yes, I'm sure. You don't need to ask again."

He took another second to search my eyes. Then his gaze dropped to do a long, slow onceover of all the flesh I'd put on display for him. At the same time, his fingers unfurled and came up to start unbuttoning his shirt and his tongue darted out to lick his lips.

I watched as he slid the first plastic disk free of its hole, his fingers deft but unhurried. Every inch of my skin felt caressed by his penetrating gaze as he took me in.

Heat simmered in my lower belly and there was an ache starting to build between my thighs. I wanted to go to him, wanted to get this part of the evening of being exposed to him when he wasn't over with, but it was like those eyes were keeping me rooted to the spot.

We hadn't even touched each other yet, and it was like he was already in control, already dominating me with nothing but his gaze. It was crazy.

A tingle ran down my spine and settled right between my legs. The dullish ache became an almost uncomfortable one as I watched him tug his shirt out of his pants once it was unbuttoned and shrugged out of it.

My mouth dried up at the sight of his ripped torso, his abdomen as chiseled and hard as the freaking pyramids in Egypt. Every block, every muscle was defined and created a distinct line between it and the next.

Lips parting so I could run my tongue along them, I managed to tear my eyes away from his body just in time to see his mouth curve into a satisfied smile. "Like what you see?"

His hands moved to the button of his slacks and there was a

noticeable bulge sitting underneath them. I forced my lips to imitate his as I gave him a small shrug. "Only about as much as you do."

His smirk turned into a grin. A vaguely wild, manic one, but a grin nonetheless. If he hadn't been in the process of taking off his pants and toeing his shoes off, I could easily imagine him rubbing his hands together in anticipation.

"Oh, this is going to be fun," he said quietly, his eyes never leaving mine even while it sounded like he'd said the words more to himself than to me.

When his pants hit the floor, my insides clenched as I waited for him to get rid of the designer boxer briefs he was wearing, but he didn't make a move to take them off. The bulge was more pronounced now, a lot more pronounced, but Cyrus didn't seem to take any notice of it.

Moving with the easy grace of a predator, he closed the distance between us and ran a single finger between the valley of my breasts. "The entire time we were together tonight, you weren't wearing any underwear."

It wasn't a question, but I nodded anyway. My gaze was transfixed on that finger, watching as it ran up and down the length of my torso. It was as if he couldn't decide where to touch me first, but the calculating gleam in his eyes told me differently.

"What if I'd said no?"

I gulped because I didn't even really want to think about that. "I'd have been humiliated beyond belief, but I would have kept helping you anyway."

"I don't doubt that." His fingers splayed and his palm ran down the center of my chest, along my stomach, and curled to cup my mound. "But what would you have done about this?"

As if he knew how wet I was already, he dipped the same finger he'd used to touch me first through my slick lips. I barely stifled my answering moan, biting my lip and letting my head fall back instead.

With his free hand coming up to grasp my chin and bring my eyes back to his, he used the other to put near perfect pressure on my sensitive bundle of nerves while his fingers found my entrance.

They were so tantalizingly close to where I wanted them, but he didn't move any farther than that. "Answer my question, Luna. Would you have touched this slippery pussy of yours all by yourself? Would you have rubbed your hard clit while imagining it was me doing it?"

A whimper escaped me. I'd never had a man talk to me like this before, though I had known some people were into dirty talk. I just never would have thought I'd be one of them.

Cyrus slid only the tips of his fingers into me, using the heel of his hand to make me moan again. "Still waiting for an answer, gorgeous."

His voice was a low rasp and I could feel his hardness pressing against my stomach. I was learning that he was some kind of master of self-control, though. If I didn't give him an answer, I doubted he'd let it go.

"Yes, I think I would have. Eventually. Once I'd gotten over the mortification." I was proud of myself for getting the words out at all.

I'd been right, though. At my response, he finally slipped the finger all the way in. "I want you to show me what you would have done, how you would have touched yourself."

"What?" My eyes opened wide through the haze of lust that'd had them at half-mast. "You want me to show you how I…"

I couldn't even say the word out loud, but Cyrus didn't seem to have any problem doing it. His eyes were heated on mine, but they were also serious. "I want you to show me what you would have done to this pussy if I wasn't here."

"Why? You *are* here, so—"

Seemingly sensing my alarm, a small frown appeared between his eyebrows and his hand cupped my jaw and cheek. "Have you never shown anyone before?"

Suddenly mute, I could only shake my head.

He muttered a curse. "I don't know who you've been with, babe, but I'm willing to apologize on behalf of my entire gender."

"Why? Don't you know what to do?" It was my turn to frown, but only until I saw what had to be the very epitome of confidence in his expression.

"Trust me. I know what to do. I'd just like to see what you'd like me to do first. I'm not into making people uncomfortable, Luna. I don't fuck to get only myself off and I don't want you to feel like you have to pretend to like what I do because nothing turns me off faster than that."

A frisson of fear tightened my belly. "Are you one of those kinky types who like things that cause other people pain?"

"There is pleasure to be found in a certain amount of pain." He smirked and ran a light touch along my cheekbone. "But if you're thinking I like the hardcore, sadistic things, then no. It's not about that. I'd just like to see what brings you pleasure and I'll take it from there."

"Pain doesn't bring me pleasure," I whispered. "Just so we're clear."

"I didn't think it did." His expression was still carnal, his finger still moving inside me with expert level precision, but he also looked oddly... earnest?

"Okay." I released a shaky breath. "I don't really get it, but okay. Let's go to my bedroom."

He withdrew from me but kept a hand on the small of my back all the way to my room. Once there, he pushed me gently onto my bright purple bedspread, flicked on the lamp on the nightstand as if it was his, and kissed me until I was writhing again.

When my hand slid between my legs, it was because I just couldn't stand not being touched anymore. I'd all but forgotten I was doing this because he'd asked, and as my fingers tapped my hard bud, I groaned into his mouth.

Cyrus slowed the kiss, breaking it off to trail his lips along the column of my throat, trailing the tip of his tongue down my collar-bone and sucking a nipple into his mouth. My back arched as my hand picked up its movements.

I felt his eyelashes moving against my skin, but that was the only indication that he was watching me instead of closing his eyes. He'd angled himself so he'd have a view of my most intimate parts, but he'd done it so subtly that I hadn't even noticed it at first.

Instead of making me self-conscious or horrified about what he was witnessing, I felt strangely empowered. More than that, I was more turned on than I'd ever been and my fingers flew across my bud until my neck arched and I felt the familiar stirrings of an orgasm beginning to build.

Long fingers suddenly wrapped around my wrist to stop the movement. I cried out and my hips bucked, but then his fingers replaced mine, and before long, I was hurtling headfirst into an explosion of tingling warmth and bright colors.

My orgasm ripped through me like a hurricane, hitting me hard and leaving me feeling battered in the best possible way. My breaths came in hard, fast pants but Cyrus's mouth sealed over mine as his lips and fingers coaxed me back to earth.

As sated as I was, all I wanted to do was curl up in a ball and go to sleep. Until my eyes blinked open and I saw the way he looked at me.

His pupils had taken over almost completely now and there were dots of sweat on his skin that I doubted had anything to do with physical exertion. The muscles in his forearms were corded as he hovered above me, his throat working and his voice raw.

"God. You're beautiful when you come. I want to see it again."

My cheeks were warm from my orgasm, but I felt a rush of fresh blood joining the blossoming flowers on my skin. "I, uh, I'm not multi-orgasmic or whatever it's called. I'll take care of you, though."

Elbows finding purchase on my comforter, I tried to push myself up on my numb limbs. Cyrus's lips stopped me, just as his hand started moving again.

"We'll see about that," he murmured, then kissed a burning path down my body so slowly and leisurely that I knew he was on a mission to prove me wrong.

It was only after proving to me two more times how very wrong I was that I heard his mumbled curse as he wiped his mouth with the back of his hand. "My condoms are in my wallet out in your entrance hall. Give me a minute."

I wound my arms around his neck before he could move, bringing him back to me. "I have some. Hold on."

Surprise flickered across his face, but I rolled my eyes at him. "I might not curse, but I'm not a complete innocent. I do like sex and I believe in protection. It's not only guys who can buy condoms."

He grinned like the cat that had gotten all the cream, but I guessed he just had gotten more of mine than anyone before him. "Point me in the right direction then, princess. I need to get inside you and I need it now."

Slightly shaky and with trembling hands, I reached blindly for my nightstand. I felt him shift off me and knew he must finally be getting rid of his pesky underwear.

Cyrus got the hint about where my stash was and, moving faster than an Olympic athlete, managed to find a condom and roll it on before positioning himself over me.

All I could do was blink back my surprise at how he managed to do it all so fast when I could barely move. His broad tip rested heavily at my entrance, his strong forearms on either side of my head.

"I'm going to fuck you now, and I want to hear you. Feel free to say whatever you want. If you happen to curse, it'll be our dirty little secret."

When he thrust into me, I nearly did curse. He felt so darn good that it took everything in me not to. I moaned instead. Loudly.

Cyrus caught the sound in his mouth by bringing his back to mine and then kissed me soundly as he started to move. *Boy, could the man move.*

Every thrust of his hips was like he was trying to deliver me to heaven personally, like he was determined to drive me higher and higher using nothing but his body. His lips never left mine, even when our kisses were broken by sounds of pleasure and eventually turned sloppy.

I felt his impending orgasm as surely as I felt my own. He thickened inside me, the hard planes of his stomach dipping and his legs trembling. He mashed his mouth to mine when his thrusts became uneven, and when I felt him pulsing, I was done for.

I flew over the moon and kissed the stars before finally, grudgingly coming back to earth. Cyrus had his damp forehead in the crook of my neck when I did, his hips still moving as he drew out every last drop of our orgasms.

"We're definitely doing that again," he said, his heart racing against my skin.

I only replied when I found my voice, buried somewhere between bliss and another plane of existence entirely. "Yeah, this is going to be fun."

His breath ghosted across my heated skin as he chuckled, but I felt him nodding. "Agreed. It might not be so bad to plan this wedding after all."

I giggled because why the heck not? I wasn't looking to marry this man, and frankly, I didn't give a darn how he felt about weddings in general. "Should we make this our official reward for successful days?"

"Yes." He hadn't paused or hesitated for so much as a second. "Abso-fucking-lutely. I need to take care of the condom. I'll be right back."

As his weight lifted off me, I didn't even yearn to have it back. This arrangement we had going probably didn't include cuddling, and I was okay with that.

My limbs felt loose and languid, my mind already shutting down for sleep. Cyrus had been a lot to deal with for my poor, very deprived body—as April had called it—and I was ready to sink into my mattress and not even think about moving for the next twelve hours.

Eyes already drifting closed, I heard his low chuckle before I felt him press a kiss to my forehead. "I'll get what we need from the bride and come by the shop soon, okay?"

"Okay," I murmured as I rubbed my cheek against my pillow. "Let me let you out."

"Just come lock the door when you're ready. I'll close it behind me." I listened to his footsteps as they moved away from my bedroom, then forced myself to get up so I could go do as he'd asked.

There had been nothing awkward between us after the sex, none of those "I'll call you" lies that only ended in despair and self-doubt. No, things with Cyrus had been easy.

At this point in my life, with all the troubles at the shop and the uncertainty about how I was going to be able to keep it, easy was exactly what I needed. One day, I'd meet the guy I was going to marry, but that guy wasn't Cyrus, and I was completely, one hundred percent okay with what I had with him in the meantime.

CHAPTER 12

CYRUS

"Hey, bro, you got time to go to lunch?" Peter asked when I opened my front door.

I had the penthouse in an exclusive apartment building that had excellent security, but I still frowned at the sight of my brother at my door. "Peter? Why aren't you at work? You haven't taken a day off in forever. Everything okay?"

The doorman at my building had a list of exactly one person who was welcome anytime, who he didn't have to call ahead about, and that was my brother. Logically, I knew this meant that the man I was looking at who wore Peter's face had to be him, but I was confused as fuck as to why or how he would be here in the middle of the day.

He chuckled as he walked into my place, shooting me a grin over his shoulder. "What? Does a guy need an excuse to see his brother?"

"If that guy is you, then yes." I let the door slam shut and ran an eye up and down the length of his body. "Are you injured? Because I gotta tell you, I don't like blood."

"I know." He lifted his shirt with the grin still on his face and gestured at the unmarred skin of his torso. "See? No injuries. I'm good."

"Why are you here then?" A quick search of recent memory

revealed that this visit was unprecedented. I felt the blood drain from my face. "Is it Jenny? Is she okay?"

I didn't know why he'd be smiling the way he was if she was the one in trouble, but I was genuinely confused about his presence. His expression sobered and he dropped his shirt. "Chill, dude. She's fine. Why are you so worked up?"

"I'm not worked up. I'm concerned about why you're here in the middle of a fucking work day." I shoved my hands into the pockets of my jeans to keep them still. "The last time—"

Understanding dawned in his eyes and he shook his head hard. "No, this is nothing like the day Mom had her accident. Jenny said you'd been sending her a bunch of questions about the wedding and I took the day off to answer all of them."

Relief pounded through my veins, leaving me slightly dizzy. It took me a second to fight off the deluge of memories from the last time Peter had appeared at home when he should have been working, but I gritted my teeth and got through it.

"That's why you're here? Wedding stuff?"

He nodded with a contented smile spreading across his lips. "Yeah. Why wouldn't it be? I told you, Jenny and I both take this very seriously. We might not be able to get days off all the time for wedding stuff, which is why we've asked you to help, but the least I can do is to take one day to make sure you've got it all."

"So, lunch, huh?" Blood had resumed its flow through my limbs, making me able to move again. Grabbing everything I needed, I opened the door again. "A little warning would have been nice. How did you even know I was available today?"

"Your calendar is still synced to mine, dumb ass," he said, smirking as he walked out into the hall again. "I've told you a hundred times to undo it since we're no longer living together, but you never did."

"That's because you're the only person I have left in the world, dumb ass," I joked as I jabbed the button for the elevator. "Between you and my virtual assistant, I'd rather you know where I am than that guy."

"You know you could and probably should get a real assistant, right? Like a flesh and blood person who could help you."

"This person is flesh and blood. I just don't have to see them twenty-four seven. Besides, Scott's great. I don't need to see him to know him."

Okay, so maybe I was a bit reclusive, but it wasn't like I was a hermit. Having people around constantly just wasn't really my thing.

I'd done fine by myself. Leased office space with a receptionist and conference rooms whenever I needed them worked well enough. My business was all done online, so all I needed was my laptop and I was good to go. Even Scott had only been hired as a matter of necessity.

"Trust me, if I'd had a real assistant, they would be dealing with your wedding," I said as a digital ding signaled the arrival of the elevator.

Peter rolled his eyes at me, shaking his head. "In that case, I'm sorry you don't have a real assistant. They might have been more enthusiastic about all this."

"It could have been an octogenarian who would have seen you married before you'd spent a night together or a millennial who might have created an overly complicated wedding hashtag for you."

He groaned as he put his head in his hands. "Scott's great. You should keep him."

"I was planning on it." I smirked at my brother as the elevator descended. "But hey, if you want an overly complicated wedding hashtag, just let me know. Also, you're welcome to move in with me until the wedding if you want the no-sex thing."

"You're insane." He narrowed his eyes at me. "And unusually chipper now that you're over your freak out. You're not a chipper kind of guy. What gives?"

A night of unadulterated pleasure with the woman helping me plan your wedding. "Nothing. I'm just in a good mood."

"I'd say." He gave me a suspicious side-eye, then started laughing. "You got laid, didn't you?"

"I did, but that's not exactly something I'd be in a good mood about. Stop making me sound like I was celibate before."

"Dude, if I didn't know any better, I'd say this woman had to come glitter for you to look like this the day after."

She didn't come glitter, but she might as well have. Fuck, one night with Luna and I already knew I needed a lot more of her. I was borderline addicted to the way her body writhed beneath mine, to the way her beautiful face contorted in pleasure and she looked almost guilty about it.

I didn't tell Peter any of this, though. He was riding the high of being in love and planning his wedding. A few words out of my mouth and the pussy-whipped fool would be suggesting we make it a double.

"It's no big deal. We had fun and that was all there was to it." The elevator let us out, and as we made our way out of my building, I realized I had a problem. "I need to stop so I can get a notebook."

"What for?" His face screwed up. "You have your phone, don't you?"

"Yeah, but handwritten always feels better." I could write faster than I could type. Plus, I had a feeling that with Luna by my side, whatever list I made today was going to have babies. It was always easier to keep track of those on actual paper. "What? You could take the day off but you can't spare two minutes to buy a fucking notebook?"

"You didn't even need a notebook at school," he grumbled, then threw his hands up. "But okay. Let's stop for a notebook and pretend there's nothing weird about it, even when the guy who wants it made his fortune off electronics."

I shrugged as we slowed near a stationery store. "Yeah, let's do that."

A few minutes later, I emerged with a pitch-black, faux-leather notebook with the words *Nothing like planning a wedding to make you want to punch every person you've ever met in the throat* emblazoned across the front of it.

Peter took one look at it and burst out laughing. "I kind of feel like you ordered that off the internet especially for today and that was what the whole notebook thing was really about."

"If only." I shrugged, but I really should have thought about doing just that. "I think it was the universe just knowing what I needed and giving it to me."

My brother stopped laughing and dragged his hands though his hair. "The fucking universe? What is with you, man?"

"Nothing. I just feel like karma won this round, putting this particular book in that particular store right when I needed it."

We kept talking shit as we made our way to our favorite bar, ordering a pitcher of beer and some wings before taking up residence in our booth. I spread the pages of my brand-new notebook and took my newly purchased pen out of my pocket.

"Okay, so you said Jenny talked to you about the questions I've asked. So why don't you start by going through them and giving me the answers?"

Peter lifted his ass to get his phone out his pocket, but his eyes never left mine. "You're taking this really seriously."

"You took the day off work, so you are too."

He rolled his eyes. "Yeah, but it's my wedding. You didn't want to be involved at all, but now this?"

"If I'm going to do it, I'm going to do it well. You know me. I don't waste my time." It was true enough, but it only made him more suspicious.

He held my gaze for another minute before he blew out a breath and rubbed his hands over his face. "Yeah, okay. Thanks, bro. I know you didn't want to do this, but I appreciate that you're putting so much effort into it."

"Whatever," I said gruffly. "Just answer the fucking questions." Peter already knew that I'd do anything for him. *I mean, case in point.* I didn't need to spell it out for him. "Start with those I sent you, but feel free to add details you think I might need."

The words came *this fucking close* to choking me, but I said them anyway. Luna had told me that we needed as much detail as we could get to make their day perfect, and since that seemed to be up to me, I was going to make sure I got everything she could possibly need to give my brother the best fucking day of his life. It was nothing less than he deserved, even if I didn't agree with how he was choosing to get it.

"Jenny has forwarded all your messages to me, so I figure we go through them point by point." Peter tapped on his screen. "But it doesn't make me less curious to know why you've suddenly had a change of heart when it comes to wedding details."

I sighed, wishing I could close my eyes and teleport to anywhere but here. God, the last thing I wanted was for my brother to get married. It couldn't end in anything other than heartache and destruction, at least not in my experience, but I couldn't stop him, either.

"I haven't had a change of heart. I just want it to be a nice day for you. That's all." I pressed the tip of my pen into the paper so hard it nearly tore. "Just give me the information, asshole."

"A nice day for me?" He blinked in surprise, his head jerking back. "Since when do you care about my wedding day being *nice*? Last I heard, you were raving about how I was making the worst mistake of my life and begging me not to do it."

"I wasn't begging," I scoffed, "and you made it plenty clear you were doing it anyway. If you're so determined to tie the noose around your own neck, the least I can do is to make sure it's the best fucking noose there ever was."

"That makes no sense."

"Maybe not to you," I grumbled.

Peter sat back against the leather vinyl of the booth, dipping his head to the side. "Is there some woman helping you with this, telling you what to ask us? Because it sure as shit can't all be coming from you. Jenny and I went through all your questions last night and there's a certain... finesse and knowledge to them I know you don't possess."

"I have a friend helping me." It was close enough to the truth.

A friend who made me come harder than ever and become desperate to corrupt that innocent little body, but a friend nonetheless. If there were more *rewards* like *that* down the line, I would plan the shit out of this fucking wedding.

Peter scoffed at me. "Bullshit. A friend? As long as I've known you, friends have never been a part of your life. You don't do friends. So who is she?"

"A fucking friend. Do you want my help or not?" I slammed my elbows down on the table and pushed the notebook closer to him. "Because if you do, I need the answer to the fucking questions."

For a beat, he didn't respond. Drawing his hands slowly away from the table, he showed me his palms with a smile spreading on his lips. "Okay, buddy. Let's do this. I'll answer your questions without asking any more of my own. For now."

"Just give me your answers," I said, feeling exasperation scratching at the inside of my chest.

It was amazing how things had ended with no weirdness or need for conversation with Luna, and yet my brother, who was the fucking reason I'd met her, was the one making it annoying. Yes, she was helping me, and yes, we had a great fucking night together, but why couldn't it be left at that?

We'd agreed there were no strings attached and I'd really believed it. She certainly hadn't acted like there were, so why should I have to explain anything to anyone?

Thankfully, Peter didn't press any further. He kept looking at me curiously, but he didn't ask again. He answered all of Luna's questions instead and elaborated where he felt it necessary to do so.

By the time our beer was drained and our wings were nothing but a pile of bones, he smirked at me. "If your *friend* has any more questions, I'll be happy to answer them, Cy. Tell her thanks, by the way. We really appreciate both of you."

CHAPTER 13

LUNA

"Adi and I are going shopping for new clothes for summer," April said when I answered my phone. "You want to come? Please say yes. She's asked me four times if I thought you'd be able to join us."

"In that, I don't think I have much of a choice." I laughed and drained the last few drops of tea from my mug. "When and where? I'll meet up with you."

April gave me the details while Adi sang a song in the background, made me promise again that I would be there, and hung up shortly after. I stood up from my couch, still smiling over Adi's antics.

She had me wrapped around her little finger and she knew it. Whenever she wanted me to go somewhere with them, I went. I wasn't even ashamed about it. I adored both her and her mother. Spending time with them was never a hardship.

Besides, I was in such a good mood today and hadn't really felt like being by myself all evening anyway. Sunshine warmed my skin when I stepped out onto the sidewalk, and a light breeze lifted strands of my loose hair, but the sunglasses on my head kept it out of my face.

The shopping complex where I had to meet up with them wasn't too far away, so I decided to walk. Pedestrians filled the sidewalk, all eager to take advantage of the fine weather in the late afternoon.

Since it was Friday, many people were dressed up and probably heading out for drinks with friends. As I walked, I admired some outfits and frowned at some of the more eccentric ones.

Mostly though, my mind was on Cyrus and what had happened between us last night. I still couldn't quite believe I'd actually gone ahead and asked him, but the lingering soreness of body parts that hadn't been touched or used for a long time reminded me that I had and that being with him had surpassed every one of my expectations.

Seriously, the man was a God in bed. The end result had totally been worth the anguish and anxiety in the run-up to asking him.

All day long, it had been difficult to keep him off my mind. Whenever I had a minute of spare time at the shop, which unfortunately was pretty often, I'd found myself thinking about our night together and got all hot and bothered again.

On the plus side, the memories had kept an ever-present smile on my face and not even my worries about my debt had been able to get me down. Around midday, I'd realized that the feeling of actually being happy and not worried for once was somewhat freeing and I wanted to hang on to that feeling for as long as I possibly could.

"Luna," Adi called, jumping off the low wall surrounding the parking area where she and April had been waiting for me. "Over here."

Her arms waved in the air and a grin split her face into two. I raised my hand in a wave and crossed the side street to get to them. "Hey, guys. Excited to do some shopping?"

"Yes," she cried and ran toward me, throwing her arms around my waist for a big hug.

I returned it, squeezing her little body tight before letting go.

She looked up at me with wide eyes. "I'm so glad you came. You wear the coolest clothes."

Glancing down at my floral-print sundress, I lifted my shoulders and ruffled her hair. "Thanks, kiddo. I'm not so sure I agree, though. Either way, I'm happy to be here."

April came to stand beside me, her brows pulled together and curiosity burning in her eyes. "You look different."

"What do you mean?" I asked as Adi slipped her hand into mine and started dragging me in the direction of the mall.

April followed after us, studying me intently. "You're in a good mood. Like, better than normal. We spotted you as soon as you came around the corner and you haven't stopped smiling since."

"Can't a girl be excited about a shopping trip?" I turned to look at her as we walked, batting my lashes innocently.

She snorted and narrowed her eyes at me. "Sure, but I know this is about more than that. I'll get you to spill the beans sooner or later, so you might as well tell me now."

"There's nothing to tell." I darted my eyes toward Adi, who was still a few paces ahead of us even as she held on to my hand.

"Got it," April murmured, "but now I'm expecting juicy details about whatever this is."

I chuckled but nodded as we pushed our way through the double doors into the air-conditioned mall. It was busy inside, but the first shop we went into a few doors down from the entrance was relatively quiet.

"Okay, ladies," April said. "You know the drill. Everyone picks three options for round one. Adi tries them on and models each one for us to decide."

"I'm assuming you still hold the power to veto any choice?" I asked, remembering the winter clothes fiasco of the year before.

She rolled her eyes at me. "Of course. Unless you're offering to pay, the final decision-making power lies with me."

"One day, Adi, you and I will hold that power," I said, hoping against all hope that one day, I really would be able to take Adi on a shopping trip.

Our tastes tended to be similar, whereas April loved bold colors but hated print. To be fair, she also had to make more sensible choices in clothes she knew Adi would end up wearing to school. One pair of decent jeans paired with a few different shirts went a lot further than one more expensive skirt, for instance.

"That's okay," Adi said, giving my hand a small squeeze before releasing it. "We always end up getting at least one or two of our choices."

I nodded, warm fondness spreading through my heart as I looked into her soft brown eyes. In so many ways, Adi was much more mature than the average six-year-old. Try as we might, April and I had not been able to shield her from certain realities, such as the fact that money was generally tight for us both.

"Let's make those one or two choices count then." I smiled but promised myself that once I got out from underneath the hill—since luckily it wasn't quite a mountain—of debt, I'd spoil Adi a bit.

April stuck close to me as Adi wandered off down the aisle we were in. We moved slowly after her, not wanting to let her out of our sights but hanging far enough back that we weren't completely obvious about it.

"So." She bumped her shoulder into mine. "What's all the smiling about?"

"I took your advice." I shot her a glance before pulling a bright purple shirt off the rack. "About Cyrus."

"Are you serious?" Her voice rang out in the quiet store. She cleared her throat and had the decency to flush when a shopper in the aisle next to us scowled at her. "What advice? About sleeping with him?"

"Yes, but keep it down," I whispered. "I don't want everyone in here knowing about it."

"You're never going to see them again, but okay." She took the shirt from me and hung it over her arm as I rummaged through some more. "Are you going to make me go fishing for the details? Because I will raise my voice again. And use your name loudly."

I shook my head at her. "You're impossible."

"I'm curious." She lifted her shoulders and flashed me a coy smile. "Plus, you're not exactly loose lipped with details. Since I'm living vicariously through you, I do what I need to in order to get you to talk."

"How are you living vicariously through me?" I plucked another shirt from the rail and handed it over. "If that's true, I'm going to have to apologize for being so boring recently."

"Apology accepted, but it won't get you out of telling me what happened. And when it happened."

"Last night." I bit my bottom lip to stop another smile from spreading. "You were right. He didn't say no when I proposed some no-strings-attached fun."

She lifted her hands and gave me a slow, soft clap as she smirked. "I didn't think he would. You're hot and you're a nice person, which he would know considering that you've spent some time with him out in the real world."

"Yeah, I'm helping him with his wedding stuff and sleeping with him. If that's not real world, I don't know what is." I meant it as a joke, but April's expression grew serious.

"It's not his wedding, right?" She cocked her head, her eyes on mine. "I'm sure you've talked to him about it, but I just don't want you to have to go through the same thing you did with Landon. Especially if you're actively participating in the wedding planning."

"He hates the idea of marriage and he straight up laughed in my face when I thought it was his wedding, but you're right. I guess it can't hurt to just make sure."

A sliver of dread opened in my stomach. I was ninety-nine point nine percent sure the wedding wasn't his, but what if it was? If I'd just slept with a guy who was about to get married inadvertently—again— I didn't know if I'd ever be able to trust any man ever again.

I drew in a deep breath, trying to dislodge the icy tendrils of dread spreading from my stomach to my lungs. They wrapped around them, constricting my next breath.

No. Cyrus isn't the one getting married. I repeated the words over and over again, but I couldn't help the uneasiness now flowing through my veins. "You don't think he'd lie to me about it, do you?"

"I don't know," she mused, concern etched into the tightened lines beside her eyes. "But after what we've both been through with men in the past, I think it's best to ask him pointblank."

"What if he lies?" Panic flared through me. "Darn it. I really hoped

I wouldn't let what happened with Landon end up with me being at this point. I can't question everything every person with dangly bits tells me forever."

"Look." She brought her hands to my shoulders. "I'm not saying I think he has lied to you, nor do I think he will. I just think both of us tend to have shitty taste in men and I don't think asking him again could hurt."

"What we have is supposed to be fun," I muttered. "It suddenly doesn't feel like so much fun anymore."

She brushed my hair behind my ears when I tucked my chin to my chest, dipping to maintain eye contact. "None of this now. You haven't done anything wrong. If it is him getting married, you didn't know. You're not the cheating scumbag. He is. But if he laughed in your face, I'm pretty sure he's not lying. It's just a bit strange that he hasn't given you much details about a wedding he's planning, don't you think?"

"Yeah, I do think." I had thought about it, but I had ignored those little doubts because I wanted to believe him so badly. *Scratch that. I'd wanted him so badly.*

Also, I genuinely hadn't wanted what had happened with Landon to scar me in any permanent way. I wanted to say I was over it and mean it. If I second guessed men all the time, that wouldn't bode well for truly having moved past it.

"I dated one jerk, but that doesn't mean they're all jerks," I said in a quiet voice when I noticed Adi heading back toward us. "That's been my mantra for the last two years and I'm sticking with it."

"Atta girl." April smiled, but I saw the remaining worry in the depths of her chocolate brown eyes. "Just be careful, okay?"

"Okay." My phone chimed as Adi reached us. She was holding a bundle with way more than her required three first picks, but since April and I hadn't gotten around to picking much yet, we headed to the changing rooms with all of Adi's choices instead.

As they chatted to the shop assistant handing them a card with the number of items she was about to try on it, I tapped out my pass code on my screen.

A smile formed automatically on my lips when I saw Cyrus's

name, but then I remembered the conversation I'd just had with April and it slipped right off.

Cyrus: Hey, you. Got that info we needed. When can we meet up?

The text itself was innocent enough if someone else had to read it. There was no nickname or kiss and hugs in it, nothing to suggest we were anything more than two people planning an event together.

Doubt threatened to close my throat, but I wouldn't let it win. As far as I knew, I had no reason to mistrust Cyrus. I'd never caught him in a lie and he certainly seemed honest and forthcoming enough.

I swallowed past the lump, determined not to let the Landon thing stand in the way of something new, something that could be light-hearted, fun, and unbelievably orgasmic.

April was protective of me, as fiercely as ever after everything that had gone down. I knew she hadn't meant to plant this doubt in my mind and I had to take her suggestion at face value.

All she'd said was that I should ask him, and ask him, I would. But I wasn't going to let it eat at me. I had to keep my faith that not all men were untrustworthy jerks until they proved otherwise. I had to trust that while I knew Cyrus could be a jerk, he wasn't necessarily an untrustworthy one.

Luna: Sunday will be good. Shop will be closed. Still working out the extended hours. That work for you?

His reply came in not a minute later.

Cyrus: Sure. See you then.

I released the breath I'd been holding through my nose. On Sunday, I would get my answers.

For better or for worse. *How ironic is that?*

CHAPTER 14

CYRUS

"Hey," Luna said as she walked up to my car. "I really don't need you to chauffeur me around, you know?"

"What? No 'thanks for picking me up'?" I joked as I opened the door for her. "Because you're welcome, Luna. I've already told you, you're helping me out. The least I can do is to pick you up."

Dropping her head against the seat, she nodded as she let out a heavy breath. "Yeah, I guess so. That's what you keep saying."

"Yeah, because it's true." My brows knitted as I glanced at her in the rearview mirror. "You okay?"

"I'm fine," she said, but she still didn't look at me. "Just had a long weekend."

"What? You party it up last night or something?" I reached into the cupholders behind my center console. "Because if so, I have what you need right here. I wasn't sure how you take it, but it's extra strong and extra large." I held out the cardboard takeout cup of coffee I'd stopped for on my way over and smirked. "You can thank me later."

She dragged her lower lip into her mouth and raised an eyebrow as she took the drink from me. "Thanks, but even if I was hungover, this wouldn't be the way to cure it. I'm not much of a coffee drinker."

"You're not a…" Fuck, this woman was an anomaly. "Let me get this straight. You don't curse and you don't drink coffee? How do you not kill people on a daily basis? And why did you suggest we go for coffee the other day?"

"Places that sell coffee usually sell tea as well." She smiled and finally darted her eyes in my direction, holding them on mine. Something still seemed off about her, but I knew she'd let me in on what it was when she was ready. "If you hadn't been so focused on getting the planning 'out of the way,' you might have noticed I ordered tea when you ordered coffee."

"But coffee is the nectar of the gods." I frowned deeply. "It's my emotional support beverage. If it wasn't for coffee, I'm pretty sure I'd have fists flying in every second of the meetings I attend."

"I don't have anger management issues," she said as she shrugged, then chuckled. "Now you, on the other hand, I could imagine needing a dose of caffeine to get the day started. I'm assuming you don't wake up well?"

"I wake up just fine. The problem comes in as soon as I connect with the world outside my bed. In case you haven't noticed, I'm not exactly a people person."

"Oh, I've noticed," she said, her tone teasing. "Thanks for the emotional support beverage though. I might just need it to get through the morning with the Wedding Grinch."

"You're welcome." I pressed the ignition button to start the engine and plucked my sunglasses out of the neckline of my shirt to slip them on. "Where do you feel like going to talk about all of this?"

"There's a park nearby. Since you already got us drinks, why don't we go there? It's so nice out."

She wasn't wrong.

Wispy white clouds sat high in the bright blue sky. It was a perfectly windless day, and New Yorkers seemed to be taking to the streets in droves, but I hadn't noticed any of it until she'd pointed it out.

"Yeah, sure." I shifted the car into gear and pulled out to join the light morning traffic, following her directions to the park. "How has your weekend been so far? Why did you say it's been a long one?"

"Just work stuff, I guess." She picked her purse up out of the floorboard and rummaged around in it until she found her own sunglasses, then slid them on.

I was strangely disappointed that I couldn't see her eyes anymore. They were so deep and expressive that I found I'd come to rely on looking into them to try to determine what was really going on behind them.

Guess I'm just going to have to go with my gut for now. It told me something was up with her and waiting her out was getting to me. "Work stuff?"

"Yeah." She sighed. "I told you I wanted to extend the shop hours, remember?"

"Sure." It had come up in one of our conversations last week. "What about it?"

"I'm just not sure how to go about doing it. I'll figure it out, though. Don't worry about it."

My eyes slid to the side as I slowed for a red traffic light. "Want any help figuring it out? I don't know if I've told you this, but I'm good at business."

"You haven't been as modest as you seem to think." She smiled. "So I assumed even if you haven't said it, but I'll be fine."

"Are you sure? I wouldn't mind." I wasn't even only offering because she was helping me. Business was something I enjoyed and figuring out what she needed in hers would be fun.

Luna shook her head, a small smile still playing on her lips. She moved her hand to cover mine on the gear shift. "Thanks for offering, but I really will be fine."

"Okay." I let out a breath and rolled my lips. Obviously, something was going on with Luna's shop, but I couldn't help her if she wouldn't talk to me about it.

Deciding to ask about it again once we knew each other a little better, I pulled into the parking lot she directed me to. "The park is right around the corner. We can walk the last few blocks."

"You got it." I found a space and carefully pulled into it, then turned in my seat to face her and pushed my sunglasses to the top of my head. "Before we go anywhere, are you going to tell me what's bothering you?"

"Why?" She sighed and dropped her head back, letting it loll to the side to watch me as she pulled her own sunglasses off. "It's not a big deal."

"Whenever somebody says something isn't a big deal, it's usually because it is a big deal."

"I thought you didn't want a relationship. This sounds a whole lot like relationship talk."

"I thought we'd agreed to keep sleeping together for the time being. That may not constitute being in a romantic relationship, but it does mean we have some kind of relationship with one another. Even if it doesn't mean we're a couple." I lifted my hand to her cheek. "As always, you can tell me to fuck off. If this is really about work, then fine. You don't have to talk to me about it, but I can't sleep with someone who has so much trouble looking me in the eye all of a sudden."

"Well, I can't sleep with someone if he's the one getting married." Her eyes blew wide open. She sucked both of her lips into her mouth, like she hadn't meant to say that and was trying to seal her mouth against saying anything else.

I lifted my eyebrows and lowered my chin, keeping my gaze on hers. "I thought we'd established I'm not the one getting married."

"Yeah, we did," she said, her voice so low I could barely hear her. "But I told you about my ex and what happened. It just occurred to me that you said it wasn't you getting married, but I still don't know who it is."

"I'm not your ex, Luna. If I wanted to sleep with a woman behind my wife's back, she wouldn't be called my wife." I wedged my hand into the pocket of my jeans and extracted my phone. "Here. Let me prove it to you."

I unlocked the device and clicked into a social media app I didn't use often but Peter loved. He'd signed me up for it because apparently everyone under the age of eighty had a profile on it these days.

"This is Peter, my brother." I turned the screen toward Luna and scrolled through his photos. "That woman with him is Jenny, his fiancée. They're the people getting married. Take the phone, scroll through his profile. There are photos of their engagement and I'm pretty sure I got an email saying he tagged me in something where he thanked me for agreeing to help."

Tentatively taking it from me, she spent the next minute or so looking at pictures and whatnot until she gave it back. "I believe you. Peter and Jenny are the couple we're planning a wedding for, not you. I'm sorry for sounding like a lunatic."

"Well, to be fair, the word does have your name in it, so maybe I should have expected it." My lips curved into a grin as I unbuckled my seatbelt and opened my door. "Are you coming, Luna the lunatic?"

A low groan fell from her lips, but she nodded and let herself out. "That nickname isn't going to stick, is it?"

"I don't know. Are you going to keep coming up with the crazy thought that I'm the one getting married? Because that's the second time I've told you it's not me."

"I know. I guess I just wanted to be sure." She offered me a small smile as we started walking out of the parking lot. "I didn't really believe it was you getting married, but after what happened before..."

"I get it. Better safe than sorry." Emerging onto the street, we joined the people on the sidewalk and settled into a slow pace as we headed toward the entrance of the park.

The very faint and sheer lilac and rose scent of blossoming cherry trees wafted in the air, accented with vanilla and an almost nutty aroma. Beside us in the park we walked along, all sorts of flowers were in bloom, and trees were budding with bright green leaves. Luna pointed it all out to me, marveling in naming certain flowers and getting excited about spring.

She tipped her head back and inhaled deeply, letting out a contented sound. "I love this time of year. All this new life is like a gift from nature, don't you think?"

"Can't say I've ever thought about it that way, but it sure beats everything being gray and dreary." I opened the latch on the low gate leading into the park and held it open for her, then followed her through and shut it again.

There were people all over, sitting on the grass or under the canopy formed by the light pink cherry blossoms. Luna led me away from the main area just inside the gate, walking back in the direction we'd come from.

Our arms brushed together as we strolled through the park, but neither of us made a move to touch the other more than that. It was comforting that she wasn't trying to cling to me or lay some claim to me despite what we'd agreed to.

In the past, I'd been burned once or twice by people claiming to be okay with casual sex when what they really wanted was everything but. "Are we done talking about this thing with your ex then? Because I promise you, Luna, I'm not him. I might be an asshole, but I'm not an insecure or attention-seeking one. When I have been in a relationship, I've always been faithful."

Crossing her arms under her breasts as we walked, she angled her head to look up at me. "You were faithful to the gold-digger?"

My lips pressed into a tight line, but I nodded. "Until the very end. After the very end even." I hooked my thumbs into my pockets. "I know you and I haven't made any promises to each other and that we're not planning to, but you can trust me."

A soft sigh escaped her. "Yeah, I'm beginning to see that. I'm sorry. I didn't mean to make things awkward. I just can't get caught up in another situation like that."

"I really do get it." I nudged her shoulder with my arm. "We've both been in shitty situations before, but this isn't anything like that. Let's just agree to be honest with each other if something's up and with whatever we say to each other. Sound good?"

"Sounds good." She pointed at a concrete bench situated underneath the gently swaying vines of an old willow. The clear blue sky reflected in the still waters of a pond beside it. "Wanna have a seat so you can tell me what information you got for us?"

"Sure. I even bought a notebook to document this process in." She laughed when she saw the inscription on the front but didn't comment on it. "Okay, Grinch. Show me what we're working with."

"Okay, so apparently one of the big items on the list is finding a venue. They've found a few they liked on the internet, but I have to go check them out in person."

"If they haven't booked one yet, I think we need to prioritize that. A lot of other things will be dependent on the venue. For example, some will only allow natural and biodegradable confetti and others will provide the DJ with their fee."

I used the pen that came with the notebook and fitted into a small elastic sleeve on the side of it to make a note. "Okay. What else?"

For the next hour or so, Luna and I went over every detail I'd gotten from Peter in meticulous detail. She also asked me more about them as a couple, but this time, it felt like she was asking me to get a clearer idea of what they might like instead of asking to make sure they really were the couple getting married.

In between wedding talk, we got to know each other a little bit better. I told her I hated teal as a color but loved black and gray, and I learned that she loved just about every color as long it was bright. Except for orange. She hated orange, which I found strange considering how many flowers came in that color.

We talked about music we liked and disliked, briefly about our families and friends and what we'd like to spend our days doing once we retired. Luna grinned when I asked that question. "I want to visit every floral show in the state and I want to walk through parks just like this one every day. You?"

"I don't know. Travel probably. I'd like to buy a one-way ticket to the country of my choice and just stay there until I was over it before moving on to the next one."

She laughed. "I wouldn't mind doing that, but I'm trying to be more realistic."

"I am being realistic." I wagged my eyebrows at her and sat back against the bench, spreading my arms along the top of it. "But I like your plan too. It's nice here."

"It sure is." A serene smile curled on her lips as she leaned back as well, ending up being basically under my arm.

If this had been some rom-com or teen movie, I'd have been slowly inching my arm forward until it was draped over her shoulders. I didn't, of course, but the thought made me appreciate what we had even more.

Before I could ask about her plans for later, her gaze dropped to her watch and she straightened up. "Come on. It's time for us to go."

"Go?" My dick took notice as I wondered if it was *reward* time yet. "Go where?"

Luna laughed and rolled her eyes at me, though I didn't know what had given me away. "Go to look at some flowers, silly. We'll talk about what else you can look at later."

CHAPTER 15

LUNA

"Where are we?" Cyrus frowned and he slowed his car when I told him to, his eyes flicking to the side to take in the greenery-filled sidewalks, the leaves and stray petals lining the streets, and sellers dragging potted plants along as they dodged the pedestrians.

My smile was wide and genuine as I opened my arms. "Welcome to the New York Flower District. We got here a little late so it'll be busy, but boy, is it worth it."

"New York has a Flower District?" he asked, narrowing his eyes at the hustle and bustle happening right there on the street.

I hummed my confirmation under my breath, bursting at the seams to get out and get started. "We do. Isn't it great? It's like a little paradise, a lush garden so close to the crowded Manhattan streets. I love it here."

"Okay, but why are we coming here?" Cyrus pointed his frown in my direction now, flicking a hand toward the market.

"We've come here because the market is nothing short of legend. It's the busiest flower market in the country and it also happens to be where I first realized I wanted to be a florist." Some of my fondest memories of my childhood had been made right here on this tiny stretch of city block. "It's like a sweet-smelling heaven. This is where I was going to get my wedding flowers from."

Cyrus had slowed the car but hadn't stopped. He pulled over onto a narrow shoulder where nursery trucks usually filled up all the spaces, and ignored the annoyed honking coming from all around us.

"Okay, that's great. I'd love to hear about it sometime, and you and I could even come back to walk around if you want, but why did you bring me here to look at flowers?"

"Because we're looking for flowers for your brother's wedding, aren't we? This is the best place around to get them from. In the mornings, they only sell wholesale, which is why it's such a circus right now. We can use my shop to order what we need, though. A lot of people around here know me and all you need is your card, which I've got."

For some reason, his jaw clenched and those green eyes flashed with irritation. "Only one problem with that. Peter and Jenny are getting their flowers for the wedding from your shop, Luna-tic."

"There's so much more choice here," I said and saw a spot opening up down the street. "There. Quickly. Go. It's like a sign. No one ever gets parking right at the market."

"We don't need parking because we don't need to visit the market. If you want to walk through to see what you need to order for the wedding, fine. But the flowers are still coming from your shop." His lips curved into a smirk. "Unless this is your way of trying to get out of doing the work?"

"Never. I love my work." I was being serious, but I could see Cyrus was too. He didn't want to get the flowers from here if it meant my shop would lose the business. "Fine. Let's just go do a walk-through and take some pictures for your brother and Jenny."

"I can do that," he agreed, then gunned it off the shoulder and cut off another car aiming for the parking spot. Again, he totally ignored the other driver and shut off his engine, giving me a shrug. "What? We saw it first."

"You know, I was just thinking that you had such a good side to you for not wanting to order flowers from here instead of from the Watering Can, but then you go and do something like that."

"Racing into a parking spot we really did see first negates an entire wedding I want your business to attend to?"

"It's a matter of principle." Amusement tugged at the corners of my lips, but I didn't give into it.

"You want me to give the spot up and you and I can just go?" His broad shoulders lifted on a shrug, but I knew that he knew he had my number. "Because I'm okay with that, too. Like I said, we're getting the flowers from you. If you get them from here, that's your prerogative, but I don't need to be here for that."

"Let's just go." I opened my door and jumped out of the car, giggling when I felt his strong arms grabbing me around the waist.

"There are better things we could be doing with this time, you know?" he murmured against my ear.

My heart skipped a beat and then started racing, my nipples beading against the lace of my bra. I shook my head and turned to face him, his hands sliding down to my hips. "Wedding planning before fun, remember?"

Cyrus released a long groan and brought his head down to rest on my shoulder, his fingers flexing. "But we've done hours of wedding planning already."

"We still have a few more hours to go," I said but looped my arms around his neck and lightly scratched his scalp with my fingernails as I turned my head toward him, keeping my voice low. "If we can get through it, we can always claim our reward later."

"Fine." He groaned again and gave me a mock pout, his head still on my shoulder and his lips only inches away from mine. "But then we get as many hours for fun as we got for this, deal?"

I smiled and closed the distance between our mouths to plant a chaste kiss on his lips. "Deal. Now come on. I'm dying for you to see this. I love this place."

Exhaling a heavy sigh, he nodded against my skin and withdrew from me before motioning for me to lead the way. Although my nerves were lit with his closeness after our brief discussion of *later*, I refocused my attention on the market.

It didn't take long before my arousal was tamped down enough that I could revel in our surroundings, pushing all thoughts about *later* to the back of my mind. "This is a historic market. It started over a century ago and has been in this very spot since the eighteen nineties."

"How very interesting," he mused, falling into step beside me.

I pursed my lips and punched him gently in the shoulder. He didn't even bother to pretend it needed rubbing. "What?"

"You promised not to be down on wedding stuff all the time."

"I haven't been," he protested, then sighed again and turned to survey the vendors all around us. "Talk to me about the business side of this. How does it work? It's busy as fuck."

Potted plants, flowers in every color of the rainbow, and trees lined the street. Vendors and customers danced around each other in a choreography of weekly negotiations and transactions. "Most people here at the moment are either vendors or people buying wholesale, so they've built up close relationships over the years, but obviously, it's still important to plan ahead."

"Do they only sell wholesale then?" he asked, and the tone of his voice had changed completely. It was like he'd gone from a horny friend to professional businessman in the space of one minute.

I'd seen this side of him before, but it still intrigued me. "No. A few hours in the morning they only do wholesale, but then they open up to the general public later. We only have about another hour or so before that happens. Then it really becomes chaos."

"Are all these vendors from different shops?" He stopped in front of one of the more iconic stores, thumbing a hard, olive-green leaf with one hand.

I nodded. "Some are family-run shops that have been here since the beginning. Others are specialty niches, like tropical or faux flowers. This shop, for instance, has been here since the eighteen hundreds."

Cyrus whistled under his breath and cocked his head, surveying the storefront with renewed interest. "That's pretty cool."

"Yeah." I smiled. "I think so, too."

He looked up and down the street, his gaze suddenly snapping to mine. There was something unfamiliar in the green depths of his eyes, almost calculating. "So this is the place where you decided you wanted to become a florist?"

"Yeah, it was. It's just, like, this perfect representation of actual nature right in the middle of the world's most well-known concrete jungle. I loved coming here as a child, just walking along and learning about all the different flowers."

"Why don't you have a shop here then?" His brow furrowed, and suddenly, the calculation made sense.

"If you're thinking of turning this into a business visit for me, think again. It's not that easy to get a spot here, and honestly, I love my shop. We're here to do wedding stuff, mister."

Hands planting on his hips, his button-down shirt pulled just tight enough across his chest to reveal thin slivers of smooth skin beneath. My fingers itched to touch each little part of him I could see, my core dampening when my eyes traveled to where his sleeves gave way to muscled forearms, big hands, and long, thick fingers.

Cyrus chuckled suddenly, bringing one of those fingers to my chin and making me look up at him. Humor mixed with heat in the bright green of his eyes, his businesslike expression gone.

"I'm ready to go whenever you are, Ms. We-have-a-couple-more-hours-ahead-of-us."

"We do." I cleared my throat when my voice came out breathy. "Sorry. I didn't mean to do that."

He smirked. "Feel free to check me out anytime you like. Just know I'll be doing the same to you."

He tapped my behind once, jerking his head at the street behind me. "Get going so I can return the favor. I'm ready to get out of here."

Laughter bubbled out of me, but I felt his eyes on me like lava-hot pinpricks when I preceded him into one of the stores. My core clenched again, and I bit my lip. *Get it together, Luna. You're working here, remember?*

Shaking off the lingering desire, I made a few inquiries about flowers and greenery I thought were good options for the wedding. Cyrus and I snapped some pictures so he could show the bride, but before I could do anything else, he grabbed my hand and led me back to his car.

"What are you doing?" I asked, trying and failing to get my heels dug in to stop him. "That last place had the most perfect arrangement. It was almost exactly the picture you showed me. All I was going to do was place a provisional order. We would have been able to cancel it, but the vendors need to know well in advance so they have enough stock if it's something that contains blooms as rare as that."

"I told you the flowers and the arrangements are coming from your shop. If you want to come order them here, fine. But I don't want to know about it and you'd better add your own mark-up on top of that."

"But—"

"No buts. It's all taken care of Luna. Don't worry." He only stopped when we reached his car, the lights flashing as he unlocked it. After opening the door for me and waiting like a darn bodyguard for me to get in, he shut it and hurried around to his side. "Good. Thanks for not making a dash for it."

"You really thought I was going to try to outrun you?" My chin came down. "That'd be crazy."

"Yeah, it would be, but we already know you're a lunatic." He winked as he turned over the engine and shifted the car into gear, but he twisted at the waist to face me before easing out of the spot. "Do you want to go get something to eat?"

"Yeah, sure. I'm starving." My stomach grumbled its agreement, and while my cheeks went beet red, Cyrus chuckled and pulled out into the traffic.

"Don't worry. You're not the only one. Let's get some food in. Then we can decide what we want to do after."

CHAPTER 16

CYRUS

"Okay, so now it's my turn to ask, but where exactly are we?" Luna asked when I parked in a darkened alley. It was lined with dumpsters and a trickle of water ran down either side of the road.

There were a few other cars parked here and there, but we had definitely left the bustle behind. I chuckled and turned off the ignition. "It's not as pretty as the Flower District, but I guarantee you're going to love it just as much."

Her nose scrunched up when she opened the door and the smell of garbage hit her nostrils. "Doubt it. Are we having sewer rat for lunch or something?"

I climbed out of the car and double checked that it was locked before rounding the hood to offer her my arm. "I'll keep you safe, and no, no sewer rat today unfortunately. I'll put it on your bucket list of things to eat before the wedding."

Although I had known it all along, it suddenly really dawned on me that my time with Luna was limited. Sure, there was nothing saying we couldn't keep spending time together or sleeping together after the wedding, but it felt like it was sort of implied that we wouldn't.

Good. A clean break.

I shook off the random thoughts of how I hadn't had nearly enough of her to let her go yet, reminding myself that there were still many weeks left before Peter and Jenny tied the knot.

Luna shuddered at my side when a low noise rattled in one of the dumpsters. She grabbed my arm in a tight grip and pushed into my side. "No, thank you. I'm okay without eating sewer rat or getting eaten by one. Shall we go? I have a sneaky suspicion we're going to be lunch instead of eating lunch if we don't get out of here."

My answering laugh bounced off the walls of the narrow alley. "Relax. I've got you. It might seem scary, but it's okay because this is the back. It's the easiest place to find parking."

"The back of what?" she asked, craning her neck like she was checking to see if she'd missed something.

"You'll see in a minute." I led her out of the alley and around into a quiet side street. There were signs for several small businesses, including a laundromat, a coffee shop, and a bookstore.

Luna frowned when we came to a stop outside a solid wooden door with only a small plaque hanging above it. "Jimmy's Killer Pizza? When I said I didn't want to be killed by a sewer rat, I should have mentioned that I'm okay with not being killed by a pizza either."

"Don't worry. I told you I'd keep you safe. I'll defend you from the pizza if it's necessary, but I think the pizza here is going to need defending from you. Trust me. I know it sure needs to be defended against me."

"What are you talking about?"

My head dipped to the side as I laughed and reached for the brass handle on the door. "Let me show you."

The heavy door swung open and Luna and I stepped inside, the scent of baking oregano, dough, and melting cheese overwhelming the stench from outside. Jimmy's voice filtered out of the kitchen, the clipped tones of his Italian accent reaching my ears and making me smile.

"Welcome to the first investment I ever made." I pried Luna's fingers off my elbow and settled my hand at the small of her back instead, steering her into the small hole-in-the-wall restaurant.

Once we'd traveled down the short hallway and stepped into the dining area, conversation around us ceased for a second before picking up again. Soft Italian music flowed through the speakers on the walls and every table in the room had at least two diners at it.

The space inside had been renovated when Jimmy and I first went into business together, and now, despite the dingy facade and carpeted hallway, the restaurant itself was all exposed beams, brick walls, and hardwood floors.

Heat came off the white-painted pizza ovens and warmed the entire space, making it perfect for winter but a little uncomfortable for summer. It didn't bother me, though. "Jimmy makes the best pizza in the city."

"You invested in a hole in the wall?" she asked, a shallow V between her eyebrows. "Why?"

"I just told you it's the best pizza the city has ever known." I led her farther into the back, to a table situated in a small alcove between the kitchen and the dining area that was pretty much reserved for me.

Jimmy let his family members use it sometimes, but otherwise, it was just mine. Luna sat down in the seat I pulled out for her, taking in the space as her gaze wandered from one side of the room to the other. "This is not what I was expecting when we parked."

"I know, right?" I grinned at her as I took my seat, motioning to the fresh chilis, Parmesan, and garlic standing in small bowls on the kitchen counter. "The whole point of this place was that knowing about it puts you a step above the rest of the people in the city. Jimmy sources everything he uses from local suppliers, and he and his guys cut every chili and grate all the cheese themselves. He has two guys who spend their lives just making and rolling the dough. They're all cousins. I loved the concept."

"Because it was elitist and exclusionary?" Her brows raised. Then she shrugged and a smile ghosted across her lips. "I'm just kidding, but it is kind of elitist and exclusionary."

"Nope, check the prices. Everyone and anyone can afford to come here, but they have to know about it to be able to do it."

"This is pretty cool actually."

"Thank you." Before I could say anything else, I heard my name being called and rose to my feet, turning just in time to see Jimmy's big hand being extended toward me. "Cy! I didn't know you were coming in today. And who's this pretty lady? I'm happy to see you're finally bringing someone here."

"This is Luna," I said. "Luna, Jimmy."

Jimmy's dark eyes tracked up and down Luna's body when she stood up to shake his hand, but he was looking at her with curiosity instead of interest. The urge to pour acid in his eyes for looking at her at all still rose in me for some fucked up reason.

"She your girlfriend?" he asked, his fat lips spreading into a wide grin as he reached up to pat my shoulder. "You landed yourself a looker, man. Congratulations."

"She's not my girlfriend," I said.

At the same time, Luna shook her head. "We're just friends. I'm helping him with his brother's wedding."

Jimmy's eyes widened, his bottom lip came out, and he swung his gaze from me, to Luna, and back again before shrugging. "Sure, sure. Whatever you say. Let me know when you're ready to order and I'll make sure it gets to you fast."

Luna sat down again, shaking her head almost as if in disbelief. "This was really your first investment?"

"Yes, it was. The day after the money from the sale of my system showed in my account, this dude I used to work with told me to come check this place out. I guess he'd heard from somewhere the ballpark figure I'd gotten and he knew what Jimmy had here."

Her lips tilted into a smirk, but on her, it still kind of looked like a full-blown smile. "So even you weren't always in the know, huh?"

I laughed as I relaxed into the seat, letting the familiar scents and sounds of the place infuse my senses. "I guess you can say that. I practically lived in Peter's basement in those days. When I wasn't at work, I was working on my system."

Her black hair shimmered under the exposed, orange-hued bulbs hanging from the ceiling. "It's really hard to imagine you like that."

"Yeah, well, I've come a long way. That's what I've been told anyway."

"By who?" She leaned forward and scooped a bit of the parmesan Jimmy's cousin had just set down into a small spoon, bringing it to her nose. "I hate the smell of this stuff just as much as I love the taste."

"You and me both," I said. "And by Jimmy actually. The last time I was here, he told me I just needed to bring a girlfriend by now to make the transformation complete."

"Which is obviously not why you brought me. So why did you bring me?"

Half rising off my seat, I bent over the table to whisper in her ear like I was letting her in on some big secret. "How many times do I have to tell you? Best. Pizza. In. The. City."

She pulled away from me, blinking for a beat before she burst out laughing. "Oh my God, you totally had me going there. I thought you were going to say something cheesy."

"Funny that you thought that, considering where we are. There's plenty of cheesy to go around this place, but I'm not it." I sat down again and took a deep breath, letting my own eyes track around the space and really take it in for the first time in forever. "This place was my cheapest investment by far, but it's also my favorite."

"I'm surprised you didn't have them move somewhere more—you know—hip."

"Never." I crossed my arms and shook my head firmly. "This place is perfect exactly the way it is. Jimmy and the guys only needed some money for the renovations. No matter how good the food is, people aren't going to come out in any meaningful numbers if it looks as ratty inside as out."

"True." She nodded, her lips pursed in thought. "It's something I should keep in my mind for my business, as well."

"There's nothing ratty about your shop."

"Maybe not, but there's nothing that makes it special either," she mused. "I've always dreamed of creating a fairy-garden-like space on my sidewalk or somewhere, you know? I thought I could maybe create this perfect little romantic bubble of space in this crazy city where a couple could just sit and drink a glass of champagne. Sounds kind of stupid now, but the point is that I had plans."

"Had?" I asked. "Why past tense?"

A smile tilted her lips, but it didn't quite reach her eyes. "Maybe I'll still do it eventually. But there's a lot that needs to happen before I'll be able to."

"The old, 'the bills need to be paid before the magic can happen' thing, huh?" I put air quotes around the words, and Luna laughed.

"Look at you, using those like a pro, but yes, that. Although I can't really complain. Just being in the shop day to day is pretty magical already."

"We're both lucky in that way, getting to do what we love doing every day." When the fuck had I become profound? "Anyway, what do you think you'll have?"

Luna and I looked over the menus, placed our order, and ended up staying at Jimmy's for hours. We talked to each other, to Jimmy, and some of his cousins and, unfortunately, went through some more wedding shit. Thankfully, Jimmy and the guys kept sending over enough bites to eat that I could lose myself in the food whenever the wedding stuff got to be too much.

When my eyes caught on the clock above his register at one point, my jaw nearly dropped. "Wow. Did you realize we were coming up on dinner time?"

Luna groaned and clutched her stomach. "I don't think I can eat another thing. We haven't stopped eating since we got here."

"Yeah. Same." I felt the shift in the atmosphere between us as we both seemed to realize at the same time that it was now *later*. My insides clenched with anticipation and I felt the wickedness of it seeping into my gaze. "Are you ready to go?"

"Sure," she said, a breathy quality to her voice that wasn't normally there.

I got up and placed a wad of bills underneath the small pots and plates left on our table. Jimmy hated it when I paid, so he never brought me a check, but it was only right that I did.

Luna got to her feet as well and let me wind our fingers together before pulling her out of the restaurant.

"I want to end the night my way," I said once we were in the car. "That okay with you, or do you want me to take you home?"

"No," she replied. "I don't want to go home. I'd much rather end it your way."

The drive back to my place nearly lit my tires on fire, but it had been a long-ass fucking day of keeping my hands off her and now it was finally time for that to change.

As we walked into my penthouse, I saw her eyes go wide as she took it all in. She was impressed, but I really didn't want to talk about it. I didn't really want to talk at all.

All I wanted to do was taste her until she screamed, then fuck her until she couldn't walk tomorrow without feeling me between her legs. With that sole purpose in mind, I kicked my door shut and grabbed her wrist, hauling her into my arms.

My mouth crashed into hers and my hands slid up her back, tangling into her hair before I tightened my grip. Angling her head up, I kissed her harder, deeper, until all the wedding bullshit disappeared and all that remained was Luna.

CHAPTER 17

LUNA

C yrus kissed me like a man possessed. The force of his kisses was almost bruising but I loved every second of it. The slight burn where he tugged on my hair seemed to spread from my scalp to my core, igniting every nerve ending in between.

The opulence of his penthouse was completely forgotten as I surrendered my mouth to him, winding my arms around his neck and giving as good as I got. Lust had been simmering in my belly all day, and now it flowed like liquid heat through my veins.

I moaned into our kiss and pressed my body flush to his, feeling the bulge of his hardness against my belly. One of his hands gripped my hair even harder and the other slid down to my hip, his fingers splaying out across my lower back. He used the leverage to pull me closer to him, his hips bucking when I rolled mine.

"Fuck, we're not making it to the bedroom this time," he said between kisses, his voice a low rasp. Releasing my hair, he dropped both hands to the backs of my thighs and lifted me against him. I wound my legs around his hips, hanging onto him like a koala.

I couldn't imagine I looked extremely sexy like this, but at least no one could see us. Without breaking our kiss again, he moved until he was lowering me onto something.

Soft leather hit my bare thighs as my sundress rode up when he set me down. Then he knelt in front of me and roughly shoved my thighs apart. I stared down at him, my lids hooded and my breaths coming fast as he jerked me to the edge of the seat.

"What are you doing?"

"What I've been wanting to do all day." He didn't offer any further explanation, pushing the hem of my dress up until it was resting at the very top of my thighs.

A low growling sound came from him as his eyes raked along the skin he'd exposed, his hands following their path. Goosebumps pebbled on my skin as he trailed his fingers over it, his touch light before his gaze reached the apex of my thighs.

"Keep your legs spread for me, baby." He groaned as he hooked his thumbs into the waistband of my panties and managed to free them without me even having to lift my behind.

I nodded when he looked up at me after issuing his command. "Fine, but you're next."

He smirked, but his eyes gave away how turned on he was. Embers burned in the emerald depths as his fingers sought out my heat. I dropped my head back against the couch when he pushed the first thick digit into me.

The only sound in the room was our ragged breathing, and I heard his breath hitch when he felt me. "God, Luna. I love how wet you get for me. It drives me crazy."

"You drive me crazy," I managed to bite out as I writhed under his hand. His movements were too slow, the palm of his hand curling up to brush against my sensitive nub on every stroke but never quite touching it properly. "Please, Cyrus. Just…"

"What?" His fingers continued their slow assault, his head tilting to the side. "Move faster? Didn't I say earlier that we were going to have fun for as many hours as we did wedding planning today?"

An almost feral cry escaped me when he hooked his fingers deep inside me, but then he stopped and looked up at me.

"What, then?" I asked. "Are you going to make me wait ten hours?"

For one torturous minute, I thought he was going to say yes. Then his fingers bent again and he shook his head. "No, but you get the point. Next time you tell me I have to wait a couple more hours, I might say the same thing to you later."

"You wouldn't." I gasped when he finally picked up some speed, my head dropping back again and my chest rising and falling as my breaths became pants. "Cyrus. Please."

"I've got you, baby." His gaze was smoldering when it met mine, but then he finally touched me in all the right places, and I splintered around his fingers. My hips jerked up and loud moans spilled from my lips as I came undone.

When I started coming back to earth, he was watching me with a hunger and an edge of desperation in his eyes. Seeing that look on him sent sparks of arousal going off like fireworks through my body once again.

"I want you," I whispered as I reached for his head and wound my fingers into the strands of his soft hair. Bending over to bring my mouth to his, I kissed him passionately as I reached down to unbutton his shirt.

He let me, but before I could push it off his shoulders, he pulled back from me and tutted. "Oh, no you don't. I wasn't done yet."

With one arm reaching up to press gently against my chest, the other pushed my legs apart again, and this time, his mouth joined his fingers in sending me hurtling to the stars above. I was so sensitive that it didn't take long before my next orgasm ripped through me, leaving me trembling all over again.

Before I could come to completely, I felt him looping one arm around my back and the other underneath my knees, lifting me as if I weighed nothing. *Again.*

He carried me down a dark hallway and used his shoulder to nudge open a half-closed door at the end of it. I couldn't make out much of what I assumed was his room, only that it was large and sparsely decorated just like the rest of the house seemed to be.

My attention was riveted on the bed, though. A massive thing with a broad, high headboard towering behind it. It looked plush and soft, the ambient light from the city and moon shining in from outside making spots of it look shiny.

That was about all I had time to absorb before I was deposited onto the mattress with far more care than I'd have expected from a man like Cyrus. Once he'd set me down, he looked at me from where he stood at the edge of the bed and slowly started working on his clothes.

When he finally stepped out of his black boxer briefs, his last remaining item of clothing, he licked his lips and wrapped his fist around his long hard shaft. In the low light, I could make out the shimmery wetness on his tip and a shiver raced down my spine. *I did that to him.*

Or rather, what he'd done to me had. Whatever the technicalities, I had been involved and I loved seeing the evidence of how much he wanted me.

Feeling bold and wanton, I sat up and whipped my dress over my head, throwing it into the depths of the darkness beyond his bed. In only my bra, I sat up on my knees and beckoned him over.

Cyrus muttered a string of curses but came to me as if I had him tied to the other end of a string I was holding. He walked over to me and got on his knees, the mattress dipping and moving as he did.

I had plans for what I wanted to do to him now, but his big hands cupped my face as soon as he was near enough, and he pulled me in for a deep kiss as he pressed his hard body to mine. We made out just like that, both on our knees on his bed as we devoured each other and touched wherever we could before he finally lay down on his back and brought me with him.

"Ride me, baby. I want to watch you come all over my cock as many times as you can." His voice was so rough that the need in it was almost palpable.

Moaning as I tugged my lip between my teeth, my head fell back and I wasn't even on him yet.

"Yeah," Cyrus grunted. "Just like that, only I want you to do it on top of me."

"Smartass," I mumbled, but I couldn't really muster any heat behind the words. I was too far gone to care about his smart mouth, except of course for whatever dirty things were going to spill from his lips next. "Condom?"

"Nightstand."

Surprisingly, the box I found was still closed. I didn't want to think about it right now, though, so I just tore it open as fast as I could, extracted one of the ragged-edged packages, and bit it open before rolling the latex down his length.

As I sank down on him, my hands found my breasts and I pinched my nipples as I heard him moaning beneath me. His muscles were tense and his jaw was clenched so tightly, I'd have thought he was filled with red-hot rage if I hadn't known it was red-hot lust instead.

Encouraged by his expression and the feel of him stretching me out and filling me up in the best way, my hips started moving and didn't stop until I was falling apart around him just like he'd told me to.

"Fuck, Luna. Baby. Yes. Fuck." Cyrus gripped my thighs in a vise, his voice strained before I felt him pulse deep inside me. His entire body shook and his eyes screwed shut as his neck arched.

Sexiest view ever.

I collapsed on top of him when my muscles relaxed, staying like that until he finally rolled us over.

He kissed my forehead, then hovered above me. "I'm just going to go get cleaned up. Be back in a minute."

After taking care of the condom, he came back to bed and arranged us so I was lying against his side.

"I didn't get to see much of it, but your house looks awesome," I said when my breathing finally returned to normal and my heart no longer felt like it was flying out of my chest. "Want to give me a tour?"

Cyrus shook his head against the pillow. I felt more than saw the movement from where I was cradled with my head in the crook of his neck. I was using his arm as a pillow, but the bottom of his actual pillow rested against the top of my head.

"Let's do it in the morning. I'm really not in the mood to get up right now." He burrowed deeper into his mattress and draped his dark charcoal sheets over our naked bodies.

I looked up at him, his strong profile illuminated only by the moonlight filtering in between his bamboo blinds. "Do you mean you want me to sleep here?"

"Sure. If you haven't got any other plans, why not? I mean, I'll take you home if you really want to go, but you need to tell me soon. I'm about to fall asleep."

"No, it's fine. Go to sleep. I'll get the tour in the morning. Then I'll go home." I felt his breathing even out a minute later, but I didn't fall asleep quite as fast.

Instead, I let my mind drift to the day we'd had together, to everything I'd learned about him and the events that had led us to sleeping in his bed together. I wasn't entertaining any delusions about what this may mean or whether he'd changed his mind, though.

Cyrus was very vocal about what he wanted, and it wasn't a relationship. What we had together was fun, and I wasn't going to let his willingness to have a sleepover blur those lines for me.

Just because I was a romantic didn't mean I was naïve. Cyrus was a good guy underneath all the asshole. It felt like he was becoming a friend and the benefits weren't bad either. I couldn't start thinking that he was going to become anything more than that, and besides, all that was more than enough for me.

For now anyway.

When it ever stopped being enough, that would be the day I walked away.

CHAPTER 18

CYRUS

L una stirred in my arms, a slight smile on her lips even in sleep. *God, she's beautiful.*

She lay on her side, facing me with her pitch-black hair spread out over the pillow and comforter behind her. Her legs were entwined with mine and one of her arms rested over my abdomen.

Not wanting to wake her and still too lazy to move anyway, I rested my head back on my pillow.

In between watching her sleep and relishing having her in my bed, I made mental notes of everything I had to get done today.

There were no meetings on my calendar, but I had several ventures to check in on and a few others who had sent proposals I needed to sift through. None of it was too pressing, though, so I also ran through my kitchen inventory and wondered what we could make for breakfast.

Before I reached a decision, Luna's eyes blinked open. She stretched out like a cat, lazily pressing her breasts into the air and lifting one arm high above her head. For a beat, confusion marred her brow and then she remembered where she was.

"Good morning," she said, her voice thick and scratchy from sleep. She slid a hand under her cheek and brought her eyes to mine. "Have you been awake for long? You should have just kicked me in the shin or something to wake me up."

"I've only been awake a few minutes," I assured her, dipping my head down to catch her lips in a soft kiss.

She kissed me back, obviously not minding morning breath so much either. "Good morning to you, too."

Chuckling as she sat up and rubbed her eyes, she looked around the room. "What's the time? I should probably get ready to leave."

"Not yet." I wound my arms around her waist and put my head down in her lap, facing up. "I owe you a tour of the place, right? I'm also pretty sure I can manage to rustle something up for breakfast."

Looking down at me, her long lashes fanned out over her cheeks from this angle. "So you cuddle and you make breakfast? You're terrible at this one-night-stand thing. Aren't you supposed to kick me out before I've even had a chance to open my eyes properly?"

"One problem with that. It isn't a one-night thing. Don't tell me you've forgotten our first time already?" I smirked and reached for the soft skin of her inner thigh. "I'd be happy to jog your memory."

She squealed when my fingers tickled her, and wormed her way out from underneath me. "I may not know what the time is, but if you're serious about breakfast and a tour, I don't think we have time for memory jogging this morning. Sadly."

"Okay then." I shrugged one shoulder against the warm mattress before rolling over. "Your loss. Up and at 'em it is."

Luna grabbed my shirt from the floor, slipped it on, waited for me to grab a pair of pajama pants from my dresser, and motioned for me to lead the way. I paused at the door, eyes raking over her bare legs and my shirt covering up her curves. "You look sexy as fuck in that. It's really not fair, considering you just told me we don't have time for another round."

Laughing as she ran her hands up and down the length of her torso, she batted her eyelashes. "What? This old thing? I guess I could go shower and cover up properly before breakfast if you insist."

"Don't you dare." I grabbed her hand and led her out of the room before she could make good on her threat. "Stop talking crazy. I enjoy starting my Mondays with a case of blue balls."

"In that case, remind me to shimmy later. Unless twerking is more your thing? Personally, I don't think it's super sexy, but I'm happy to help you start your week out right, however you prefer."

I groaned. "Trust me. None of those extras are necessary."

We stepped out of the hallway into the main room and she stopped dead in her tracks, pulling me to a halt as well.

"This is the billionaire's version of a bachelor pad then, huh?" she asked as her eyes tracked around the room. "A TV half the size of my bed, couches, a bar and one rug."

"It's one hell of a rug," I said, eyeing the navy blue and light gray monstrosity that covered a generous portion of my open-plan living area.

The bar, TV room, dining room, and kitchen were separated only by weight-bearing pillars placed evenly throughout the room. Jenny had insisted that I needed something to give the place some warmth and, when she saw the rug, had declared that it would be a great start.

"It is. I feel like the gray floors and white walls would have felt a bit stark without it." Luna gave me a playful nudge with her foot. "Tell me, is there a Bachelors-are-us store somewhere that sells these dark leather couches and giant TVs?"

"Yeah, there's one right around the corner actually. You should pop in sometime. They have great specials on hardwood bar counters and stools."

She laughed, the light and melodic sound amplified by my high ceilings and lack of general decor.

Peter had helped me choose some artwork shortly after I'd moved in and there were mirrors with thick black frames that had been here when I bought the place, but other than that, the walls were bare.

One entire wall was made of stackable glass doors and opened up onto a large balcony. Luna headed toward it, trailing her fingers just about an inch away from the glass as she walked from one side to the other.

"Is that a hot tub out there?" She shot me a look over her shoulder, eyes lit with excitement and maybe a little bit of heat again. "Can we try it sometime?"

"If we do, it'll be the first time it gets used since I bought this place."

"Really?" She frowned, wrapping a lock of loose hair around a finger and twisting it absently. "Why?"

I shrugged. "I'm just not a big fan."

"But you've got such a beautiful view. I mean there's the city, park, and water. What could be better than relaxing in your private hot tub with a cold drink on a warm summer night?"

"Uh." I flicked my finger toward the air conditioning unit. "Lying on the couch underneath that with a cold drink in my hand. No water, no humidity."

"Do you have zero sense of adventure?" She turned away from the window and came to stand in front of me. Instead of putting her hands on my chest, purring, or attempting any of the other methods of seduction I'd been treated to the morning after, she simply crossed her arms.

With her eyes on mine, she seemed to contemplate something before holding out a pinky finger to me. "If you and I are still friends by the time summer is in full swing, we're having a beer under the stars in that hot tub."

I linked my finger with hers, even though I couldn't remember the last time I'd been made to pinky swear on something, and added a condition of my own. "Fine, but only if you're naked for the duration of our dip."

Her lips parted in surprise and I practically saw the objections running through her mind before she shrugged. "Only if you're naked too and all the lights are off."

My hands snaked around her hips and I tugged her closer to me. "Now who doesn't have a sense of adventure?"

"There's a difference between having a sense of adventure and becoming an exhibitionist. I mean, to each their own, but that's just not my kink."

I freed the lock of hair she was still toying with and wrapped it around my own finger. "Pray tell, what is your kink then?"

Our mouths were so close together now that we were breathing the same air. My cock began hardening again just as Luna's eyes dropped to my lips. "At the moment, it's just you."

"Good. Because you're mine too. At the moment, like you said." I captured her lips with my own, drawing her in for a kiss that quickly escalated. It was only when I moved to lift her again that I remembered neither of us had eaten since the last time we'd done this.

Groaning into the kiss, I gently shook my head and lifted it away from hers. "We were going to make breakfast, remember?"

"Right," she said slightly breathlessly, sounding about as dazed as I felt.

My head didn't work right around this woman. At times, I could ignore it and focus. Especially when we had to talk about the wedding.

But we hadn't talked about that at all this morning and she was wearing only my shirt. I couldn't even blame myself for not being able to think straight.

Inclining my head toward the kitchen, I waited until she was a step ahead of me before adjusting myself and following behind her.

"I'm assuming Bachelors-are-us also regularly run specials on stainless steel appliances and industrial coffee machines?" Luna teased as she ran her fingers across the marble countertop.

Looks like she got her head back a lot quicker than I did. Fuck, I was still waiting for blood to resume a flow in the Northern direction and here she was right back to kidding. "Yeah, it's a two for one special. Buy a dishwasher, get the coffee machine with it."

"That actually sounds pretty good." She laughed, carefree and relaxed. As she settled with her hip against the counter, she looked around the space again. "This is a really nice place, Cyrus. Thanks for showing me around."

"As long as you don't go getting any ideas," I joked, but her face fell and her expression hardened.

"I don't care about your money or your house. I'm not interested in material things." She straightened up and jerked a thumb over her shoulder in the direction of my bedroom. "I have to go get dressed or I'm going to be late opening the shop. Thanks for offering to make breakfast."

She spun on her heel, very clearly offended by my comment. Stalking off to my room without a backward glance, Luna disappeared down the hallway.

I shouldn't have said that to her, but why do I even care if she's offended?

Before I could figure it out, Luna was dressed and breezing past me on her way to my front door. She lifted her hand in a wave. "Bye, Cyrus. See you when I see you."

The door slammed behind her. I was still standing right where she'd left me, holding a pan in front of my stove.

Rolling my lips into my mouth, I realized I wasn't hungry anymore. I stashed the pan back in its drawer and went to take a shower.

If I'd expected it to clear things out for me, it didn't work. By the time I was dressed and ready to go, I was still confused.

There was only one person I could think of that might be able to help me make sense of this, and that was my brother. A glance at the watch on my wrist told me he'd be at work by now, so that was where I headed.

Gallagher Plumbing and Electrical where Peter worked operated out of the basement of an old warehouse. I'd always found their offices surprisingly bright and cheerful and the people were so friendly they made me uncomfortable.

I found my brother on the stairs descending into their offices, his toolbox in hand as he chatted with one of his coworkers. His brows rose in surprise when he saw me. Then a frown tugged them together.

"Hey, bro. What's up? What are you doing here?"

"Brought you some coffee." I held out the cup I'd picked up from a truck down the street. "Do you have a minute?"

"Of course." He said goodbye to the other guy, who gave me a friendly wave before jogging down the last few stairs into their office.

Peter took the coffee from me and sat down on a low wall

surrounding a patch of flowers beside the stairs. "Thanks for the coffee, but I'm assuming you didn't come here just to fortify me for the day ahead."

I sighed and dragged a hand through my hair before taking a seat next to him. "No, I think I fucked up."

"What did you do this time?" He gave me a side-eye as he blew into his cup. "And to whom?"

After giving him a rundown of what had happened earlier, I took a sip of my coffee and shook my head. "It was a joke, kind of, but she knows where we stand. I don't know why she got so offended."

"Seriously?" His brows knitted so tightly together, I wasn't sure if he'd ever look normal again. Then he let out a dry sounding laugh. "You're so full of shit sometimes."

"Why?"

His light green eyes opened wide and his jaw slackened before it tightened. "Because not everyone cares about money, dude. I know they do in your world, but this chick doesn't sound like she lives in that world. If anything, she lives in mine, and down here on the working-class level, we care about making ends meet."

"But—"

Peter held up his callused hand, already showing signs of having had grease on it at some point in the morning. "I've never taken you up on any of your offers for money and it doesn't sound like this girl would either. To her, as someone who doesn't know what you've been through these last few years since you made your money, you just sounded like an insensitive dick."

"All women want money," I said. "Just because *you* haven't taken mine doesn't mean *they* don't want it."

His brows jumped up as he got to his feet, his eyes narrowed and his head shaking. "If that's really what you think, you're so much more jaded than even I gave you credit for, man. When you really think about it, has this girl ever given you a reason to think she's just after you for your money?"

Peter didn't wait for me to answer. He just picked up his toolbox and tapped two fingers against his temple. "Think about it, bro. Once you get your head out of your ass, I hope you've got a fucking good apology ready because you're going to need it."

Watching him walk away, I took another sip of my coffee and turned everything he'd said over in my head. If I was being honest with myself, Luna never had given me the impression she wanted my money at all.

As hard of a time as I had believing that I may have found the one woman in this city who didn't want a piece of my bank balance more than they wanted me, I had to admit that Luna seemed different. Like maybe, just maybe, she really didn't give a fuck about money.

CHAPTER 19

LUNA

A blonde woman with French tips and a salmon-pink dress pranced into my store a short while after I opened it. She had her eyes glued to the screen of her phone but snapped her fingers in the air as if rudely requesting a check from a server.

"I need twenty-four bunches of pearl-white roses for a wedding," she barked in a clipped tone. "Can you help me?"

Narrowing my eyes as I tried to determine if I'd ever seen her before, I waited until she glanced up from her phone. "Twenty-four, you say? That's a lot. When is the wedding?"

"A couple of weeks." She planted both hands, one with her phone still in it, on her hips. "Can you help me or not?"

Something about her made me skeptical. I didn't know what it was, but it left me feeling uncharacteristically unhelpful. "No, I don't think so. Pearl white isn't a common color. An order would have had to be placed weeks ago for the quantity you want."

If I'd been so inclined, I probably could have helped her. Truth be told, an order of that size, of that species, and on such short notice would have meant making a pretty penny, but I just couldn't find it in me to agree to do it for her.

Her bright blue eyes became slits as she gave me a sharp glare. "Are you saying you can't do it?"

I lifted my shoulders on a shrug and pressed my lips together as I shook my head. "I don't believe I can. Best of luck trying to find someone who can."

Blood rushed to her face and she turned an unnatural shade of red. "I have money, you know? I can pay whatever it's going to cost, but I won't be paying it to you now."

She stomped a high-heeled foot on the floor like an entitled toddler dressed up in her mother's clothes and then marched out of the store, slamming the door behind her.

I let out a deep breath, frowned at her retreating back through the window, and went back to the work I was busy with on my computer. Open on the screen was a spreadsheet I'd compiled outlining my loan, repayments, interest, and projected targets for the next few months. In another column, I had the actual targets I'd need to make to be able to keep up with the payments.

Darn it. I shouldn't have sent her business elsewhere.

There was far too much red on the screen for comfort. If I didn't exceed my projected target every month—and I'd set them on the higher side of what I could expect to reach as it was—I was in a world of trouble.

Half considering hauling my behind out of the shop and down the street to call the customer back, I was stopped by the bell above the door tinkling again. When I looked up this time, a graying man in an ill-fitted suit stood just inside the shop.

He looked around like he was surprised at what he saw, then cleared his throat when his eyes landed on me. "Ms. Willet?"

"That's me." My throat tightened. This guy looked like a lawyer, a banker, or some other profession that could only spell bad news. "What can I do for you?"

"I'm with Capital Finance," he said and my throat tightened even further. "You took out a loan with us some time ago."

"Yes," I practically squeaked as I tried to force my voice through my constricted airways. "Is there a problem?"

His thin lips lifted in a sympathetic smile. "No, not a problem as such. I'm here to make a courtesy call."

"A courtesy call?" My chin lowered as my shoulders came forward. I had no doubt I looked like a scared little mouse, but I didn't care. Banks didn't just make courtesy calls for nothing and I had a feeling I was about to have the carpet yanked out from underneath me.

"Yes." He pulled a handkerchief out of his pocket and dabbed at his forehead. "We're at a point where we have to increase the rate of interest on your loan."

"What?" I croaked. "Why?"

At least he had the decency to look genuinely sorry. "It's tough times out there. We all have our parts to play. This is mine."

"Is there anything I can do to stop this?" Black spots danced in my vision. "I'm barely keeping up as it is. I just can't afford to pay more."

He held up a perfectly smooth palm to stop me. "You shouldn't tell me things like that. I know it's going to be hard, okay? That's why we're going around making these personal courtesy calls. You'll be able to plan for the hike, and hopefully, that will make things easier."

"But I—"

"I'm sorry, miss. There really isn't anything I can do." He dabbed his brow again and shot me another tight smile. "Good luck, Ms. Willet. This truly is a beautiful store. I hope you do find a way to keep up with the repayments."

Giving me a shallow bow, he ducked out of the store. I blinked after him, my eyes filling with tears.

Just when I thought my day couldn't get any worse, Cyrus's face popped up outside my window and he held up two cups. With a heavy sigh, I wiped at my eyes to make sure he wouldn't see I was on the verge of crying and frowned when he stepped into the store.

"It's tea," he said. "Not coffee."

"Okay." Well, as much of a jerk as he could be, I guessed the silver lining was that he'd remembered what my first choice in hot beverages was. "Thanks."

"What's wrong?" Concern tightened the corners of his eyes as they swept over the expression on my face. He handed over the tea, taking a step closer to me to do it and then bringing his hand to my shoulder. "What happened?"

"Nothing you need to worry about. Just a bad day. What are you doing here?" My voice was flat, but I couldn't help it.

Snippets of my conversation with the banker kept playing over and over again in my mind. I could practically see the red notices being slapped against my door right now.

Cyrus kept his vivid green eyes on mine, seemingly warring between pushing me to find out what was really going on and letting it go. Thankfully, he chose the latter.

"Okay, well, if you want to talk about it, you know I'm here." His hand dropped away, and despite how we'd left things earlier, I still missed his touch almost instantly.

"What do you want, Cyrus? Is this about the wedding? Because I'm not really feeling up to it right now."

"It's not," he said, his shoulders slumping as he huffed out a breath. "It's about what happened this morning."

"What about it?" I walked back around my counter, needing to put some distance between us. Being too close to him muddled my brain with hormones, which was the last thing I needed right around now.

Cyrus strode up to the other side of the counter, set down his cup, and braced his hands against the concrete top. "I was a dick this morning and I'm sorry."

Arching both my eyebrows, I folded my arms. "Is that a real apology or do you just need my help today?"

"I don't, okay? It's not because I need help. I mean it. I was an asshole and it was uncalled for."

Something that had knotted in my stomach this morning started loosening at his apology. I felt the fight draining out of me. I just didn't have the energy for it right now.

"It was, and you were, but bringing me a tea isn't going to make up for it." After all the times I'd insisted on paying my own way since I'd known him, I'd been genuinely hurt by his insinuation that I was somehow after his money.

I'd also been perfectly clear about my expectations of our relationship, and not once had I hinted at wanting anything more, never mind moving into his cold palace of Bachelorhood. Cyrus had the good sense to look properly chagrined, only the very tops of his cheeks turning just one shade darker.

But still, it was something.

He flashed me a sheepish grin and lifted his shoulders. "I know, which is why I came prepared with something so much better than tea. I have to make a trip to Italy next month and I wanted to know if you wanted to come with me. Free of charge, of course."

"Your way of making up for a comment about how I'm after your money is an offer to spend more of it on me? So what, if I accept, then that was what I was after all the time, and if I don't, then at least you took another shot of flaunting that you have so much money you'd be able to afford to take me with you?"

The words came out sharper than I'd intended, and something flashed in his eyes before they narrowed. It looked like he had a retort on the tip of his tongue, but then he scrubbed his hands over his face and relaxed his posture. "I should have thought through how to phrase that because you're right. That's exactly what it sounded like."

He rolled his eyes, but then his expression shifted as his lips curled into a gorgeous smile that showed off his rows of perfectly straight white teeth. "Okay, look. Let me try this again. I'm sorry for being a first-class dick to you this morning."

"Then why did you just roll your eyes?"

"That was at myself for coming across as a dick yet again and at you for assuming my offer wasn't genuine."

"Can you blame me?"

"No, but I can roll my eyes at both of us." He rounded the counter then and took one of my hands in his, stroking his thumb over my knuckles and watching the point of contact for a second before lifting his gaze to mine. "I'm going to Italy and I'd really like it if you could come with me. I was a real asshole and I'd like to make it up to you. Can't think of a better way to do it than Italy. I mean, come on."

I couldn't stop a smile from breaking through. His sandy brown

135

hair fell over his forehead and his eyes were softer than I could remember seeing them, his touch on my hand so gentle and sweet.

This was the man I'd spent hours flirting with and talking to, the one I felt was becoming my friend. The jerk on his high horse from this morning was nowhere to be seen and my resolve to stay mad at him crumbled.

Just a little.

"I'll think about it," I said.

His eyes swept down to my lips. "I can see that smile, you know?"

"I know, but it doesn't mean I'm going to say yes."

A soft sigh fell from his lips and warmed me from his close proximity. Nodding as he pressed a chaste, sweet kiss to each corner of my smile, he gave me another of his own.

"Yeah, I didn't think you were going to make this easy on me. That's okay, though. I was prepared for it. Promise you'll think about it?"

"I promise I'll think about it," I repeated.

"Okay, good." He let go of my hand and went to reclaim his cup from the other side of the counter. "I've gotta go, but I'll speak to you soon."

My head bopped up and down. Then he blew me a kiss and disappeared out the door. I sank down in my chair and pressed my forehead against the cool concrete of the counter, but despite the morning I'd had, I couldn't quite shake the smile from my face.

Freaking Italy. He was crazy, but I liked it.

Whether or not I ended up going with him, at least my day had definitely gotten significantly better after his visit.

CHAPTER 20

CYRUS

"We have three different packages to choose from," Andrea, a representative from the venue Luna and I were checking out, said. She had dark brown hair and her lips were painted in a very unappealing shade of plum.

Despite the fact that I was here with a woman and looking at a wedding venue, she kept running the tip of her tongue over her lip and shooting me these obscene little glances. It was ridiculous.

"Okay," Luna said, scooting to the tip of her chair. "Would you be able to walk us through each one?"

Our meeting was taking place in one of the conference rooms at the hotel we were looking at. The room was on one of the higher floors and opened up to a wide balcony with cocktail tables set out on it. If I had to guess, I assumed it was where the staff took their breaks.

Obviously, this woman hadn't been trying very hard to impress us when she'd booked this room, but that seemed to have changed as soon as I told her my name. She'd smoothed out the plum skirt of her uniform and assured us she'd give us a proper tour of the facility later, but that unfortunately the other, better meeting rooms were occupied.

I'd rolled my eyes at her, but Luna had tugged on my hand and convinced me not to walk out. After reminding me that this venue was one I'd actually chosen for us to look at, she'd given me a pointed look that said *behave* and then followed the not-nice lady into the elevator.

Andrea gave Luna a wide smile now and nodded. "Sure thing. Although I'm sure you two wouldn't be interested in our Bronze package. It's the lowest one," she added in a stage-whisper, following it up with an annoying giggle.

I opened my mouth to tell her we weren't looking for ourselves, but Luna cut me off. "Actually, we're interested in hearing about every package you have."

For the remainder of our discussion, Luna played along with the woman's assumption that we were the couple looking for a venue. She even put on an old, rich woman's voice and used words like "pish-posh" and "marvelous".

It was too entertaining watching her like this to worry about setting Andrea straight or about why Luna had played along in the first place.

When they were done talking about the different packages, Andrea sat back in her chair. "That's what we offer at each of the four different venues we have. There's the ballroom, the rooftop restaurant, the garden, or the balcony."

She flicked a finger at the balcony leading off of this room and let out that giggle again. "Not this one, of course. There's a much bigger, more suitable one several floors down."

"Let's have a look at them all," Luna suggested, then laced our fingers together and brought our joined hands up to plant a kiss on the back of mine. "What do you think, darling?"

"I think you're absolutely right." I curled my lips into what I'd been told was a charming smile and leaned over to kiss her temple. *Two can play this game.* "Whatever you want, dear."

Luna snorted in her attempt to hold back a laugh, then rolled her eyes at me when Andrea's back was turned. To be fair, her demeanor had changed since Luna had decided to play along. She no longer looked at me like she wanted a bite of me.

"Right this way, Mr. and soon-to-be Mrs. Coning." She held the door for us and led us down a richly carpeted hallway to an elevator.

"I'm surprised I haven't read about your engagement," Andrea said as we stepped in. "Given my line of work, I keep a close eye on the announcements."

"We haven't made an announcement," Luna said without skipping a beat, then gave her a simpering sweet smile. "We'd prefer to keep it quiet. I trust we can count on your discretion?"

"Of course." She looked affronted that Luna even needed to ask. "I was simply surprised I hadn't read about it."

Yeah, because even though I'm known to be reclusive, I'm still on the eligible bachelor lists. Whoop-dee-doo.

Changing gears, Andrea pressed the button for the top floor. "Let's start at the rooftop restaurant and work our way down from there."

"Sounds good," Luna said.

It had been a week since I'd invited her to Italy, but she staunchly refused to talk about it. While she and Andrea walked around the restaurant once we got off the elevator, I trailed along next to her and wondered why she hadn't answered me yet.

It was a no-brainer if anyone asked me. An all-expenses-paid trip to Italy? *I mean, come on.*

Once again, though, Luna hadn't acted at all like I'd have expected her to. At this stage of our relationship, she'd shown me to expect the unexpected when it came to her, but I still hadn't been prepared for this.

It's fucking Italy! Venice, baby.

But no.

Luna could spend hours looking for a wedding venue for a couple she didn't know, but she refused to take ten minutes to talk to me about the trip. It was a little infuriating, but for some crazy reason, it was also hot. So I left it alone.

Andrea showed us the other three venues, and by the time she was done with the tour, I'd had enough time to stew about it that I was horny as fuck and wondering if she'd let me take her in one of the rooms here.

"Okay." Andrea clapped her hands and offered Luna a bright smile. "Please feel free to take a look around yourselves and let me know if you have any questions. There are some services we offer that aren't part of the packages, but that we can arrange for you. Flowers, for—"

"We're all good on flowers, thanks," I said. "Thank you for the tour. We'll let you know if we have any questions."

We'd ended said tour in the garden, and as soon as Andrea left, I slid my hand into Luna's and pulled her around a corner where we were away from the prying eyes of all those on the balconies. We were also covered by a large bush on one side and the hotel's outer wall on the other.

"What are you—"

I cut her off by claiming her mouth with mine, walking forward until her back hit the wall. I broke the impact with my arms around her waist, kissing her hungrily as I caged her body against the hotel.

She was breathless by the time she managed to break the kiss, a naughty smile playing at the corners of her lips. "What was that for? Since when does wedding planning get you hot?"

"Who says it got me hot?" It was a stupid question and I knew it. When she reached down to cup my rock-hard cock through my slacks, I dropped my forehead against hers and groaned. "It wasn't the wedding planning. I swear. It was just you. It's been days since I've been inside you, Luna. Days."

"Days?" She gasped in mock surprise and ran her palm up and down my shaft, making me hiss when she suddenly removed her hand. "Okay, I get it. I'll come over soon, I promise, but we can't do this here. Anyone could see us."

"As far as the only person who knows who we are in this hotel is concerned, we're a newly engaged couple hunting for a venue. I'm sure she'll understand if we get caught fooling around in the garden."

Luna laughed but shook her head and put some more space between us by ducking out from under my arms and stepping away from the wall. "Maybe she would understand, but I've told you before that I'm not interested in exhibitionism."

I slammed my fist into the brick and dragged in a deep breath, then forced thoughts about rotting garbage and clubbing baby seals through my head until my erection waned. "Fine, but never say I don't respect your wishes."

"I never would," she said. "In case you were thinking about using this little incident against me later, just remember that I was in no way teasing you at all today. I was simply there and you got horny. No need to take it out on me."

I couldn't help but chuckle and wag my brows at her. "Yeah, we'll see. Anyway, if we're not going to have a quickie, can we get out of here?"

"We need to talk about the venue first and see if there's anything specific in any of the venues here we like. Otherwise, we might just end up having to come back."

I squeezed the back of my neck but nodded and led her to a small metal table placed in the garden. In full view of all those prying eyes I'd been trying to escape, thank you very much. I really was trying not to push her on the public-sex thing.

"What do you think?" she asked as she extracted some pamphlets Andrea had given her from her purse.

"I like it. As far as I'm concerned, it's between the garden and the rooftop. The view from up there is incredible and I think Jenny would like to have the ceremony in a garden."

Luna looked impressed, widening her eyes as she dipped her head to the side. "You were actually paying attention? Because it kind of looked like you were stuck in your own head while we were on that tour."

"I was, but I'm very good at assessing things while thinking about others. What do you think?"

She sighed and lifted her shoulders as a sad smile spread on her lips. "I like it too, but it's outside of the price range we were given. The only reason I even came here was because you insisted, but it's not within budget, so it's a no. I was actually hoping that lower package of theirs would be in the budget, but even that is way above what they can afford."

"But you like it?" I made a vague gesture toward the building. "Out of all the venues we've looked at, do you like it best?"

She chewed her lip but eventually nodded. "Yes, I do. It's gorgeous. I love that the ceremony could take place in a garden as lush as this. It really feels like we've escaped the city when we're down here, but then the rooftop has that classic urban, city-wedding feel to it. I really do love it."

"Then we'll take it."

Luna let out an exasperated sigh and frowned at me. "No, we won't take it. I literally just told you it's not in budget. Those are a real thing, you know? Budgets."

"I know." I rolled my eyes at her and sat back. "I need to get them a gift anyway and I think this would be a nice one."

"You want to get them their venue as a wedding gift?" she asked slowly, her eyes widening as far as they could go. Then she laughed. "Two things. Firstly, only you. Secondly, good luck with that, buddy."

"Thanks." A smirk curved on my lips. "I'm taking both of those as compliments. Anyway, what are you doing tonight? Want to come over?"

"I can't. I'm sorry." She averted her gaze and dropped it to her lap. "I've got to work out a few things for the shop, but soon. Is that okay?"

"Yeah, of course." If she had to work, it really was okay.

Not for the first time, though, I had a feeling there was something she wasn't telling me. It had been pretty clear the other day that she was upset, but I'd stuck to my guns not to interfere in her business if she didn't want me to know what was going on.

I couldn't help wondering what it was, though. For some reason, it was really starting to bug me that she hadn't talked to me about it, even if she had no obligation to tell me and I had no right to know.

What the fuck is wrong with me?

CHAPTER 21

LUNA

The scent of chicken and potatoes grilling in the oven wafted through April's apartment, children's songs Adi loved playing on the TV. I sat on the floor in the living room with the little girl, both of us staring hard at the puzzle pieces spread out on the coffee table.

April flipped through the magazine on the couch, getting up every so often to check on dinner. "Are you two making any progress?"

Adi looked at the piece she held in her hand, then pursed her lips. "No, Mommy. I think this one is too difficult."

"It's not too difficult, honey. We'll figure it out." I slipped a piece into place. The picture on the box was of a beautiful country cottage set against a forest, and while it wasn't exactly an easy one, Adi and I loved to challenge ourselves by building these. "It's just the outer edge giving us some trouble because it's grass and forest. As soon as we move on to the cottage and the ducks in front of it, we should be okay."

Adi sighed at the piece in her hand again but then nodded. "You're right. We'll figure it out. We always do. Have I told you about Todd?"

My ears perked up and I exchanged a look with April, who was trying to hide her smile. "No. Who's Todd?"

"He's a new boy in my class," she said, her tone becoming almost dreamy. "He moved here from Arizona. Did you know Arizona is in the desert?"

"Yeah, I did." I smiled at her and leaned forward a little, lowering my voice. "Do you like Todd?"

Adi paused for a beat, then flushed beet red and nodded. "I think I do. Mommy says it's okay to have a crush at my age. Do you have a crush on anyone? None of my friends have crushes."

"None of your friends have crushes they've told you about," April said gently. "You haven't told them about your crush, either. Remember?"

"I guess so," she said, her teeth sinking into her lip as she looked expectantly at me. "So do you have a crush?"

An image of Cyrus that day when he asked me to go to Italy with him jumped into my mind. He'd looked so darn handsome and sweet.

It was more than that, though. I loved how playful and gentle he could be with me when he was generally so commanding and alpha with everyone else.

Unfortunately, I knew I wasn't allowed to have a crush on him. "No, not at the moment. I have had crushes in the past, though. Do you want to tell me about Todd?"

She nodded enthusiastically, then proceeded to spend the next ten minutes telling me everything there was to know about Todd from Arizona. When she was done, my heart was practically bursting with excitement for her. "He sounds like quite a catch, sweetheart. You have good taste."

"Unlike the two of us," April murmured, but Adi didn't catch it in all her excitement. Eventually, she jumped up to go wash her hands before dinner and left April and me alone.

I sighed wistfully as I popped my chin down on my elbow where I sat cross-legged on the carpet. "I hope I have a daughter someday. You're so lucky to have her."

April set the magazine down on her legs. "If you want a daughter so badly, you can always have Adi."

She came back into the room at that exact moment and made the same face that April made so often, which made my friend sigh. "Fine. You can't have Adi. She's all mine."

"Gee, thanks, Mom," she retorted.

April chuckled and caught Adi's wrist as she walked past, pulling her down into her lap and tickling the little girl until she was limp from laughing so hard. "It was just a joke, pretty baby. You know I'd never really give you away."

Adi gasped for air and tried to swat her mother's fingers away from her as she squirmed. "Maybe I'll give you away."

"Maybe you should." April threw her head back as she joined in her daughter's laughter. The two of them made the perfect picture of happiness, despite the occasional difficulty in their circumstances.

Unable to resist, I picked my phone up off the table and snapped a quick shot of them, then texted it to April before locking the device again. I giggled at their antics as they wrestled on the couch, April let Adi get some tickling in as well before she lifted her hands in surrender.

"I give up. I give up." Adi punched the air in victory, hopping off her mother's lap and taking a lap around the room.

April's brown eyes sparkled with laughter. "Okay, okay. Jeez. We get it. You won. Come on back over here quick, would you?"

Adi eyed her suspiciously but did as she asked. When she got close enough, April took both of her hands. "You know I love you, right?"

"Right."

"Then you know that everything I say comes from a place of love?"

"Sure." Adi frowned. "Why?"

April pointed toward the bathroom. "Because I'm about to say you're a big liar who hasn't washed her hands yet. I didn't hear the tap and you weren't away nearly long enough to have washed them."

Adi opened her mouth to argue, but when April arched a brow, she let out a deep sigh and hung her head as she marched out of the room again.

April tapped the side of her nose. "I know things."

"We've already established you have Mom powers," I said as I stood up and brushed off my behind. "We've also already established that Mom powers are better than superpowers every day of the week."

April got to her feet as well, then reached out to squeeze my arm. "You're going to be a great mother someday. Just, you know, get the sperm from the donation bank so you don't have to deal with a man who had to ejaculate for you to get it."

I wrinkled my nose and groaned. "Thanks for that lovely visual."

"Hey, you're the only one around here getting some on the regular, so don't give me that. Don't pretend you've never seen a man ejaculate. I bet you've seen it at least once this week."

"Not this week actually." I sighed. "I've been really busy at the shop."

I didn't elaborate because I didn't want her to worry, but I'd spent most of my nights this week in front of my computer. Trying to come up with ways to reach my targets wasn't as easy as I hoped it might be, and in the meantime, all that red on the spreadsheet kept blinking at me.

"Uh oh," April said, eyebrows raised. "Trouble in paradise already?"

"It's not paradise and there's no trouble with Cyrus." Except that he wanted to take me to Italy and I didn't know how to turn him down without telling him I couldn't close up shop for an entire week. Especially not now.

I also couldn't afford to hire someone to stand in for me while we'd be gone, so I was bang out of luck with that trip. April narrowed her eyes at me. "What's going on then? Why haven't you seen him this week?"

"I've seen him. I just haven't hooked up with him for a few days." In fact, it had now been almost a whole week since the last time we'd slept together. Not for lack of trying on his part, but I was struggling with putting my worries aside for long enough to take him up on any of his invitations to come over.

My best friend clearly wasn't buying what I was trying to sell, though. "I thought all you had with this dude was a friends-with-benefits relationship. So where are all the benefits?"

"They're..." I tried to think of a way to answer her that wouldn't

146

make her suspicious but came up blank. "They're just on hold for a while. We're both super busy at the moment."

"Too busy to fuck?"

"April," I admonished her, sending a pointed stare down the hallway. "Adi's going to be back at any moment."

"That girl washes her hands more thoroughly than a surgeon before he, or she, performs open heart surgery. That's how I knew she hadn't washed them earlier. Don't worry. We have time."

"Yeah, well, there's nothing to talk about anyway. Like I said, we've seen each other. Everything is fine. We're still friends. We just haven't gotten together for anything outside of wedding planning this week."

"How are things going with you two then?" She crossed her arms but jerked her head to show me she wanted me to follow her to the kitchen.

"It's good. Like I said, we're just friends who hook up from time to time. It's actually really going well."

April got some plates and silverware out, shooting me a look as she handed it over so I could set the table in the breakfast nook while she got back to the food. It was an almost seamless routine for us by now.

"I know it was my idea to sleep with him, but I didn't mean you should keep doing it. You know that, right?"

I frowned at her as I set out the plates. "What are you talking about? Why shouldn't we keep doing it? I just told you it's going really well. We have a lot of fun together and he really is a friend."

April sighed and stopped moving after pulling the tray out of the oven. She turned in place to look at me, her protective mittens coming up to grip the back of her neck.

"That's a terrible relationship for you to be in. Sooner or later, you're going to want something more. Fucking a really hot friend repeatedly without developing feelings isn't easy, Luna. Not even for me. Why do you think I never sleep with anyone I actually like?"

"That's ridiculous." I set the silverware down with a clatter and rolled my eyes at her. "This is the first time that I'm happy with someone without any delusions of it being or becoming something more. Trust me. I've got this. I've even already got my exit point planned if it should ever come to that."

Worry clouded April's eyes. "I just hope it's not the other one who has delusions then."

I stared at her for a beat, then burst out laughing. "Cyrus? No. You can trust me on that, too. He's not the type to harbor any of that particular kind of delusion. Stop worrying about us, April. We're fine. I swear it. Totally and completely delusion free."

CHAPTER 22

CYRUS

There was something seriously wrong with me. It was the only thing that explained why I was driving all the way over to Luna's shop to invite her to dinner when I could have just texted her.

I parked in her loading area around the back of her shop, reflecting briefly on the day I'd met her when she'd been arguing with that delivery driver right there, but then pushed the memories back and let myself in.

More and more often these days, I found myself having to push thoughts and memories of her aside. *Fucking only one woman for an extended period of time is messing with my head.*

I knew it, but I had zero motivation to do anything about it. Late one night earlier this week, Luna had turned me down again.

Frustrated that she kept dodging me and wouldn't tell me what it was about, I'd considered calling up one of my regular hookups from before I'd met Luna. Janet was a flight attendant who had texted me that very morning telling me she was in town for a night.

As I'd started typing up a reply, knowing that she'd have been there in the blink of an eye if I'd actually sent it, I deleted it instead. Needless to say, I was confused as fuck about what was going on with me.

If I hadn't known any better, I'd have thought I was developing feelings for Luna. Since that was out of the question, I chalked it up to spending so much time with her lately—both in and out of bed.

Luna was startled when I emerged through her inner door, pressing her hand to her heart when she realized it was me. "Holy crack in a reindeer-shaped cracker. What are you doing here and why did you come in through the back?"

"I like to use the back door from time to time." I couldn't help the smirk that formed on my lips or the wink that followed.

Luna's brows rose and she shook her head fast as she let out a nervous-sounding laugh. "Not with me, you don't. Still doesn't answer my other question. What are you doing here? We didn't have plans to meet up today."

"No, we didn't," I said and closed the door behind me before sauntering over to her. She was behind the counter, but I figured we were way past the point where she stayed behind it and I was on the other side.

Walking right around it like I had so many other times now, I slid my hands up her back and into her loose hair, then angled her head and brought mine down to greet her properly.

Our kiss was almost bruising in its intensity, Luna's arms winding around my neck as if she, too, was operating on pure instinct instead of what was best at this stage.

When I eventually broke the kiss, her nipples were hard under her soft pink T-shirt, her lips were swollen, and both of us were breathing a little harder than normal. I flashed her a grin and nipped at her lower lip. "See, now that's a good, 'hello, buddy.' What's with all the 'what are you doing here' stuff?"

"That's not how one says hello to a buddy." She tried to level me with a glare, but it just made me laugh.

While Luna could be pretty damn fierce when she wanted to be, right now, she just kind of looked like a kitten who had slipped on some fake claws. We were still so close together that I ran my nose along the length of hers. "It is when you've got the kind of relationship we do."

She rolled her eyes and shrugged. "Fair enough. What are you doing here, though? Or did you just get tired of waiting and decided to come claim a quickie in my arrangement room?"

"You know, I think that would be a way more fun arrangement to use that room for, but no. Well, it's not what I came for but if you're offering…"

"Oh my God, I wasn't offering." She laughed and put both of her hands on my chest. "It's just that you don't usually come by when we don't have plans."

"I was kind of hoping we were about to have plans, though." I took a deep breath and realized that we were standing much too close together. If a customer came in and saw this, Luna would never forgive herself for her lapse in professionalism.

"How so?" she asked.

Taking a step back, I ran a hand through my hair and forced my racing heart to calm the fuck down as I kept my eyes on those blue ones of hers.

Fuck. *Tropical ocean blue. I wonder if that's a thing. I—*

"Cyrus?"

I cleared my throat. "Peter and Jenny have invited me to dinner tonight. They asked me to bring you because they know you've been helping me with everything. They want to say thanks."

Luna paused, a guarded look entering her eyes. "Are you sure going won't make it weird between us? I mean, they know we're not dating or anything like that, right?"

"Absolutely. They know you're just a friend and that you're helping me. It won't make things weird. I promise."

"Okay then." A smile spread slowly across her lips, her eyes lighting up as she relaxed. "It would actually be pretty cool to finally meet them. I feel like I know them already and it's going to be so much easier to help you once I get a feel for who they really are."

"Great. They're really excited to meet you, too. I'll pick you up at six thirty?" *Why the fuck does my heart keep racing like that?*

Luna's smile spread even wider. "Sure, but would it make any difference if I reminded you that you really didn't have to come pick me up all the time?"

"Nope. I'll see you tonight." Before she could argue or my heart could randomly explode from whatever the fuck it was pulling in my chest, I got the hell out of there.

After spending the rest of the day checking out some potential new investments and having lunch with Jimmy to discuss the growth of his business, I went back home to get ready to pick Luna up.

Despite having gotten out of the shower literally two minutes before I put on my shirt, my palms were sweaty and my heart was thudding again. Although it wasn't quite racing like it had earlier, it was definitely up to something in there.

Scowling at myself as I thought back to the last time I'd felt like this, I realized that it had been when I'd taken the woman who had eventually become my wife on a first date. *Fuck that.*

I'd planned on dressing down for dinner with my brother and his fiancée, but I donned another suit instead. It was better this way, almost like it would help me keep my guard up around her.

Though fuck even knows why that's necessary. I shouldn't have been feeling any of these things at all.

Since I couldn't bring myself to call dinner off, considering that they were all really excited to meet one another, and I also still couldn't quite convince myself to text someone else to come over after, I decided to just roll with it. Whatever it was, it would blow over. That much, I was one hundred percent sure of.

When I got to Luna's apartment building, she was waiting again. A pretty, electric-blue sundress brought out the color of her eyes and complemented the shiny, loose waves of her hair. *Oh God, did I really just think that?*

"You're looking ridiculously smart for a dinner at your brother's house," she teased when I got out of the car to open the door for her. "Should I run back upstairs and grab some evening wear? Maybe my 'heart of the ocean' necklace?"

"You look perfect." The words were out before I could stop them.

Luna's forehead creased on a soft frown before she laughed it off. "Sure. So perfect. You look good, though, I'll give you that. You wear these suits so well."

"Thanks." I brushed a whisper of a kiss against her cheek and felt her shiver against me. I knew it wasn't because she was cold, though. Whatever chemistry had been brewing between us since day one seemed to have matured into something much more... dangerous.

Luna climbed into the passenger seat without another word, turning to face me once we got on the road. "Peter and Jenny, what are they like? I know we talk about them a lot, but what should I be expecting from them tonight?"

"A ton of questions. Definitely. But they're nice people, so they won't make you feel like you're facing the inquisition."

It was true, but then why did I feel like I might be after this? Peter knew Luna was just a friend. I'd made it clear to him again when he'd called with the invitation, but I knew he was hopeful my relationship with Luna would turn into something more.

Between the two us, Peter always had been the more optimistic one. Even when I'd sworn off all women just after the divorce, he'd been the one insisting it was just a temporary thing. He had this idea in his head that one day, I'd meet the right woman for me.

Given everything he knew about Luna and about how she was helping me, I suspected he thought she was the elusive and mysterious "one" he was more determined than ever I would eventually find.

Considering how I felt like I was about to introduce her to my mother when we pulled up to his house, I knew I was going to have to be careful to hide my nerves. If Peter so much as saw a tremor or a bead of sweat on me, he'd go into matchmaker mode faster than I could even blink.

That would be a very, very bad thing for him to do. Luna still hadn't answered me about Italy, hadn't slept with me in a week, and was a little more skittish about seeing me than she used to be. If Peter pushed things now, I might just lose her.

Why the fuck does that thought bother me so much?

CHAPTER 23

LUNA

I 'd lied to April.

Well, not *lied* lied, but just lied. Sort of.

It was true that I wasn't under any delusions about getting more with Cyrus. We had what we had and that was fine. What I had fibbed a little about was making it sound like I didn't sometimes *want* more from him.

I knew I wasn't going to get it, but that didn't stop me from thinking about it every once in a while. A prime example of such a time was when I walked into his brother and future sister-in-law's house.

Peter and Jenny must have been waiting for us because Cyrus had hardly shut off the engine of his fancy car when the front door to their small, suburban-looking single-family home was jerked open and the couple themselves spilled out onto their lawn.

Jenny was a beautiful, curvy woman with intelligent hazel eyes and long blonde hair. The photos Cyrus had shown me of her to prove it wasn't his wedding really hadn't done her justice.

She was tucked under the arm of a man who had to be Cyrus's brother. Even if I hadn't known who we were having dinner with and even without having seen him in the pictures, I'd have been able to tell the two were related.

The sandy brown hair, the green eyes, and even the shape of those eyes matched too perfectly for them to be anything other than related. There were also obvious differences, though.

Peter's face held the finest lines around his mouth and eyes. I knew he was the older brother, but those lines also made it clear that he was the one who was more carefree, who laughed often and wholeheartedly.

His skin was also more tanned and his hair a little messier, giving him a more rugged appearance than his brother. When he shook my hand, his palm was also rougher. Calluses born from at least a decade in a blue-collar industry.

"Luna, it's so great to finally meet you," he said, stepping away from his fiancée and clasping my hand in a gentle but firm grip. "It's about time, too. I hear you've been putting in some hard hours with Cyrus to plan the wedding."

"It's been my pleasure," I assured him, giving him a smile of my own.

Jenny took his place when he stepped away, but instead of shaking my hand, she threw her arms around me and wrapped me in a tight, warm hug. "I'm so glad to finally get to meet you. Thank you so much for everything you're doing for us."

After only a brief pause, my arms wound around her and I hugged her like she was my long-lost best friend. "It's really no problem. I've loved every minute of it. Thank you for letting me help."

When she released me, she put her hands on my shoulders and pulled away to look into my eyes. Hers were misty with unshed tears and she swallowed once before speaking again.

"You've been an absolute angel. Cyrus would have been lost without you. I'm pretty sure we'd have ended up getting married in the bar if not for you."

"Hey, the bar would have been a great venue," Cyrus said. "No one makes better wings and the beer's always cold."

Jenny shook off the emotion and popped a hand on her hip as she turned to face him. "I love the wings there, and the beer's good too, but there's no space for a dance floor, and I'm not sure Father James would have been happy marrying us in between stacks of beer kegs."

He shrugged, humor dancing in his bright irises. "Did you ask him? I'm sure we could have convinced him to do it. As for a dance floor, I've got one word for you: sidewalk."

Jenny rolled her eyes at him but then opened her arms and hugged him as well. Peter and Cyrus shook hands and exchanged a few quiet words with their heads bent together.

A warm, small hand landed on my elbow. Jenny raised a brow at her future husband and his brother and smiled at me. "Come on. Let's leave those two gossips and go inside. I wasn't sure what you liked to drink, so I made lemonade, margaritas, and put some water with cucumber slices in the fridge. What's your poison?"

"Margaritas." My answer came without any hesitation. I was going to need something stronger than cucumber water to get me through this.

Despite Cyrus's assurances that they knew the score between us, I had a feeling these two were in the post-engagement bliss stage where they just wanted everyone around them to couple up and be as happy as they were.

"A girl after my own heart." Her smile spread wider as she led me into their modest home. It was much more my speed than Cyrus's luxury penthouse. "Let me give you a quick tour so you know where to find the bathroom and all that. Also, Peter and I are terrible hosts. We're those people who tell you to make yourself comfortable and actually want you to do it."

"Sounds good." April and I were the same. "If you show me where to find a glass, I can refill it myself."

She shook her head and gave me a knowing look. "I'm sure Cyrus can manage to keep your glass full. What I meant was, kick up your feet, grab a snack, and make yourself at home."

"I can do that." I didn't bother with the comment about Cyrus keeping my glass full. If my suspicions were correct, nothing was going to deter these two in thinking we might either be together or on our way to getting together.

The front door opened up to a small but neat entrance hall, walls covered in pictures of the two of them and people I assumed were both their families. The frames were mismatched, and in between the pictures, there were quirky sayings about love and family also framed.

"Okay, so on the left is the TV and dining room. In front of us is the kitchen, and if you go down that hallway to the right, you'll find three bedrooms and two bathrooms. One is in our bedroom, which is right at the end. If there's someone in the guest bathroom, the second last door to the left, just use ours."

"Thanks, I'll keep that in mind."

Voices filling in the entrance hall once Jenny pulled me into the kitchen told me the men had finally entered the house as well. I still couldn't make out what they were saying, but Jenny turned the volume up on her own voice anyway.

She took a pitcher out of the fridge and poured our drinks into glasses she already had waiting. "So, how did Cyrus manage to con you into planning the wedding with him?"

"There was no conning necessary. I offered and he accepted. I adore weddings, and since I'm in the industry, I feel like I have a good grip on planning them."

"Have you thought about making it your profession?" she asked, hazel eyes warm as she handed me a glass.

"No, not really. Being a florist is my real passion." It was something to keep in mind, though. Maybe I could add assistance with wedding planning to my list of services to bring in extra cash. It could work. "I'll keep it in mind. I wouldn't ever want to stop being a florist, but I do enjoy event planning as well."

Jenny beamed at me. "From what I've heard and seen, you're really good at it. Plus, doing something on the side to earn a little bit more is everyone's dream, am I right?"

"Amen to that." I raised my glass in her direction and waited until she clinked hers against it. "What do you do? Cyrus told me both of you work really hard, but he's never really mentioned what you do."

"I'm a nurse at a community outreach clinic. Our shifts are insane, but at least we're only open during the day."

"Wow. That's really admirable work." My mom used to take me to one of those clinics when I was little. I'd always admired how hard the staff worked and remembered how horrified I'd been at how little they got paid when I first found out.

Suddenly, I had a much better understanding of why their budget was so strict, why they'd insisted on Cyrus helping them and not getting a wedding planner. I also felt even greater motivation to make theirs the most special wedding ever. "Peter's in plumbing, right?"

"Right." Jenny's chest swelled with pride as she spoke about him. "With his help, his company became subcontracted to the city a couple of years ago. It was a big win for them, and he's moved up some in the ranks there since, but the amount of maintenance they have to do makes for long hours."

"I can imagine."

"I'm sorry we haven't been able to help more with the wedding. I know it's not fair to expect Cyrus to do everything we've asked him to, but Peter insisted he wouldn't mind helping out, and our working hours are just too long to get it all done ourselves."

I walked up to her and took her hand, giving it a soft squeeze. "It really has been a pleasure. I totally understand. If I may ask, though, why is that date so important to you? Wouldn't you have liked to have some more time so you could be more involved yourself?"

A wistful smile spread on her lips. "It was my parents' wedding date. Neither of us want to wait another year and I really want to share an anniversary with them. They were so nauseatingly in love and they set the example of what I want out of my life with Peter. I couldn't think of a better way of kicking off our marriage than saying our vows on the same day they did."

"Oh, wow." My voice was strained, my own throat now closing up with tears. My eyes became wet, and I tried swiping below them before Jenny saw, but she did anyway.

Reaching out to squeeze my hand this time, she lifted her free index finger to wipe under her own eyes. "You really get it, don't you?"

"Yeah, I really do."

Before we could both break down into sobbing messes for love lost too soon and the profoundness of their chosen date, Jenny cleared her throat and nodded toward the door at the back of their kitchen.

"Let's go sit outside. I've set up a picnic table for us out there. It's too nice out to have dinner inside tonight."

Peter and Cyrus came into the kitchen and grabbed a beer each before all four of us made our way into their garden. It was small but well kept. Flower beds in bloom lined the white fence, and at the center of the mowed lawn was a wooden table that had a bright pink plastic cloth over it.

Plates, silverware, and napkins were already set on it. Down the middle of the table, Jenny had placed glass jars with electric candles in them.

The sun was setting above the towering tops of the trees beyond their garden, casting a warm glow over their yard. A contented sigh fell from my lips before I could stop it. *Yeah, this is definitely much more my speed.*

"This is perfect," I said to Jenny. "Thank you for inviting me."

"I wouldn't have had it any other way," she replied, then took Peter's hand and descended the three steps from their porch to the lawn.

Cyrus came to stand next to me. The back of his hand brushed mine, but he made no move to take it. "You okay? It looked like you guys were crying back there."

"I'm fine. We just had a moment," I said and then, because I had to lighten the moment, I teased him. "You wouldn't understand. It's a romantic thing."

"You and Jenny were getting romantic? Because I'd pay good money to see that." His eyes crinkled at the sides. "Peter probably wouldn't be too happy though. I'm not sure he'd be okay with sharing Jenny, even with you. He's convinced she's the love of his life."

"I'm convinced of that, too." I shoved him with my shoulder. "And

159

you know darn well I didn't mean we were getting romantic. I meant you've got to be a romantic at heart to understand why we got a little emotional and you have no romance in your heart."

"Thank fuck for that," he muttered, then jerked his head toward the table. "Shall we?"

"We shall." I took his elbow when he offered it, like he was escorting me into an award ceremony instead of a simple picnic dinner in his brother's backyard.

Peter watched our approach with interest but didn't mention how Cyrus wrapped his hand over mine in the crook of his elbow or how close we sat down to one another. He picked up the conversational ball first, asking about my shop, my hobbies, and just getting to know me.

Although I had heard so much about them, I enjoyed asking them about their lives too and soon felt like I'd known them both for years.

"Our office moved to East Alaska Street a couple years back," Peter said, the fine lines around his mouth deepening on his smile. "I love the look of confusion people get when I tell them we're in Alaska, Manhattan."

"I know, right?" I laughed. "I live on West Alaska and even the mailman gets confused sometimes."

"Really? You're only a few blocks away from my office then."

I nodded. "You know the old boardgame shop that's been converted into a Games Cafe now?"

"Yeah?"

"My apartment is in the same building. Our entrance is right around the corner from theirs."

"We should have a games evening there sometime," Jenny said, her shoulders pulling back and a competitive gleam entering her eyes. "I finally have another girl to be on my team. We're going to annihilate you."

"You like board games?" I asked, surprise and excitement mingling in my belly.

"Love them," she replied.

"I think I may have just found a new best friend." I lifted my palm for a high-five. "I feel the same, but the only other person I know who loves them as much as I do is six."

Jenny laughed and slapped my hand, then rubbed her palms together and eyed her fiancé evilly. "You two might just finally have some competition."

Peter scoffed and slung his arm over her shoulders. "You wish, babe. I love you, but Cy and I have been dominating every game one can play as a team our whole lives. No one matches us. I'm sorry, it's just not possible."

"We'll see." She shimmied her shoulders and winked, then turned her attention back to me. "You want to come help me put the platters together? We're doing picnic food tonight."

I nodded and followed her back inside. As the evening wore on, the food kept coming and the drinks kept flowing.

When it was eventually time for us to leave, Cyrus got us an Uber and decided to pick his car up tomorrow. Peter hugged me goodbye, holding on to me for a minute longer than necessary to whisper in my ear.

"Take care of my brother, okay? He's a good guy underneath the dick demeanor. Just don't give up on him too easily."

I didn't know what to say to that, but Cyrus was eyeing us suspiciously, like he knew his brother was talking to me.

Nodding, I pulled away from him. "I won't, don't worry."

It felt like another lie, though. Cyrus wasn't mine to give up on, but I would take care of him. For as long as I could. At least he had Jenny and Peter to do it once I couldn't anymore.

CHAPTER 24

CYRUS

"A re you tired?" I asked Luna after we got settled in the backseat of the Uber.

Her hand was in mine, but her gaze was fixed on the passing city lights as we drove. She seemed to be deep in thought about something, and once more, I wondered what was going on in her head.

I'd seen Peter saying something to her before we left, but I didn't know what it was. I was curious, though.

Knowing my brother, it was probably something Luna wouldn't have wanted to hear. Like how I had the capacity to love or how she shouldn't give up on us. Some matchmaking bullshit like he'd tried with me when we'd first arrived.

The second he'd laid eyes on her, he'd pulled me aside to comment on how beautiful she was and how I shouldn't let her go. Rolling my eyes in the relative darkness of the car, I tightened my grip on her hand and lifted it to my lips to get her attention.

"Hey, you okay?"

She nodded, the expression in her eyes still slightly absent when she looked at me. As if she'd snapped herself out of her thoughts, she suddenly focused on me and blinked. "I'm sorry. What did you say before?"

"I asked if you were tired."

"Oh." She rocked from side to side, then shrugged. "No, not really. It's only just past ten."

"I know, but they've got an early bedtime for obvious reasons." Both of them started work at the crack of dawn and didn't often get home until after sunset. "They liked you, though."

"I liked them, too." A soft smile curled on her lips. "I really admire Jenny. How she can be as loving and cheerful and carefree as she is with her line of work, I don't know."

"Yeah. I've never really understood it either." I sighed as I angled myself to face her. "I might not like the idea of Peter getting married, but if he's got to do it, he sure chose well."

"It's good to hear you say that."

I chuckled. "I might be a cynic, but I'm not blind. If you're not tired, do you want to go grab a drink before I take you back to your place?"

"Sure. I wasn't really ready to say goodbye to those margaritas anyway." Her eyes stayed on me as I leaned forward between the seats and asked the driver to drop us off at a cocktail bar near her apartment.

When I sat back, she frowned and fidgeted with the material of her dress in her lap with her free hand. "This is none of my business, but what happened to Jenny's parents?"

I sucked in a breath and rubbed her knuckles with my thumb. "She told you about them, huh?"

"Just that they chose their wedding date because it was her parents'. She said they were the example she wanted to follow in her own marriage."

"Well, the date makes a lot more sense now." Peter hadn't told me why that date was so special to them, and I hadn't thought to ask. "It might not be any of your business, but it's natural to be curious. Especially since you're putting in so much work to make the wedding happen on that date."

"I probably should have asked her. I just didn't want to upset her."

Guilt crept onto her expression. "You know what? Never mind. I'll ask her myself the next time I see her."

"No, it's okay. They won't mind me telling you." I exhaled a deep breath. "Her father died suddenly of a heart attack. Her mother followed about a month later. She didn't have a heart attack, but Jenny believes she died of a broken heart. There was nothing really wrong with her."

Luna blinked as her eyes became watery. "She lost both of them suddenly?"

"Yeah. It was a terrible time. Everyone in our old neighborhood knew and loved them. Peter had only just started dating her, but it hit him hard, too."

"They've been through a lot together then."

"You have no idea," I said softly. "The three of us have faced just about all our toughest times together."

"But you still don't want him marrying her?" she asked just as the driver started to slow.

He dropped us off at the bar and I clicked into the app to give him a good tip. It wasn't often I found a driver who had given me as much of an illusion of privacy as he had.

Taking Luna's hand once I was done, we walked into the dark, crowded bar and found a table near the back. Pool balls clinked nearby, loud voices nearly drowning out the sound of the jukebox in the closed-off area a few feet away.

Raucous laughter rang out from all around us. People were obviously enjoying their Friday night.

It felt like Luna and I were in our own private bubble. We were also enjoying ourselves because we were getting to know each other better, but our conversation was anything but light or carefree.

After a quick stop at the bar, we took our seats and continued with the conversation as if it had never paused. I let my beer dangle between my fingers as I closed my eyes.

"It's really not about her. It's just the concept of marriage. Those two adore each other. They've loved each other almost half their lives, but I just can't shake the feeling that getting married is going to spell the beginning of the end."

Luna leaned across the table and took my hand in hers. "It's okay to be scared for him after what happened to you, but I disagree. I don't think it's the beginning of the end. It's a new beginning where they get to write their own, hopefully happy, middle before eventually the end comes for us all."

"That's a cheery thought."

She chuckled, but there was no humor in her eyes. "That doesn't make it any less true."

"Maybe. Let's just say my experiences with marriage haven't given me much reason to think there can be anything happy about them."

"What about your parents?" She cocked her head, her fingers running along the length of my wrist and hand. There was nothing sexual about her touch. It was meant to be comforting, and strangely, it was.

"They had a good marriage at times, I guess." I lifted my shoulders and shook my head.

"Where are they now?"

"They died in a car accident when I was eighteen. That's why Peter and I are so close. We haven't had any family but each other since. My parents were both only children, so we didn't have any extended family."

"I'm so sorry." The pain in her eyes told me that she wasn't just saying that. She bowed her head forward, tears shining in her eyes again when she lifted them back to mine. "I lost my parents when I was twenty-one. Legally an adult, emotionally still very much a child in need of her parents to help her through it."

"Sucks, doesn't it?" I let out a humorless laugh, then slapped the hand not holding hers against the table. "Enough of this. It's making me too sad and it's Friday night. Friday nights weren't meant for melancholy. What's an item on your bucket list you wish you could check off tomorrow?"

Surprise registered in her expression at the abrupt change of subject, but she didn't skip a beat. "There's this huge flower show in Dallas every spring. It runs for six weeks and it showcases more than five hundred thousand types of plants. I'd love to take off for Texas tomorrow and not come back until I've seen every plant they have to offer."

"You should do it," I said. "Seriously. Why not?"

"My piggy bank won't get me there yet." She smiled. "But it will someday. What about you?"

"If I could sit down with Elon Musk tomorrow, it would be a dream come true."

"So why don't you?" Some laughter had returned to her eyes. "Seriously. I'm sure if anyone could do it, it would be you."

"I've tried. Turns out getting a meeting isn't that easy." I let an easy smirk curve my lips. "But I'll keep trying. If I gave up that easily, I wouldn't be where I was now."

Something shuttered in her eyes at my words, but it was gone before I could pinpoint what it might have been. Moving on to the next question, I kept learning more about Luna and offering her more of myself.

Three more drinks in, her eyelids started to droop. I was seated next to her now, having moved when the bar became too noisy to hear her from all the way across the table.

Reaching out to slide a finger under her chin, I lifted it until she looked at me. "I think it's time to call it a night."

"Yeah." She yawned. "You might be right. Maybe it's just the lack of fresh air in here, but I can hardly keep my eyes open."

"Let's go." I ordered another Uber, paid our tab at the bar, and took Luna's hand as we walked outside.

We were still holding hands when our ride pulled up. Since her apartment was only a short ride away, we didn't talk much.

Her hand was on my thigh, though, and her fingers were trailing up and down in a way that was definitely sexual this time. Every so often, she even moved a bit higher and brushed my crotch with the back of her hand.

I stifled a groan and moved my hand to her leg, giving her the same treatment. Both of us stared out our own windows, neither of us making a sound that would draw attention to what we were doing.

By the time we exited the car, however, the air between us was so thick with tension that I doubted it was possible to have hidden it completely.

"Want to walk me in?" Luna asked, even though I'd asked the driver to wait for me a minute.

"Sure." I hadn't wanted to be presumptuous, despite what had happened in the car. It had been almost two weeks now since we'd last been together and I'd stopped inviting her over a few days ago.

Whatever had been bothering her seemed to have taken a back seat for the night, though. I told the driver he could go, then followed her into her building.

Once we were inside her small bright apartment, I lingered near the door. "I should probably go. Thanks for coming with me tonight and thanks for—"

Luna had kept walking when I'd stopped, but she turned around suddenly and marched back to me. Without any hesitation, she wrapped her arms around my neck and pressed her lips to mine.

Oh, fuck yeah. This is so happening.

CHAPTER 25

LUNA

B ack in the bar, I really hadn't been able to keep my eyes open. When we'd hit the sidewalk hand in hand, that changed. Fast.

It was like with my first breath of fresh air, my body became supremely aware of Cyrus's. He'd let me into his life and his world in a way he never had before tonight and it did things to me that he was opening up.

Plus, my body had grown addicted to his and it was done with the denial I'd been putting it through. With his heat radiating into me as we sat close together in the back of the Uber, I just hadn't been able to keep my hands to myself.

My panties had grown damp just by feeling his hard body so close to mine, smelling that intoxicating scent, and remembering how good things were between us. At first, I hadn't meant my touches to be a tease in any way.

Since my hands insisted on touching him in some way and my inhibitions were slightly reduced by the amount of alcohol I'd imbibed, I figured putting a hand on his leg was perfectly acceptable at this point in our relationship.

Too bad it hadn't stayed there. Like it had been possessed, my hand went rogue and did what it really wanted to do. So it ended with practically feeling him up in the backseat of a car being driven by a total stranger.

It was so unlike me that it actually felt like I was breaking free from some mold which, in turn, turned me on even more. *Vicious, vicious cycle.*

I'd had to bite my lip to keep from moaning all the way back to my place and, once inside, had immediately started heading to my bedroom. Having assumed we were on the same page, I was shocked when he said he had to leave and all I knew was that I couldn't let him.

I knew I was to blame for him feeling like I might not want him in this way anymore, but it was time to show him how much I really did want him in any way I could get him. With that in mind, I didn't let him take control this time.

Instead, I pulled his usual trick and walked him back while I kissed him hard, only stopping when he hit the wall. Since I didn't have his finesse, I hadn't thought to break the impact with my arms, but Cyrus didn't seem to mind.

If anything, it seemed to make him even hotter. His mouth warred with mine, our teeth clashing and our tongues dancing as intensely as a tango.

When I abruptly stopped kissing him and dropped to my knees, my hands already on his belt, a growl ripped out of him as he looked down at me. "What are you doing?"

"Turning the tables." I flashed him a satisfied smirk and yanked his belt free. Once that was done, I undid his button and unzipped him, then carefully lifted his boxers over his cock as I let the pants fall to the floor.

He was hot and hard in my hands, his skin smooth and his tip offering a single bead of wetness. I couldn't see much of how the rest of his body was reacting, but his fingers threaded into my hair and pulled while his head arched back against the wall.

The muscles in his neck and shoulders were tense and it sounded like he was trying to control his breathing. I grinned against his shaft, feeling a rush of empowerment running through me at how fast I'd managed to get him to this point.

Deciding it was my turn to tease, I pressed soft but open-mouthed kisses all along his hard shaft, giving his skin little sucks as I went along. With one hand wrapped around his base to keep him where I needed him to be, I reached between his legs and ran my finger along the smooth skin I found there until I cupped one of his balls.

I alternated between those and the soft line of skin while I kept my mouth on him. All my touches were feather light, and from the way he was snapping and moaning, I was guessing it was working.

"Shit, Luna. You're killing me here. Absolutely fucking killing me. I want to come all over your gorgeous face so badly right now. Fuck."

His hips twitched, and his hands tightened, but he didn't take over. He was letting me do what I wanted, just like when I'd walked him backward. I wouldn't have been able to move him otherwise if he hadn't let me. There was just no way.

"It's been a while. I wanted to make sure you knew I haven't forgotten about you or stopped wanting you."

He stilled, his eyes closing as he rested his head against the wall. A sound fell from his lips, but I wasn't sure if it was pleasured or tortured.

The next minute, he burst into action and moved so fast I could hardly keep track of what we were doing. When I caught up, I was naked on my bed and he was rolling a condom down his length.

Then he was on top of me, the gleam in his eyes nothing short of possessive as he spread my legs with his hips and thrust into me. "I haven't forgotten about you either, baby. I sure as fuck haven't stopped wanting you."

As if he was trying to drive home his point, he thrust into me with an animalistic frenzy. It was no less rhythmic than it had been before, nor did the wildness of his actions make him any less talented.

There was an edge to him tonight that was different, sure, but the end result was the same. Two orgasms blew me to smithereens before his kisses put me back together again, but it was only when I opened my eyes again after number two that he followed me over the edge.

"Fuck. Luna. I'm—" Cyrus's moans mingled with mine in the air as he tensed and his hardness pulsed deep inside me. I felt him swell and my toes curled as his pelvis ground against my clit.

"Cy. Oh, God. Cyrus." My back arched as waves of bliss spilled from my core to my extremities, caught in the powerful current of aftershock after aftershock.

Our bodies moved together in a staccato rhythm as we rode out our climaxes, holding on to each other as though trying to use the other as an anchor. When we finally stilled, I felt Cyrus's breaths warm my skin and wrapped myself around him even tighter, holding him to me for just a minute longer.

Hearts slamming against the other's chest, we lay like that for a long time before he finally pulled out to take care of business. I'd felt empty of him before but never as bereft as I did now.

During the past couple of weeks, I hadn't even realized how much I missed doing this with him until I had it again. Why had I avoided him?

Sure, the shop was having financial problems, but it wasn't like abstaining from sex was going to fix that. I also hadn't answered him about Italy and not knowing how to tell him why I couldn't go had been a big motivating factor behind not wanting to spend time with him alone.

He hadn't brought it up, though. I supposed it was entirely possible that he'd guessed my answer by now. Cyrus wasn't stupid, and if a person hadn't answered a question like that in all this time, it was unlikely they were going to say yes.

When he crawled back into bed, I laid my head on his shoulder and fitted myself against his side. "Can you stay tonight?"

"No, I'm sorry." His arms curled around me too, as if it was starting to feel as natural for him as it was for me. "I have to leave the city for the weekend for a conference upstate early in the morning and I haven't even packed yet."

"Oh, okay." I tried not to let the disappointment raging through me show. I'd been pulling away from him for weeks due to no fault of his. It made no sense to feel rejected by him. "Hope you have fun at the conference."

He chuckled darkly and his features twisted into a grimace. "I'd hardly call it fun, but it's an event I committed to ages ago. I couldn't cancel now even if I'd much rather spend the rest of the weekend buried between your legs."

"You say the sweetest things to me," I teased.

"Only because you have the sweetest pussy around, babe." He propped himself up on one elbow and treated me to his sexiest smile, that lock of hair falling across his forehead again.

It was too tantalizing to pass up, so I reached for it and brushed the hair out of his face, letting my hand linger there. "You know I was being sarcastic, right? That's really not a sweet thing to say."

His body shook against mine with laughter. "Coming from me? That's just about the sweetest it gets. I wouldn't want to spend a weekend burying myself to the hilt in just any pussy."

For some reason, his statement made flutters go off in my stomach. In his own, highly inappropriate way, Cyrus had just told me that he still only wanted me. It shouldn't have meant a thing to me, but it did. Because despite the nature of our relationship, I still only wanted him as well.

No one else. Just Cyrus.

"I have a conference call on Monday, but I'll talk to you sometime after," he said. "We'll see if we can meet up. Unless you're going to be too busy with the shop?"

"No, let's talk after. I won't be too busy." The shop wasn't too busy either, which was the problem. "Do you mind staying for a little while? Just until I can fall asleep."

"Sure, baby." He kissed my eyelids and lay back again. "I'll leave your keys in the mailbox, okay?"

"Okay," I whispered, the overwhelming exhaustion I'd felt earlier creeping up on me again.

When I woke up a couple of hours later, Cyrus was gone but his masculine scent clung to my sheets. I had a feeling I should appreciate it being there for now because sooner or later, I was going to have to start working on my actual escape plan and not just the point when I would have to do it.

CHAPTER 26

CYRUS

"Good afternoon, Mr. Coning," Eddie, the owner of one of the businesses I'd invested in, greeted me on Monday. "Thank you for calling in today."

"It was the least I could do, considering that you rescheduled the meeting for me," I said, smiling into the webcam mounted on top of my laptop.

I was at home, relaxed in shorts and a T-shirt. One of the perks of my job was that I could be naked most of the time while making million-dollar deals and no one would ever know.

I'd tried it once or twice, just to see what it would feel like, but it had been too weird. Even for me. Most of my business was done with men anyway and being naked while talking to a bunch of boring men wasn't really my thing.

Eddie's eyes flashed with surprise as he looked into his own cam, leaving me to wonder why. There was a sheen of sweat on his forehead, and now that I was looking at him properly, I realized he looked terrified.

"What's up, Eddie?" I frowned. "Have you got bad news?"

He shook his head. "No, not at all, sir. In fact, I have great news. We've doubled our profits since this quarter last year, and as of last week, we're the leading small environmental cleanup company in the state."

"I wasn't aware of that."

"We received the news on Friday afternoon, sir. Only after close of business, which is why I didn't call you right away. It's being announced this week." The man was practically sputtering. His face went red and I was pretty sure I saw sweat streaming out of even his ears now.

"Jesus, Eddie. Are you okay? Congratulations, but you look like shit. What's going on?"

"Nothing, sir. It's just that…" He trailed off, his eyes not even meeting mine on his own computer screen. "I was a little afraid of giving you feedback after last time, sir."

"What? Why?" I tapped my screen, and sure enough, he finally lifted his head up again. "Why the fuck would you be afraid of reporting back to me?"

"Well, sir…"

It dawned on me then. "I was that much of a dick?"

He flushed but nodded and laughed nervously. "Yes, sir, but I mean, it's to be expected. You invested a whole bunch of money with us and—"

"Tell you what. Let's start over today. I'm in a good mood and your company is doing better than we ever expected. Call me Cyrus and stop fucking stammering."

"Yes, sir—" He swallowed. "Cyrus. I meant to say Cyrus."

I chuckled. "Sure, you did."

Fuck. I enjoyed knowing I could strike fear into the hearts of certain others, but I'd never meant to become someone the business owners I dealt with were afraid to report back to.

My insights weren't vital to the success or failure of most of their enterprises, but I liked to think they knew they could come to me for help if they needed it. Eddie was right, even if he had said it in more of a Luna way than a me way. I had invested a whole bunch of money into most of these businesses.

I'd invested a shit ton of money into this particular business, and if it had tanked because he was too afraid to speak to me, I'd have ripped his fucking junk off and fed it to him with a spoon.

I'd rather have any of the business owners come to me than fail just because they felt they couldn't approach me. On the other hand, I'd never wanted any of them to approach me.

"If you don't mind me saying, Cyrus, you're looking well," Eddie said cautiously. "I don't think I've ever seen you in such a good mood."

I laughed and raked a hand through my hair. "Yeah, well. I had a good weekend. Relaxing."

Despite my nerves and misgivings about Luna meeting my brother and his fiancée, the night had gone better than I ever could have wanted it to. Drinks at the bar had given me insight into Luna beneath the surface and had also taught me that we shared some of the tragic events in our pasts, and then as an added bonus, I'd gotten to make her come a couple times before she fell asleep.

It had been the best night I'd had in a while and I'd ridden the high of it ever since. I'd also convinced myself to stop overthinking all the confusing shit and to just live in the moment with her.

That was what I did best anyway and I didn't see why I had to change now. I grinned at Eddie and gave him a casual shrug. "Yeah, well, finding out that you guys are climbing so fast in one of the up-and-coming industries to watch sure doesn't hurt."

Eddie's eyes slid away from mine to focus on someone off screen. When he focused on me again, he reminded me of the shy kid who had first pitched to me two years ago. "Actually, Cyrus, now that you mentioned our climbing, there's something else I wanted to talk to you about. Something that we think will give an edge over even our biggest competitors."

My brows rose and I rested my elbows on the armrests of my chair, linking my fingers together across my stomach as I inched my face closer to the screen. "Oh? What's that?"

"It's a bit of a long story to get into over a call, but maybe we can schedule a meeting sometime."

"I'm afraid I'm not going to be able to make it to your neck of the woods for at least the rest of this month. Texas isn't exactly on my way to the gym, you know?"

Eddie chuckled. "True, but didn't I see your name on the guest list for that entrepreneurial event coming up in Venice?"

"Um, yes. Yes, you did. I'd almost forgotten about it actually." Mostly because I'd pushed it to the back of my mind while waiting for Luna's answer, which still hadn't come. "Thanks for reminding me."

"Sure thing. We're going as well. Wouldn't miss it for the world. Should we find some time while we're there to meet up?"

"Great idea. I have some meetings scheduled there already, but let me check my calendar, and I'll let you know when I'll be able to see you."

"Whenever you're available, we will be," he assured me but then bit his lip. "The only presentation we're really keen on going to is the one that's being made by Landon Parker. You know the guy who—"

"I know who Landon Parker is." My good mood slipped some and the muscles in my hands tensed.

Landon Parker was the man now married to my ex-wife. Which meant that the She-Devil was going to be there in all her smug glory. *Fuck my life.*

"Let me tell you what," I said, interrupting Eddie again. "I'll send you a few times that I'll have available. You pick the one that suits you best and we'll meet then. Congratulations again. I'm proud of you guys, but I really need to run."

After he said goodbye, I ended the call and groaned as I buried my head in the heels of my hands. Why the hell did she always have to make these appearances in my life whenever I was least expecting her to?

Not for nothing, but I fucking hated my ex. If I showed up single again, she was going to wipe the fucking floor with me.

Of course, she wouldn't do it to my face where I could defend myself. No, I'd spend the entire time hearing from random strangers how I was still hung up on her, how I'd never get over her, and how she had really been the driving force behind my success.

It was bullshit. All of it.

Fury rolled through me like a thundercloud, taking my previously good mood and threatening to dissolve it for good. Clinging to thoughts of Luna since I didn't want to be taken over by the darkness that I associated with my ex, I slowly felt the cloud disappearing.

Once it was gone, there was nothing I wanted more than to see her. Luna was messing around with some arrangements when I walked up to her back door, and I watched her through the small window.

She was swaying to the beat of music I couldn't hear, a smile etched onto her face as she plucked a flower from this bucket and that to add to the arrangement. Before I could startle her again, almost as if she felt me watching her, she turned to face me and her eyes zeroed in on mine.

I saw her mouthing my name as I opened the door, unable to keep a smile off my face. "Hey, babe. Looking good. Don't stop on my account."

Bringing her in for a hug as the door swung closed behind me, I buried my face in her hair and let the sweet, floral smell of her chase the last wisps of the darkness away.

She hugged me tightly, then pulled away to look up at me. Her big blue eyes found mine, and though there were questions in them, I was stunned again by how crystalline and deep they were all the same time.

"Hey, Cyrus. It feels like I'm having deja-vu, but did we have plans for today? I thought you were just going to call me when you were done with your conference call, not come over."

"Isn't a visit better than a call?" I dropped a kiss to the tip of her nose. "I wouldn't have been able to do that over the phone, would I?"

"No." She sighed and ran a hand through the long ponytail her hair was pulled up into. "I wish you'd called, though. I'm busy with these arrangements for a corporate event tonight. It was a last-minute order, but I couldn't turn them down. I could have saved you the trip."

"Worth it to be able to hug you for a minute." I meant it as a joke, although also not really, but Luna just looked uncertain.

Eventually, she smiled up at me and pressed a kiss to the corner of my lips. "Yeah, it's good to see you too, big guy. I really need to get back to it, though. I'm supposed to deliver these just after five."

"Can I see you tonight?" I needed to talk to her about Italy and it couldn't wait any longer. "Please?"

"I'm sure I can fit you in," she joked, making a show of removing an imaginary diary from her pocket and paging through it. "Ah, here we go. It says I'm having dinner with you at my place at seven. Apparently, I'm cooking."

"Great. Just make a note on there that I'll bring the wine." I bent my knees to be at her height, then brought a hand to the back of her neck, and guided her mouth to mine for a deep kiss.

"I'll see you later," she murmured against my lips, the sweetest little dazed smile playing on her lips.

"See you then." I laid one more kiss on her, then forced myself to leave before I bent her over that table just like I'd warned her I wanted to do before. Maybe later, after we'd talked, I'd get to be inside her.

Unfortunately, and I never thought I'd even think this, but there was something I needed more from her tonight than just pleasure. I just hoped she would be as willing to give it.

CHAPTER 27

LUNA

"Have I told you how good you look when you're dressed down?" My eyes drank Cyrus in like they hadn't caught sight of him in years and had missed him every day.

When he'd come by the shop earlier, it was the first time I'd seen him in shorts and a T-shirt, and though he was wearing different ones now, he'd remained in casual wear. Maybe it was just because I'd become so used to what an absolute sexy god he cut in his suit that I didn't notice it so much anymore, but like this?

Like this, he didn't just look sexy. He looked approachable, like a hot young exec who knew how to laugh and have a good time. It was a welcome change from the intimidating, scowling businessman who looked like he hadn't cracked a smile in over a month.

In the time I'd known him, I'd come to learn there was a lot more to him than that domineering, controlling asshole he'd looked like the first time I'd met him. Having seen him in jeans once or twice, in various states of undress, and my personal favorite, stark naked, it was still jarring to see him look so young and carefree.

With an olive-green T-shirt clinging to his muscles like I wanted to be, his eyes seemed to have turned to a mossy color rather than the usual emerald. They were still electric, just in an entirely different way.

Casual navy-blue shorts with little sailboats on them and a pair of honest-to-God flip-flops completed the look. Even his hair looked lighter than usual, giving him a surfer vibe that I liked.

While I was giving him a onceover, he did the same to me. Those full, kissable lips tugged up into a smirk when his gaze came back to mine.

"You don't look half bad yourself. Did you forget to put pants on or did you mean to make me want to bend you over your kitchen counter before we even got around to eating?"

I flushed, realizing that I'd put on booty shorts that were actually part of a pajama set to cook in. With my preference for cooking by touch and taste rather than following a recipe, I'd long since discovered it was a much smarter bet for me to cook in pajamas and an apron with my hair pulled up in a messy bun.

That way, the clothes I wanted to wear stayed clean and I only needed a few minutes before a date started to change. *But this isn't even a date, so why does it matter?*

Right. My subconscious was one hundred percent correct, so I met Cyrus's smirk with one of my own and put a hand on my hip, jutting it out. "Wouldn't you like to know?"

"I would actually." Pupils dilating, he strode into my house and kicked the door shut behind him. He licked his lips a second before they descended onto mine and he groaned into my mouth. "You taste so fucking good. What are we having?"

"Spaghetti Bolognaise with Parmesan, micro-greens, and a salad. It's nothing fancy, but my mom taught me how to make it, and since we were talking about our parents on Friday, I thought it would be nice."

In an instant, his expression changed from ready to fuck to can I hold you. At my slight nod, he drew me into his arms and crushed me in the tightest, most comforting hug I could remember getting.

He might be a heck of a kisser and he definitely knew what he was doing in bed. But apparently, the man knew his way around a hug, too.

"Can I help with anything?" he asked against my ear before he released me.

I chewed on my lip before I made my decision. Cooking this dish was like a sacred experience for me, given from whom I'd learned to make it, and I usually refused help, but I wanted Cyrus to share in it tonight.

"Sure. I've got all the ingredients out, and the sauce is already simmering on the stove, but you can help me finish it off and decide when we should haul out the pasta."

"Sounds good. I'm sure I can manage that." Giving me a boyish smile I was sure I'd never seen from him before, he held up a finger and disappeared out the door for a second before he returned with a paper bag in his hand. "Told you I'd bring the wine."

Fixing his hand to the small of my back, he walked with me to the kitchen and helped himself to two glasses. He filled them with some fancy-labeled white wine and pushed one over to me.

The wine was cold, condensing on the outside of the glass almost immediately. I took a sip, moaned at the tangy crispness on my tongue, and went back for more.

Cyrus watched me, lust flashing behind his eyes again before he blinked it away and cleared his throat. "I wanted to talk to you about something."

"Yeah?" I asked, dropping my head to one side. "What?"

Please don't let him say this is over. Please don't let him say this is over. I'm not ready yet.

"A few weeks ago, I invited you to come to Italy with me for a conference. The event I told you I had to attend is this weekend, which means I need an answer. I think you'd enjoy it. Not only is it being held in Venice, but it's also an acclaimed annual event for entrepreneurs, and it's a great opportunity to network."

My heart skipped a beat. *Freaking Italy.*

"If it's an event for entrepreneurs, why wasn't I invited?" I asked jokingly, trying to lighten the mood. "I own my own floral shop. I should've made the cut."

He set his glass down on the counter and braced himself against it, not even the corners of his mouth twitching in a smile.

"It's only for the most successful entrepreneurs in the country. I need you to come with me and pretend to be my wife." He said all of this completely deadpan.

It had to be a joke, but it sure didn't look like one.

There was tension around his eyes and the muscles in his forearms were corded as he braced his hands against the counter. A tick in his jaw told me how clenched it had to be as he waited for my answer.

My own jaw slackened so much, it nearly hit the floor. "Are you kidding me? No."

"Why not?" The strong column of his throat moved. "I asked you to come with me almost a month ago, Luna. It's not like this could be coming as a surprise to you."

"You never said anything about pretending to be your wife." There was no way I'd be able to do that and not start believing it myself.

If I opened only a tiny part of myself up for believing it could happen for real, I really wasn't ready for that. Plus, he was the one adamantly opposed to relationships and marriage, so why was he trying to make this into more than it was?

"Besides," I added. "I can't go. I thought you'd have assumed that by now."

"Why not?" he asked, his voice coated in steel.

Nerves ricocheted through me, but I had to tell him the truth. I'd always been honest with him and I wasn't about to change that now. Even if I had avoided him partially for weeks because of the answer to this very question.

"The shop's in trouble. I took out some loans a couple of years ago and the interest is eating my repayments alive. That man who was there when you got there the other day, do you remember?"

"Bad suit and nervous demeanor?" he asked, eyes still laser focused on mine.

I nodded. "That's the one. He was from the bank. They're pushing my interest rate up. I can't leave the shop right now and I can't afford to get someone in to look after it. I need to be there to make every dollar I can until the bank eventually decides even that's not good enough."

The kitchen went so quiet, I'd have been able to hear a pin drop if I'd had one around to test the hypothesis out with.

Cyrus seemed to have frozen in place, and when he finally moved, it was only to fold his thick arms across his chest and lower his chin. If I'd thought he looked less intimidating and scary without the suit when he had that expression on his face, I'd been wrong. *So very, very wrong.*

Not that I was scared of him. I knew he'd never do anything to hurt me, but he was certainly all alpha businessman again. *Bye pretty surfer dude.*

"That's what you've been so busy with?" he demanded in a low tone. "That's what's been keeping you out of my bed at night? Money problems?"

His jaw was clenched so tightly now, I was worried he was going to crack a few teeth, but I nodded anyway. "Yes. I've been trying to figure out strategies to make more money."

"You know what I do for a living, right? I. Invest. In. Other. Businesses," he gritted the words out. "Why didn't you come to me? If not for money, then for help with strategizing?"

"Because it's not your problem, Cyrus." My voice was soft but earnest. "Both of us were very clear about what we wanted out of this and you helping me save my business wasn't part of the deal."

Cyrus cocked his head, his voice dangerously low. "What about a new deal?"

"What new deal?" I asked warily, not sure if I could live with an amendment of the terms at this stage without throwing the entire fudging agreement in the trash.

"This can be a solution for both our problems. I'll pay off your debt, every last cent of it, and you will come to Italy and pretend to be my spouse. You will be compensated for doing so. It'd be a business transaction, so think carefully."

I blinked rapidly, all at once shocked and appalled and awed at how fast his mind worked. What he was offering me felt like a lifeline. Heck, it *was* a lifeline.

If I took his deal, I got to keep my shop. It was as simple as that.

But at what cost? Going to a different country and pretending to be married to him? Wasn't that exactly like that movie where the prostitute pretended to be dating the millionaire and ended up falling in love with him?

Only in this scenario, I would be the prostitute. I couldn't afford to say no, but I also couldn't afford to take the chance and risk falling in love with Cyrus.

Is there any cost that's too high for saving your shop? A voice whispered in the back of my mind and I let out a heavy sigh because I knew it was right.

Broken hearts could be mended. Failed shops with heaps of outstanding debts couldn't be reopened. With my shoulders slumping, I lifted my eyes to his and nodded. "Okay, you've got yourself a new deal. I'll come with you."

CHAPTER 28

CYRUS

Loud rock music flowed from the speakers in the bar where I was meeting up with Peter. The Wednesday afternoon after-work crowd sipped on drinks, ties loosened and heels having been traded out for flats.

Peter was already waiting when I got there, a pitcher of beer and a bucket of wings on the table in front of him. He licked barbecue sauce off his fingers before wiping his hand with a towelette, then picked up the beer and poured a glass for me.

"Hey, bro, what's up?" he greeted when I slid into the booth across from him. "Where are you off to this time? Your text only said you're going out of town again."

"Yeah, that's what I wanted to talk to you about. I'm going to that annual entrepreneurship thing. It's being held in Venice this year."

He nodded slowly. "Italy, huh? You're one lucky son of a bitch. Any chance you want some company?"

"Jenny would kick your ass if you took time off to come with me when you should be saving your vacation days for the honeymoon."

"True." He grinned. "But come on, dude. It's Italy. If we take Jenny with us, it could be an early honeymoon."

I knew he was only joking, but I took a sip of my beer and

wondered if I could somehow convince him to come anyway. "We'd have a great time. That's for sure. Luna's coming with me and I know she'd love to have some company around when I have to go do the schmoozing."

His green eyes grew wide. "Luna's going with you?"

"Yeah. I invited her a couple of weeks ago, but she didn't give me an answer until yesterday."

"I'm surprised she took you up on the invitation." He lifted his glass but didn't take a sip from it. Brow furrowed, he looked at me like he was trying to solve some kind of puzzle. "I didn't think she'd be the type to go jet-setting to an exotic location with someone she hadn't known all that long."

"She wasn't exactly agreeable at first." Understatement of the fucking century. "It took some convincing, but eventually, she said yes."

"I can see why you'd want to take her. We really enjoyed having her over for dinner the other night. She's a great girl. Good sense of humor, fun, gorgeous. I bet you two are going to have a ball of a time in Italy."

"Yeah, I'm not so sure about that." I rubbed my palms over the stubble on my jaw. "Samantha and her husband are going to be there."

Peter's expression fell, his shoulders coming up and his eyes narrowing. "What?"

"You heard me. It's an entrepreneurship conference and Landon is one of the big boys, remember? He may not have made as much money as I did when he sold his first company, but he did make bank, and he loves talking about it. They gave him a slot as a speaker this year."

His lips curled in disgust. "Asshole. You really think Sam will go with him?"

"It's not his fault she set her sights on him, but yeah, he is an asshole. As for Sam, I'm willing to bet she's going to be there. I don't think she'd miss the chance to go gallivanting in Venice and prancing around at the social events with that giant fucking rock on her finger."

"Unfortunately, I think you're right. It's somewhere she can be seen and she lives for that shit." He shook his head. "I still can't believe she turned out like that. I really didn't see it coming."

"I didn't, either. Obviously." At the time, she'd had me wrapped around her little finger. She fed me so many lies and so much bullshit and I'd lapped it all up like an obedient fucking puppy. "At least she's not my problem anymore. Dodged a bullet when she left me, if you really think about it."

"Amen to that." He raised his glass to me and took a long pull of his beer. "Have you warned Luna that your ex is going to be there?"

"Not yet. I didn't think it would be a great selling point when I was trying to convince her to come along. I asked her to pretend to be my wife while we're there, so I think she knows something is up. She just doesn't know what."

My brother's jaw dropped and disapproval hardened his gaze. "You asked her to do what now?"

"I told her to pretend to be married to me. You know Samantha. If I showed up single again, what do you think she would have done?"

"So instead, you thought it was a good idea to ask Luna to pretend to be your wife?"

I frowned at his tone. "Yes. What about it?"

"Well, that'll certainly show Sam," he said sarcastically, shaking his head as he drained the rest of the beer. "I hope you know what you're doing, man."

"Of course, I do. I'm taking a friend to Italy, all expenses paid and more, and am asking her to do me a favor to keep my fucking ex off my back. Where's the harm in that?"

"You're playing with fire, bro." He ripped a piece of chicken off a wing and chewed before filling his glass again. "You've been the saving grace for our wedding, and I know I owe you for that, but I just can't get behind this."

"Luna has been the real saving grace."

"Exactly." He nodded and pointed at me with his glass. "Don't fuck it up, man."

"I'm not fucking anything up because there's nothing to fuck up," I said. "We've been over this. She's a friend who's helping me out. When

187

I first invited her, she wasn't going to say yes. Since I couldn't have her saying no after I found out Sam was going, I added a little incentive. That's all there is to it."

"You really are dick, you know that?" With another shake of his head, he finished the wing he was busy with and grabbed another one. "She's a nice girl and you can bet your fucking ass she's not going to like it when she finds out why you're taking her."

"She knows I'm taking her so she can pretend to be my wife. Does the reason why I need a wife make any difference? No."

"I don't think she's going to see it that way. It's one thing knowing your friend needs a wacky favor like this. It's another thing entirely to know they're using you against their ex." He tore another piece of meat off the bone, chewing as he narrowed his eyes in thought. "That's if she even sees you as a friend. You two looked mighty cozy the other night."

"Whatever. Both of us know the deal between us. We're friends, we fuck sometimes, and that's it. Nothing cozy about that."

"Maybe not to you," he muttered into his beer.

If only he knew that it wasn't what was going on in her head I was worried about. I'd decided to stop thinking about what was going on in mine, sure, but it was easier said than done. "Look, Peter, I know you guys like her, but she's not the girl for me, okay? She loves love. She wants hearts and flowers and a white poofy dress. I can't give that to her."

"Big difference between can't and won't, brother." Disapproval crept back into his tone. "What Sam did to you was fucked up, but I've said it once and I'll say it again. Jenny isn't Samantha. Luna isn't Samantha. There's something going on between the two of you. It's like you're doing this dance where neither of you want to admit it, and you keep going to and fro, but eventually, it's going to blow up in your faces."

"How very prophetic of you."

He rolled his eyes and shoved his hands through his hair, agitation coming off him in waves. "I know you think you've got this shit figured out, but you don't. You just can't see it yet."

"So, what? You don't think I should have invited Luna to Italy?" I crossed my arms to keep from slamming my fists down on the table. "Tough fucking luck because it's already done. I can't uninvite her now, and even if I could, I wouldn't. We're already sleeping together, and we really are friends. What difference does it make if I ask her to wear a bogus ring while we go away together?"

He ground his teeth together. "I'm not saying you should uninvite her. I'm just saying taking her with you to make your ex jealous is wrong."

"I'm not taking her to make Sam jealous. For God's sake. I don't give a fuck what Samantha feels when she sees us together. I only care that she doesn't spend the entire conference talking shit about what *I* supposedly feel. I also don't want that smug asshole husband of hers looking at me like he pities me for losing the gold-digging whore. It's been years of the same thing and I'm fucking over it."

Peter held up his palms in surrender, dragging in a deep breath. "I get that you're over it, dude. Again, I'm not saying you shouldn't take Luna. I'm saying you should take her because you want to, not to use her in front of a woman who was shit to you. Mark my words, this is not going to end well."

CHAPTER 29

LUNA

"Sorry for making you drive with me to pick Adi up," April said as she flicked her indicator on. "I really didn't realize it was this late already and I'm dying to know your great news."

"I've found a solution for my money problems." I grinned at her. "Like, all of them, even the ones you don't know about."

She turned her head to look at me and slid her sunglasses down her nose. Thankfully, we were stopped at a traffic light, so her brief glare didn't put us in any danger.

"You have financial problems I don't know about?"

"I did. I mean, who doesn't, right? I didn't want to tell you because I didn't want to worry you, but I was afraid I was going to lose the shop."

"What?" The pitch of her voice nearly pierced my eardrums. "How did I not know about this?"

"Like I said, I didn't want to worry you." I shrugged and inclined my head at the green light. "Stop looking at me and pay attention to the road. We do want to get to the school alive, right?"

A car honked behind us and April flipped the driver off in the rearview mirror as she shifted her car into gear. "I can't believe you didn't tell me you were in such deep trouble. I knew you owed some money and stuff. I kind of figured it was a problem when you started talking about extending the shop's hours and all that, but I didn't realize it was that bad."

"It was." I swallowed the lump that appeared in my throat when I even thought about the visit from that banker. "But it's all over now."

"How?" She frowned and took her sunglasses off this time, obviously deeming it important for me to see her expressions properly while we were having this conversation. "Please tell me you didn't go to a loan shark or something."

"Nothing like that," I assured her as I waved my hand. "Cyrus is helping me out actually. He's going to pay off all my debt and in return, all I have to do is to go to Italy with him this weekend and pretend to be his wife."

"What? Why?" Her frown deepened. "I thought you guys weren't anything more than friends with benefits. You said you were happy with that."

"We are and I am." Although I didn't know for how much longer. Not wanting to think about the inevitable end, though, I focused on explaining Cyrus's plan to April. "He invited me and I said no because of the shop. Then he offered to pay off my debts if I went with him."

"Is he that desperate to get fucked on foreign soil? Are you guys even exclusive with this little arrangement you've got going on? I mean, surely it would have been cheaper for him to just find a girl over there to get off with while he was there."

Something dark twisted in my stomach as my mind conjured up an image of Cyrus with some faceless Italian supermodel. Because of course the woman he picked up in my imagination would be a supermodel but one with big boobs *and* a brain between her ears.

Stop it, I chided myself. *He has every right to pick up a supermodel whether I go with him or not.*

At that thought, the dark twisted thing knotted and left me feeling a little sick. I shoved the feeling down with as much strength as I could muster and refused to pay any attention to it.

"Maybe it would have been cheaper, but I'm not sure some random person would have agreed to pretend to be his wife."

"Girl, anyone would pretend to be his wife. Have you seen him?" She gave me a pointed look before frowning again. "More to the point, why does he need a pretend wife?"

"Something about his ex being there." I sighed as I thought back to the call I'd gotten from him last night. "Apparently, she's a real piece of work and he doesn't want to show up single when he knows she's going to be there."

"It sounds like he wants to use you to make her jealous." April's nose crinkled. "How do you feel about that?"

"I don't mind." There might have been a teeny, tiny bit of untruth to that statement. "He's not my boyfriend, April. He's just a friend. If he wants to pick someone else up while we're overseas, he can do it. Though he'd have to know the benefits part of our friendship would end if he did. As for wanting to make his ex jealous, why not? It's kind of the dream, right? To be the winner in the breakup?"

She rolled her eyes at me. "Just a friend. Right. I forgot. The point isn't who's winning in his breakup. It's that he wants to use you to do it."

"That's kind of flattering, right? I think it's cool that he thinks being with me would make her jealous." *Lies, more lies. God, what's wrong with me?*

April pursed her lips. "Don't sell yourself short. You could make any girl jealous, but again, that's not the point. The point is that he wants to use you."

"So what?" I shrugged. "He's paying off my debts in return and I get to keep the shop. Who cares if I have to act all lovey-dovey with him for a couple of days?"

I had a feeling I cared, but I didn't mention it. April was already convinced that I wasn't capable of maintaining a relationship like the one I had with Cyrus. I didn't want to give her any reason to think that she was right.

All that would do was worry her. She'd think I was falling for him and want to protect me from that. Heck, I wouldn't have been surprised if she tracked down my airline ticket and burnt it to keep me away from him if she thought I was in danger of getting hurt.

I really, literally couldn't afford not to go on this trip and keep up my end of the bargain. If I didn't go, the shop was as good as gone. It was that simple and that complicated all rolled into one happy, depressing package.

Why, oh why did it have to be marriage *we had to pretend about?*

April shot me a worried glance as she waited in the long line of cars in front of the school. "Well, as long as you're sure you're really okay with it. All I know is, I wouldn't like knowing I was being used. On the other hand, knowing is better than not knowing, I guess." She shrugged. "Hell, maybe it's not that bad. At least you know what his intentions are and why. That's a ton more honesty than I ever got with my ex."

"Cyrus and I are always honest with each other." It was refreshing to know I had that kind of relationship with him, but it was also a little scary. At least he wasn't asking questions I couldn't give him the honest answers to. "It's one of my favorite things about us."

"Us, huh?" She lifted both her eyebrows and pressed her lips into a thin line. "But sure. There's nothing more going on between you guys than friendship."

The line of cars snaked slowly forward until finally, we reached the front. Adi hopped into the backseat and dumped her backpack on the floor before fastening herself in. "Hi, Mom. Hey, Luna. What are you doing here?"

I twisted in my seat to face her as well as I could and smiled. "I wanted to come with mommy to pick you up because I'm going out of town for a few days and I wanted to say goodbye."

The corners of her lips turned down. "Where are you going? How long will you be gone?"

"Less than a week. I'm going to Italy. Want me to bring you something back from there?"

Adi brightened up instantly, licking her lips as she thought. "Definitely. I want chocolate and some Italian money and pizza."

"I don't know that I'll be able to bring back pizza, sweetheart. The chocolate and the money I can do."

"Okay." She sighed. "I guess that's fine."

"Let me tell you what. I'll get what you asked for and I'll pick you up something nice as well. How does that sound?"

"Good."

"Just good?" I reached out and wiggled my fingers like I was about to tickle her tummy.

She hooted with laughter and squirmed even though I hadn't touched her. "No, not just good. Great. It sounds great."

"Awesome." I smiled and retracted my hand, tuning out April's voice when she started asking Adi about her homework.

One of the best things about being the cool aunt was not having to worry about things like homework. Instead, I let my mind drift to Cyrus and the conversation I'd just had with April.

I hated that I hadn't been entirely truthful with her, but how was I supposed to tell her that I felt sick when I thought about Cyrus with anyone else? How was I supposed to admit that she had been right and that I was finding it more and more difficult to separate my feelings from the sex?

The truth was that I didn't like the idea that he was using me but not for the reasons she thought. I didn't like it because I was jealous. Jealous that Cyrus cared enough to try to make his ex jealous when I knew he would never care about me that way at all.

CHAPTER 30

CYRUS

Luna couldn't seem to tear her eyes away from the window as we landed at Marco Polo Airport in Venice. I'd chosen seats on the right side of the plane so she'd have a good view of the islands coming in, and since it was almost mid-morning, the sun was starting to burn off the light drizzle that had blanketed the city earlier.

"That's just incredible," she breathed as we came in for our approach. Her hand reached over the divider between our seats to seek mine out. She wrapped her fingers around mine and tightened her grip, her nose still up against the small window. "Thank you for bringing me."

"Anytime." I turned my hand in hers so our palms fit together, then leaned over to look out of the same window. I'd landed here plenty of times before, but being here with Luna made me really appreciate the magic of seeing it for the first time again.

The expanse of water below was dotted with smaller islands until Venice City came into view, its larger landmass consisting of a plethora of red roofs and the legendary canals. Luna glanced down at the open guidebook in her lap, then lifted a hand to point at the city.

"Did you know it's made up of one hundred and seventeen islands?" she asked, her voice filled with awe and disbelief.

"I didn't know the exact number, no." Unlike Luna, I hadn't studied up much on the place before coming here for the first time.

Even though we were flying business class, Luna probably wouldn't have noticed if they'd stuck us in the cargo hold. Her nose had been buried in that book since I'd picked her up at her place the day before, almost all the way to Paris, where she took a temporary break to marvel at the Parisian airport where we caught our connecting flight. If she hadn't dozed off, I was pretty sure she'd have read up on Venice all the way to France.

As we'd sipped on French coffee for me and tea for her, she'd spouted off fun facts about Paris and its airport, then opened the travel guide again as soon as our butts hit our seats for the final leg of our flight.

Once we'd touched down and claimed our baggage, I whisked her through the busy terminal to the water-taxi dock. A man was waiting for us there, sent by our hotel after I'd made a booking online.

Luna's blue eyes were wide when she noticed him. "There's a person with our names on his plaque. How cool is that?"

"It's awesome." I grinned and felt a rush of genuine excitement I hadn't felt for a long time.

Traveling and even being picked up by drivers carrying my name on their boards wasn't something that had tickled my fancy for years, but it sure did now. "I booked us on a private water taxi to get from here to the hotel. It kind of makes you feel like James Bond, getting off a plane and onto a fast boat to zoom into an ancient city."

"I can't wait." She laughed, the light scarf around her neck rustling in the breeze as we stepped onto the pier and greeted the hotel representative. He was dressed in a smart suit but wasn't much for small talk.

After confirming we were the passengers he'd been waiting for, he nodded at an attendant waiting nearby and the two of them took our luggage from us. Luna wrapped her arm around mine and slid her sunglasses over her eyes.

"Assuming we don't have any bad guys to catch once we get there, what are our plans for the day?"

"Getting lost in Venice." It was something I hadn't done yet and something that came highly recommended by every travel website. "We don't have anything to do until tomorrow with the conference, so I thought we'd spend the day seeing the sights."

I practically felt the thrill running through her body. "I'm so up for getting lost, but there are a few things we can't miss. St. Mark's Basilica and Square, Doge's Palace and we have to see the Rialto Bridge."

Nudging her hip with my own as we followed the men wheeling our luggage along to our boat, I let my own sunglasses drop to my nose. "What do you take me for? I'm not a tease or a sadist and only one of those two would bring you all the way here and not visit all those places."

"I have it on good authority that you can be one heck of a tease," she said, her voice low enough that only I'd be able to hear her. The corners of her lips pressed in like she was trying to hide a smile, but her little joke was forgotten when she laid eyes on the gleaming hull of our water taxi. "That's just for us?"

"Just for us," I confirmed, stepping in and holding out my hand to help her. "The driver will drop us off at a central point on the Grand Canal and take our bags to the hotel. That way, we can use our time to explore and only check in later when we're ready."

Luna's jaw loosened. Then her arms were around my neck and squeezing me tight. "You're the best fake husband ever."

Something dark formed a pit in my stomach at her words. Truth be told, this was only supposed to be a business transaction, but I was still glad she was here and not just so she could play my wife to get Samantha to back the fuck off me.

I didn't know how to tell her that without making her worry that I'd tricked her into coming, though. I'd been honest with her when I told her I needed her help, which was why she'd eventually agreed.

Now that we were here, though, I was also just really happy to have her with me. Watching the wind whipping through her hair as she gripped the golden railing at the front of the boat once we got underway, her head turning this way and that to take in all the sights, I couldn't imagine having come here without her for this trip.

"Where to first?" she asked when we stepped off the taxi and got our first real look at the famous city.

"Let's just get lost and not think too much about where we're going." I took her hand in mine and led her off on the cobbled streets, pausing when she did to take pictures of the quaint and rustic buildings. "The basilica and the clock tower are that way. I booked us on a tour later. Told you I wasn't a sadist or a tease, so for now, let's head off the other way."

"Sounds like a plan." Luna smiled and followed me as we walked in the opposite direction to two of Venice's biggest tourist attractions. We lost ourselves in the maze formed by the city's walkways, stopping for about a million photos along the way. "I love that your first plan for the day was getting lost. There's so much to see here."

She pointed toward artists sketching on canvas right there on the sidewalk and local produce sellers at a market we were walking past. "We're really getting a feel for the place, you know?"

"That was the idea. It was recommended on just about every blog I read, so I figured we'd better do it."

"Well look at you, Mr. I'm-so-cool-about-traveling. You actually read blogs before we came here. I'm impressed."

I wagged my eyebrows at her. "Anything to impress my wife. You know how it goes. When you're married and out of that newlywed stage, the sex starts to dry up if you don't take action."

She rolled her eyes, but her shoulders shook with laughter. "Leave it to you to use arguably the most romantic city in the world to spice up our imaginary sex life."

"Unless I'm very much mistaken and have been having some very vivid dreams lately, our sex life is not imagined."

"True, but if we really were married, would you have been hoping you'd be getting lucky tonight because you brought me here?"

"Absolutely, but come on. Like you said, it's one of the most romantic cities in the world. Everyone would want to fuck here."

"I believe the term you're looking for is making love, not that other word." She laughed and rolled her eyes again. "But I see your point."

A glance down at my watch told me it was time for us to start making our way back. Luna practically had stars in her eyes as we toured the famed, towering basilica and the buzzing main square.

We fed pigeons and watched as children chased them. We saw gondolas gently lapping against the piers, chuckled at the striking ensembles worn by the gondoliers, and finally found a cafe to grab a bite to eat and do some wine-tasting.

The sun was starting to set as we got our check at the cafe and the streets were emptying out as tourists and locals alike headed inside to get ready for the night ahead. Most of them would be heading out again, but I doubted we would join them.

Luna's eyelids were getting heavier by the minute and it was obvious the excitement of the day and the jetlag were getting to her. Venice was six hours ahead of New York, and even I was feeling the effects of it being past midnight back home.

"Let's head back to the hotel," I said. "If we get hungry later, we can always order room service."

She nodded. "It feels like such a pity to miss out on even an hour of this place, but I don't think falling asleep on my feet would do either of us any good."

"Right there with you." I paid for our food and wine-tasting, thankfully without any objection from Luna, who was taking in the sight of the old-fashioned streetlights coming on beside the canal.

She let out a contented sigh as she watched the orange glow of the lamps reflecting off the water, then took my hand when I held it out to her. I'd planned it so we ate near the hotel, making it an easy walk along the ancient cobblestone paths to get there.

Luna gasped when I pointed out where we'd be staying. "It looks like a castle."

"Yeah, and it's got the best views in the city," I said. "Plus, there's a rooftop pool and terrace where we'll have breakfast in the morning. It doesn't get any better than that."

"I don't think it does," she said, her eyes wide as we stepped inside the opulent lobby. The place was all old-school charm with modern touches, a gleaming hardwood floor beneath our feet and pressed ceilings.

Overstuffed couches, thick rugs, and golden accents everywhere gave the beautifully restored hotel the feel of a place where history met with culture. I loved it here, even if it had been some time since I'd appreciated it the way I did now.

Luna looked like she was floating on air beside me, seemingly having gotten a second wind from seeing where we'd be staying for the next couple of days. It was only when I received our keys and handed one to her that the smile slid from her face.

"Two rooms?" she asked as we turned to head to the elevator. "Why did you get two rooms?"

"I told you this is a business transaction. I mean sure, we're friends too, but I didn't want you to feel like you had to sleep with me in exchange for coming."

"Yeah. Sure." She huffed out a breath as the elevator arrived and didn't speak to me again until she was standing in front of her room. "The lady downstairs said our bags had been delivered, right?"

"Right." I closed the distance between us and lowered my head to hers, brushing a kiss to her cheek. "Sleep tight, Luna. We have a long day ahead of us tomorrow and we won't be able to turn in this early again."

"Okay." Her tired eyes caught mine, and it looked like she wanted to say something before she decided not to. Instead, she pressed her lips together and swiped her room key in front of the electronic reader. "Good night, Cyrus. See you tomorrow."

Without another look at me, she disappeared into her room and the door swung shut behind her. I stood in the richly carpeted hall for another minute, wondering what I possibly could have done wrong this time.

The entire day had been lighthearted and easy, until we'd gotten our keys. She couldn't possibly be offended that I hadn't wanted to assume she'd want to share a room, even though as I headed toward my own, I couldn't deny that I would have preferred only getting us one.

CHAPTER 31

LUNA

Venice was everything I ever could have imagined and not a place I'd ever hoped to see in person. The labyrinth of canals and walkways was enchanting and the way the water sparkled almost as if it was made of molten gold was absolutely magical.

The only downside to it all was being in this city for business. I'd hoped that it would at least feel like Cyrus had brought me as a friend, and at times, it did, but finding out he'd booked two rooms was a stark reminder of the real reason I'd accompanied him here.

There had been times on our flight and once we arrived that it really felt like I was in Venice with him for the right reasons. Even if they weren't romantic ones, it felt like he at least *wanted* me with him.

But I'd been right before. I was really going to have to watch myself here. It would be way too easy to fall for him, especially while we sipped wine side by side and soaked up the Italian zest for life that seemed to be present in every molecule of air we breathed.

All day, we'd spent together with hands linked loosely as we wandered around some more. It had only been about an hour and half ago that we'd gotten back to the hotel to get ready for the gala that would kick off his conference.

Cyrus had gotten me a dress—without my knowledge—that had

been wrapped in a white box with black and silver ribbons wrapped around it. He'd had it delivered to my room while we'd been out and it fit me like a glove.

It was an electric-violet color, a floor-length gown with sheer straps and according to the embossed paper note from the designer that had come with it, handmade beads and sparkling crystals sewn onto the bust. The skirt cinched around my waist, then kicked out just enough to provide balance to the width of my shoulders.

I'd never had the perfect hourglass figure, but the dress was a masterpiece that sure made it look like I did. After my shower when we'd gotten back from another day of sightseeing, I'd braided my hair into the fanciest plait I could do. Then I'd tucked it up into an elaborate twist behind my head.

It had taken a lot longer than I'd thought it would, but I'd used the bathroom mirror and a small compact I carried in my purse to check it out, and I thought it was more than worth the time. Going with smoky eyes and a neutral shade for my lipstick, I only just had enough time to give myself a final onceover before a knock came at my door.

I hardly recognized myself, and I smiled as my heart stammered in my chest. *Let's see how you keep it all business tonight, Cy.*

I'd managed to put all those weird emotions I'd had before we left into a box, and though I was disappointed about the two-room thing, I was genuinely excited about going to this event with him. I also hoped seeing me in this dress would inspire him to use only one of the rooms tonight.

Because hey, why not get laid while in the city of love with your friend, right?

When I opened the door, a lot of those weird feelings came punching out of the box and they most definitely were not friendly. Cyrus in a suit was beyond hot, but I'd gotten used to that. Cyrus in a tux, however, was just plain beyond. There were no words for how good he looked.

Fire burned in his eyes as they raked down the length of me before coming back up. His lips curved into a smile as he hooked his thumbs into his pockets.

"You look stunning," he said, a rasp I usually only heard in the bedroom in his voice.

"Thanks. You look okay, too." I lifted the dress and dipped into a silly curtsy. "Shall we go to the ball?"

He chuckled, the sound rumbling from his chest when I straightened out again. "We shall. There's just one thing we need to complete your outfit."

I titled my head. "Yeah, what's that?"

One of his hands slid into the inside pocket of his jacket, and when he pulled it out, a small velvet box came with it. My breath caught in my throat and my heartrate kicked up a few notches.

No. That can't be what I think it is, right?

But, of course, it was.

Cyrus lifted the top of the box and presented me with a ring that managed to be dainty and flashy all at the same time. It had the finest filigree work around the band and wasn't gaudy, but the center stone was large, and the smaller ones inlaid around it weren't exactly subtle either.

"With this ring, I thee wed." A slow smirk spread on Cyrus's lips. "For the night, anyway. What do think? It looks pretty legit, right?"

My hand came up to my chest and I tried to smile, anything not to show the inner maelstrom of emotions from showing on the outside. There was no way I could let Cyrus see how him presenting me with a ring, especially a ring that was so close to the one I'd always wanted, and hearing him say those words affected me.

A part of me that was wholly too big had leaped in joy and it wasn't just because of the ring or the idea of marriage this time. It was because the man in question was one I would have given my all to if he'd have let me. Or if I'd have let myself, for that matter.

While we hadn't been intimate since we'd been here, we'd hardly stopped touching. We laughed and talked and walked hand in hand. I'd seen glimpses again of that man I now knew lived inside, the one Peter had alluded to when he'd said there was good guy beneath all that dick demeanor.

Even now, with that one unruly lock of hair refusing to stay back and falling across his forehead, his eyes shining with humor and his posture radiating that cool, calm confidence I'd come to expect from him, I felt connected to him. Almost like I belonged to him.

Well, technically, you do. For tonight, anyway. Just like he'd said.

"Yeah," I said, blinking back the harsh reality that Cyrus wasn't really anything more than a friend at most, and forced a smile. "It's pretty darn legit. You ready to get this show on the road?"

"Let's," he said, then reached for my left hand and slid the ring onto it, even bringing it up to his mouth to kiss my hand once he had. "Perfect."

For one moment—just one moment in time when our eyes connected again—it felt like this wasn't temporary. Feeling the weight of his ring on my finger felt right, even though I knew it wasn't right, and for that one moment, I imagined he felt it as well.

Then he opened his mouth and shattered the illusion, or as April would have said, the *delusion*. "God, am I glad you agreed to fake marry me. I would have hated to have gone to this thing on my own."

Right. I closed my eyes and sucked in a quiet breath, fortifying myself for the night ahead. "Sure, because you made it so easy to say no."

He shrugged and held his arm out for me. "Hey, tell me you aren't glad you said yes. Aren't you having fun? Doesn't knowing you're going back debt free and having seen all this make it a little easier to be fake married to me?"

It left a bitter taste in my mouth actually, but I didn't mention it. "Well, if there's anything that makes it worth putting up with you, I guess it's that."

Laughing as he gently rested his hand over mine in the crook of his elbow, he shook his head at me. "At least now I know there's something that makes it worth putting up with me. How about Greece next time?"

"I don't know," I said dryly. "What's the next favor you're going to need from me?"

"Don't know yet." He smirked and pushed the errant hair off his forehead with his free hand. "I'll let you know, but Greece?"

I sighed but couldn't hold back just one small smile at how genuinely enthusiastic he sounded. "Sure. Greece, it is."

It turned out the gala was being held in our hotel. When the elevator let us out in the lobby, it was swarming with elegantly dressed people holding champagne flutes and waiters carrying big silver trays of hors d'oeuvres around.

My eyes slid to the front door and I noticed a sign outside the massive glass windows stating that the hotel was closed for a private function. *Holy cow. I didn't realize this is such a big deal.*

As the night wore on, however, I learned a lot of things I hadn't realized before. Firstly, this event was not only such a big deal, but it was ridiculously fancy as well.

Secondly, Cyrus was as much of a big deal to these people as the event itself was. He was the center of attention and he absolutely rocked the role. More than ever, he practically oozed power and dominance.

Even in a room full of the most successful entrepreneurs of our time, Cyrus didn't blend in. He stood out like an impeccably dressed sore thumb. He kept me close to his side, boasting about how he'd married the most amazing woman in the world, and even though I knew none of the compliments were real, I still found myself proud to be next to him as people fawned over him.

"Let's go find our seats," he said as we walked into an actual ball-room. It came complete with chandeliers, about six thousand different pieces of silverware on the tables, and what looked like real diamonds as part of the centerpieces. "We'll sit for dinner while some speakers take the stage."

"Are you a speaker tonight?" I asked because he hadn't mentioned being one but after seeing how revered he was around here, I wouldn't have been surprised if he was.

He chuckled and shook his head as he led us to one of the tables right up front. "They asked, but I've spoken two years in a row. I'm pretty sure everyone around here is as bored of listening to me as I am of speaking to them."

"Only you," I mused, taking a seat in the chair he pulled out for me.

Cyrus chuckled again and took the seat next to mine, then leaned over to say something in my ear only to stiffen before a word came out. I turned my head, our mouths so close together that we were breathing the same air.

"What?" I asked. "What's wrong?"

"Nothing." A faint grimace tightened his impression. "Don't look right now, but the woman who just walked in wearing the red dress? That's my ex."

My breathing faltered and my mouth went dry. I was about to get my first look at the only woman Cyrus had ever loved enough to make his wife, the very woman who was the reason I was in this magical place to begin with.

When I finally did turn slowly to take a peek at her, I almost wished I hadn't. My eyes nearly fell out of my head and I suddenly felt nauseated.

The former Mrs. Coning was beautiful, as I'd imagined she would be. She was simply breathtaking, the kind of gorgeous that had most men in the room turning toward her, even those with what I suspected were models on their own arms.

Blonde hair fell in a sleek curtain around her shoulders, her pale skin perfectly set off by her blood-red dress. Everything from her makeup, to her figure, to the small silver clutch she carried was perfect.

On her left hand, the same one carrying the clutch, sat a ring that was only just on the smaller side of the size of Australia. She flashed a dazzling, red-painted smile at the room, as though she was royalty we had all been waiting for.

A strong arm wrapped around her waist and she turned into it like a flower toward the sun, one graceful hand landing on a broad chest as she turned that smile on the man she had married after Cyrus. It was once my gaze finally left the stunning creature who was apparently as soulless as she was beautiful that I realized who her next target had been.

It was no wonder I'd immediately known the arm was strong or that I'd recognized the broad chest even without really taking him in because I'd had that arm around me plenty of times before. Countless nights I'd set my own hand or head on that chest before falling asleep.

Because the man she had married after Cyrus was the one I'd thought I was going to marry once. He was none other than Landon Parker himself.

In this one instance, I was giving myself a pass. Mentally, at least.

Fuck. Fuckity. Fuck. Fuck.

This was just my fucking luck.

CHAPTER 32

CYRUS

"Well, that was just as boring as ever," I said as I led Luna to the bar. "I'm going to need something stronger than wine to shake myself out of the stupor those idiots put me in. What do you feel like drinking?"

Her arm was linked with mine, but Luna was staring off straight ahead like she was in a stupor. All through the speeches, she looked like she'd seen a ghost and had had some kind of mind control exercised on her to forget it.

Every movement she made seemed robotic, automatic. The dessert had been out of this world and she'd hadn't even made a sound. It was almost like she hadn't tasted it at all.

I'd chalked it up to her tuning out the speeches, which I totally got, but now I was starting to think there was more going on. I faced her when we reached the bar, propping one elbow on the counter and snapping my fingers in front of her eyes.

"Earth to Luna. Where'd you go, babe? I mean, I know that was boring but it's over now. It's okay to come back."

She didn't even almost crack a smile at my attempt to joke, but at least she blinked away the glossed-over look in her eyes. "I'm sorry. What did you say?"

I smirked at her and reached up to cup her cheek. "I said—"

"Well, well, well." A familiar, booming voice interrupted us. "Look what the cat dragged in, and with Cyrus Coning, no less."

My head swung to face Landon fucking Parker, a scowl taking over my expression. "Landon. Meet my wife, Luna. Luna, Landon Parker."

"Oh, Luna and I are old friends," he said, reaching out to take a hand she hadn't offered him and scraping his lips along the back of it. "How are you doing, Luna? I didn't expect to see you here."

Finally seeming to come fully back to earth, she pulled her shoulders back and lifted her chin. Her hand withdrew from his and a cold smile spread on her lips. *Holy fuck.*

"Of course you didn't. If you had, I have no doubt you'd have left your wife at home. It wasn't nice to see you, Landon. When I told you I never wanted to speak to you again, I meant it. Please leave my husband and I alone now unless you want me to start talking. Loudly enough that everyone around us will know how you and I know one another."

I got seriously fucking hard watching and listening to her standing up to him like that. I'd always known the woman had balls, but for her to take on my arch nemesis like that was the hottest thing I'd ever seen.

Landon floated away from us like a balloon that had been punctured without me even having to step in, and Luna released a heavy sigh. I grinned at her and held up a hand. "That was fucking awesome. Just one question, though. How *do* you know him?"

Luna arched a brow at my unspoken request for a high-five but slapped my palm with one of hers anyway. "That's my ex. The guy I thought I was going to marry."

My amusement and libido took a backseat fast. Jealousy flared up instead, dark and angry as it pulsed through my veins and infected my brain. I had no reason to be jealous. I knew their relationship had ended two years before I'd ever met her, and even if it hadn't, friends had no right to be jealous of ex-lovers, but the thought that she'd been with him drove me to the brink of fucking insanity.

It made me want to hulk out and smash things. Just the thought of him seeing her naked or her waking up with him or speaking to him the way she did to me was enough to make my vision blur and my muscles tighten.

"That's the guy you thought you were going to marry?" I asked, managing to keep my voice deceptively calm.

Luna nodded and blew out an exasperated breath as she grabbed a flute of champagne from the tray of a passing waiter. She downed it in one go before slamming it down on the counter beside her.

"Yes, he was. Silly me, huh? Thinking a guy like that was going to marry me."

Suppressing the urge to tell her how distinctly *not* silly she was and how every guy would be more than fucking lucky to marry her, I crushed my lips to hers instead. Maybe it was intense possessiveness that had taken hold of me as soon as I saw him touching her hand, but I suddenly couldn't keep my hands off her.

Luna moaned into the kiss, her arms coming up around my shoulders and her fingers tangling into my hair. Both of us seemed to forget where we were and even what we were to one another for a minute, but we remembered at the same time.

She pulled away from me, careful to keep up the act by keeping her arms around me and smiling sweetly as she looked into my eyes. "Do you think I should tell his wife what he did? I've always felt like she deserved to know he was seeing another woman for the first few months of their marriage. I never thought I'd have a chance to meet her, but looking her up on social media to tell her just seemed tacky."

I took a minute before I answered, absorbing the earnestness in the deep blue depth of her gaze. Her expression was open and vulnerable. She was really asking me if I thought she should tell Sam, not because she was vindictive or as a method for me to exact revenge.

She honestly wanted to know what I thought, whether I thought it would be the right thing. As I let memories wash over me of the time we'd spent together, I pulled up instances in which I'd seen how badly the asshole had damaged her.

The damage wasn't too bad, but there were some scars. I also thought back to Luna asking me if I'd ever cheated on Sam, and I remembered the revulsion I'd felt at the idea. Whatever she had done to me, no one deserved to be cheated on.

I still didn't know if Samantha had cheated on me, but this wasn't about us. It was about them. Whether or not she had cheated on me, Landon had cheated on her. If he'd done it then, he was likely to do it again.

Hell, even if he hadn't, I was almost entirely certain Sam didn't know she'd been cheated on. As far as I was concerned, cheating was one of the most despicable things a human being in a relationship with someone else could do.

And despicable as Samantha Parker herself was, she did deserve to know that while he'd been married to her, Landon had been seriously dating another woman. To the point that he'd discussed marriage with her and had led her to believe they were on the brink of getting engaged.

"Yeah, I think you should tell her," I said, splaying my fingers on her hips and bending over to plant a kiss on her lips. "I'll be at the table. I think I just saw her heading into the ladies' room, if you want to get it over with."

I hadn't been watching Samantha at all this evening, but the color of her dress made her impossible to miss in a sea of mostly black and white. Strangely enough, despite all the beautiful women around, I only had eyes for Luna.

I'd only seen Sam heading into the bathroom because there were a bunch of men in the required black and white that had parted for her to move through. And they happened to be standing right behind Luna.

She gave me a small nod, took a breath, and turned to move in the direction of the restrooms herself. I watched with rage simmering in my stomach as the leering group of men stepped aside to let Luna through as well, making a mental note of each of their faces and vowing right then and there never to do business with anyone who looked at her like that.

Unfortunately, that vow was the worst thing I could do to them in here. Physical violence wasn't an option, despite how badly I wanted to punch someone.

With a resigned sigh, I ordered a single-malt whiskey, knocked it back, and then ordered another to take back to my table. Someone sidled up to me as I did, and when I looked back, I seriously reconsidered making physical violence an option.

"Luna the little florist, huh?" Landon smirked as he nudged my elbow on the counter with his. "Great fucking lay for a peasant, isn't she?"

"Excuse me?" I cleared my throat, my grip on the empty crystal glass tightening to the point where I was afraid it would break. "What did you just say about my wife?"

Landon paled, but his eyes darted around like he was aware that people were starting to watch us and didn't want to be seen backing down, even if neither of us could be heard by anyone else as of yet.

I supposed it was the principle of being seen backing away from me that made him stupid. With a sneer on his pathetic face, he shrugged. "You heard me. She's a fucking great piece of ass, but she's just not good enough to really make it permanent. I don't know what you're really doing with her, but I'd be willing to bet you're only playing with her, too. Just like I was."

"She's my wife, asshole." My voice rose along with my temper. "If you ever talk about Luna that way ever again, I will come after you personally and I will fucking destroy you. You hear me, Parker?"

The blood that had remained in his cheeks drained from it when I got in his face, literally vibrating with rage. A small hand on my shoulder pumped a sense of calm through me, and when I turned, I wasn't at all surprised to see it was Luna who'd had that instant effect on me.

"I mean it, you fucking coward," I growled at Landon before grabbing Luna's hand and walking out with her.

Just before we hit the exit, I heard Samantha screeching in front of everyone. "You fucking cheated on me? You bastard!"

CHAPTER 33

LUNA

C yrus looked smug as all hell as we walked into the bar on the rooftop of our hotel. "I'm glad we decided to have drinks. I could use a couple to unwind after all that."

"Yeah, it was quite something." I was still trembling slightly, nerves and adrenaline over confronting Landon's wife not quite draining out of me as fast as the fight had. "I can't believe I did that, but I really felt like she needed to know."

If Landon had been my husband, like he almost had been, I knew I'd have wanted to know. No matter who she was to Cyrus, she was still a woman and we had to stick together. If she decided to work through it with her husband, that was her business. I'd done my part and given her the information she needed to make her own informed decisions.

"Samantha might not be the best woman in the world, but I'm proud of you for standing up and doing something to the guy who made you feel like shit."

"Yeah, I guess there's that, too." I licked my dry lips and a waiter came by as if summoned by magic, dropping off a complimentary bottle of wine and one of water. "Is that really free?"

Cyrus laughed and shrugged his shoulders. "Considering how

much the room rate is here, nothing they serve is really free. As for whether it's going to show up on our check this evening, no. It won't. Let's just say it's included."

"That's..." I trailed off when I spotted a familiar, ravishing woman walking in. She marched up to the bar, her long, red-tipped fingers swiping underneath her eyes as her shoulders shook.

Slamming her silver clutch down on the counter of the bar, she held up four fingers as she spoke to the bartender.

"Wow. I guess she's all for drowning her sorrows tonight."

Cyrus frowned when his gaze followed mine and he saw his ex standing at the bar. "Yeah, it looks like she is."

"I wonder where Landon is," I said. "I'd have thought he'd at least come after her after the blowout they just had downstairs."

"He's probably still down there, trying to fix his reputation and telling more lies," Cyrus said distractedly.

I shifted in my seat so I was more in his line of vision but without making it obvious what I was doing. "That sounds like him. Have you known him for a long time?"

"Yeah, I guess you could say that." He dragged a hand through his hair, bringing his gaze to mine. The expression in his eyes was almost absent, though. "If I'd known he was your ex, I never would have asked you to do this."

"That's okay. It felt like we both kind of got our own back, you know?"

"Sure, yeah." He laughed, but the sound was humorless, and his eyes tracked back to where Samantha was sitting at the bar.

In fact, regardless of how many times I tried to drag him back into conversation with me, he kept one eye on Samantha the whole time, and at a point, he even let out a small sigh.

When I'd first realized he'd booked us each our own room, I felt discarded. Like he was treating this as nothing more than a business transaction, and that had stung but not nearly as much as the realization I had as I watched him now.

He'd brought me here to make her jealous. I knew that, but what if there was more to it than that?

What if he'd known all the time that Samantha and Landon would get into some kind of fight if he brought me, even if he hadn't known about my past with Landon, and he'd brought me specifically so they would fight?

What if he'd wanted them to fight so he'd be able to find her once she was alone after and that was also why he'd gotten us separate rooms? So he could take her to his and make love to her after their big fight?

It was pretty diabolical, sure, but I couldn't put it past him. I'd seen how ruthless he could be firsthand and, over the last few months, had learned that there wasn't much that could stop Cyrus from getting what he wanted.

If that was his ex, it was entirely possible he'd planned this whole thing out. It was unlikely he'd known what their fight would end up being about, since I really didn't think he knew about my history with Landon, but his ex had seemed like a catty, jealous type when I'd confronted her.

Cyrus showing up with a wife had been enough to set her off as it was before I'd even opened my mouth to her about Landon. The things she'd said to me just because she'd seen me with Cyrus and had obviously noticed a ring on a very specific finger had been unwarranted, to say the least.

She'd snarled at me and very obviously staked a claim on him, making it sound like he was still an option to her and like she'd be his first choice even though she was married to someone else.

It was disgusting actually, considering that she really was married to someone else, but I felt like she deserved to know the truth anyway. It had just made it easier to tell her once I'd learned she wasn't some sweetheart I'd been a party to hurting.

If Cyrus had known all that about her, which I had to assume he did, given that he'd been married to her, it wasn't unthinkable that he could have orchestrated all this to trigger her, make her jealous, which was guaranteed to cause a fight between her and Landon, then take her up to his room.

There were a lot of what ifs, but I knew Cyrus, and if anyone could make it happen, it was him. With the way his eyes were tracking her every move, watching the curve of her throat as she swallowed back some shot or another, it really wouldn't have surprised me if even his ulterior motives had ulterior motives.

Since I'd dealt with my fair share of ulterior motives when it came to relationships, I wasn't keen on being part of the ulterior part of the motives any longer. Angling myself so my elbow was on my armrest and my body was now smack in the middle of his view of her, I waited for him to look at me.

When he did, there was a slightly hazy look in his eyes that made me feel sick for the second time tonight. *Oh, God. He wants her.*

"You told me to tell her the truth because you knew they'd fight, didn't you?" I asked, fighting to keep my voice from cracking.

He cocked his head at me, sitting back with his hands in his lap and one ankle crossed over the opposite knee. *Oh, ew. No. He's definitely trying to hide what going on in his pants.*

With the urge to vomit making blood roar in my ears, I barely made out his response. "Well, I knew there was a decent chance they were going to fight after you told her. It was pretty obvious."

"Pretty obvious, huh?"

He frowned at me but nodded. "Sure. Of course, it was going to happen."

Well, there you have it, ladies and gents. Confirmation of his intention when he told me to tell her the truth.

I'd inadvertently done the dirty work for him. Tears closed my throat, but I cleared them away. I wouldn't let him see me cry. I couldn't.

"You and I are just friends, though, right?" I asked.

When he nodded, I stood up and grabbed my purse. "Well then, you go do what you need to do. I'm tired and I've had enough of all of this. Good night, friend."

Cyrus opened his mouth to say something, but I didn't stick around to hear what it was. Walking as fast as my insanely high heels would allow without literally needing someone to lean on, not that I'd ever literally or metaphorically lean on Cyrus ever again, I left the bar.

I didn't know exactly when my feelings toward him had changed, but they had. I'd been feeling the shift for some time now, but things became crystal clear in that moment. The way my heart cracked open as I headed down to my room and let the realities of what was going on here really dawn on me told me that I'd missed my exit point somehow.

I didn't know how I'd let it happen when my eyes had been wide open all this time, but I'd sure as heck missed the exit and was speeding along the freeway to the majestic yet heartbreaking city of "Fallen for Him."

Because I had. I didn't know how I could've been so dumb, but somewhere along the line, I'd let him charm me into believing that this could be real. In the meantime, I'd also thrown my last bit of caution to the wind and had decided to trust him with my heart.

To be fair to him, it was a heart he'd always been clear on not wanting. At least now I knew the real reason why. It wasn't because he was too hurt by his ex. It was because despite everything, he still wanted only her.

It had never been only me he wanted, despite what I'd let myself believe. It had been her all along, and tonight, he was finally going to have her again.

What sucked even more was that he was going to have her in the room right next to mine, while I cried my eyes out over him and hoped to everyone who might be holy that this hotel had thick walls. If it didn't, I wasn't sure what I was going to do.

But clearing out my bank account and skipping out of Italy in the middle of the night was one option. Even if it meant not fulfilling my end of the bargain by pretending with him for the rest of his trip.

All I knew was that despite our deal, nothing would be the same after tonight. Whatever real friendship might have developed beneath it all was gone. I would never be able to look at him the same way.

I didn't know if I was going to be able to look at him at all.

CHAPTER 34

CYRUS

When Luna marched away from me without so much as a backward glance, I was truly baffled. I'd thought we'd definitely been the couple to come out of that gala on top, not that I was really counting on it, but I didn't get what she was angry about.

I'd just poured us each a glass of some of the finest Italian wine. The moon and the city lights were reflected on the surface of the canals. It was fucking beautiful up here. Why the hell did she leave?

Everything had been okay when we'd left the ballroom, I was pretty sure. When we'd sat down, she'd seemed fine. But then Samantha had walked in and everything had changed.

Just before Luna had stormed off, I was pretty sure I'd even seen tears in her eyes. *What the fuck?*

As I got up to go after her, a dainty hand planted on a red-clad hip blocked my path. I didn't need to look up to know who those things belonged to. "Samantha. I saw you hit up the bar."

She sat down in the chair Luna had just vacated and the thought of her sitting in it instead left me feeling slightly revolted.

I inclined my head at her. "I didn't say you could sit."

"I didn't ask." She pouted when I looked up at her, blinking her soft green eyes as if she was trying to hold back tears. She wasn't.

Samantha wasn't capable of crying. It was a little known secret, but it was also a fact.

"I should never have left you for him, Cy," she simpered, crossing one knee over the other and leaning forward. She knew what she was doing, all right.

Sitting the way she was, she was offering a fantastic view of her tits. If it was any other man sitting in front of her, he'd undoubtedly have dropped his eyes. Even if just for a second.

Samantha had a fantastic fucking rack on her and she knew it. But it wasn't any other man sitting in front of her. It was me.

Not only did I know exactly who and what she was, but I also had eyes for only one pair of breasts, and they sure as hell weren't here. "What do you want, Samantha?"

"I want to talk to you."

"Why?" I held my glass to my lips, my eyes on hers. "What could you possibly want to say to me?"

"Why are you being so combative?" she asked almost demurely. "I just want to talk."

"You never 'just'," I put finger quotes around the word, "want to do anything. You've had years to talk to me. Why now?"

"You're married," she said, her eyes never leaving mine as she dropped the seductive pose and relaxed back in the chair like she owned the place. Although considering who she was married to, I supposed it wasn't impossible.

I'd invested in a few hotels around Europe myself. Parker might have done the same. If he hadn't, it wouldn't be a bad—

"Are you even listening to me?" Her shrill voice cut through my thoughts.

When I refocused on her, I shrugged. "I'm not really sorry to say I wasn't."

"I just told you your wife has been sleeping with my husband. Does that not bother you?"

"She's not sleeping with him. She has slept with him. It's very much past tense."

"So you married my husband's ex?" That knowing gleam I hated entered her eyes. "Were you that desperate to get my attention, Cyrus?"

"No, but if that was what you were so desperate to talk to me about, I'm out of here. I would suggest going to find your husband and talking to him about it."

"No, I—" She released a sigh. "That's not what I wanted to talk to you about."

"What is it then, Sam? As you pointed out, I'm married. I should get back to my wife." There was nothing I wanted to do more than to find Luna and figure out why she'd left before we'd even gotten around to having our nightcap. And why she'd seemed pissed off when she had left.

"I was so stupid to have left you for Landon. I never should have done it." Emotion cracked in her voice, but I didn't buy it.

Even if it was real, it wouldn't have mattered. Whether or not she genuinely believed that she shouldn't have left me for him was irrelevant. Because she had left, and just as surely as she had, I was over it.

Seeing her tonight had solidified it for me in a way it had never been before. I'd realized that I had never really loved Samantha. The knowledge was as terrifying as it was empowering because I'd married a woman I hadn't loved.

What was it that Luna always said about doing it for the right reasons? Because I was sure now that I hadn't. Everything she, Peter, and Jenny had said to me about marriage and why they believed in it was swirling around in my head, making me question if I'd been right about the institution after all.

What had happened with Samantha was what had disillusioned me about it, but if I hadn't loved her, if I really had married her only because of infatuation or in some desperate attempt to cling to one more person, to make a family with her just so I'd have one again, maybe I needed to re-evaluate.

I swallowed a lump in my throat, but it wasn't tears that had put it there. It was all the unsaid shit that needed to be said to Luna and yet Samantha was standing in my way of getting it done. Or sitting in my way, more accurately, but she was the reason I wasn't with Luna right now.

"I have to go," I said abruptly.

"No, just listen to me for one minute," she begged, and it was only the glassiness of her eyes that made me agree. Because whatever she needed to get off her chest, if there was any chance it was going to keep her away from the bar for the rest of the tonight, she needed to say it.

I wasn't a monster, and only a monster would leave if it meant driving her to drink even more than she already had. *With her family history...*

"Fine." I crossed my arms over my chest. "You have one minute. Go."

"Leaving you was the worst mistake I ever made," she started. "Landon's an asshole. You wouldn't believe the things he's done to me. I should have known cheating wasn't something that would be off-limits with him. He's terrible."

She sniffled, and I almost genuinely believed she was about to burst into tears. Even so, I felt nothing but a pang of empathy for a fellow human being. No regret, no want or need to have her back. Just that one little stab of empathy.

I remained silent, though, as I mostly had since this conversation started, and I motioned for her to continue. Again, not a monster. *An asshole, maybe, but not a monster.*

"You should hear the way he speaks to me. It's like I'm a piece of shit who should be grateful that he's speaking to me at all. He parades me around like a show pony, but as soon as the attention of the room shifts away from us, he's gone."

A choked sigh escaped her. "He's never home before the early morning hours and he's almost always drunk when he gets there. You know that's a trigger for me. He gets high in front of me and he flirts with other women."

When a tear rolled down her cheek, I stood up. I might not be a monster, but I didn't particularly feel like being manipulated either. She grabbed my wrist and rose to her feet as well. "If I leave him, I get nothing, Cyrus. We have a pre-nup drawn up by his lawyers that I can't beat. Unless you help me, baby. If you and I get back together—"

I jerked my arm free of her grip and narrowed my eyes. "Don't touch me, Sam."

"Don't you dare walk away from me." Her nostrils flared. "You owe it to me to have this conversation, you—"

"I don't owe you shit. Hearing you out tonight was far more than you ever had a right to expect from me. Am I glad he treats you like shit? No. You should be happy, Sam, and one day, I hope you will be. For now, you got what you deserved. Good luck getting yourself out of it."

Just before I turned to walk away, I sighed and dragged both hands through my hair. "For God's sake, stay away from the bar. Find your husband and try to work things out with him. There had to have been a reason why you chose him. Whatever happens, just leave the bar, okay? He's not worth the risk."

Wetness I truly hadn't believed she was capable of appeared in her eyes, and her shoulders slumped, but she nodded. "This isn't over."

I let my hand drift from my chest and motioned to hers. "If you mean us, then yes. It's over. Move on, Sam. I sure as fuck have."

Without a doubt in my mind that I'd made the right choice, I finally turned away from her and left Samantha well and truly behind. Perhaps for the first time ever, it felt like she really was where she belonged. In my past.

It still didn't mean I was ready to get married again, nor did I know if I ever wanted to. But it did mean that for the first time since she'd left me, I was free to make my own decisions. I was done letting her and the baggage she'd caused dictate my actions.

Deciding that waiting for the elevator was a waste of time, I flung the door to the stairwell open and took them down two at a time. Since Luna and I were on the upper floors of the hotel anyway, it took me almost no time to reach her door.

I lifted my hand and started to knock before her final words played through my mind again. *We're just friends, right?*

Like the idiot I was and because I'd been so wrapped up in

watching Sam down shot after shot, wondering why the asshole wasn't there to stop her, I'd said yes. Although it wasn't like I could have said no at the time.

Things might have changed for me, or at least I thought they had, but they obviously hadn't for Luna. Whatever crazy shit I'd been trying to convince myself I didn't feel for her, she really didn't feel for me.

All she wanted was to be friends, and I didn't know if I could be that for her any longer. If I knocked and she opened her door, invited me in? Fuck.

I didn't know if there would be any coming back from that for me. When I'd booked our two rooms, I'd done it in an effort to preserve our friendship despite what I'd asked of her to convince her to come here.

Perhaps it had been unknowingly at the time, but it might just have saved our friendship for another reason as well. I just wasn't sure it was one she wanted to hear, and if I went in there, I couldn't guarantee I wouldn't say it anyway.

So I didn't knock. I braced both hands against her door, hung my head, and silently apologized for being a shitty friend in the days to come. Then I went back to my room. Alone.

For the rest of the nights we were on this trip, that was the way it would have to be. Unless Luna decided otherwise.

CHAPTER 35

LUNA

Cyrus was always busy for the remainder of our time in Italy. During the day, I explored by myself and tried not to wallow in misery.

Instead, I got lost in the sights and sounds of the magical place he'd brought me to, doing my best to soak in every moment despite the fact that I'd rather have had him beside me. Before we'd boarded the plane to come here, he'd warned me that the couple of days after the gala would be rough for him.

Meeting after meeting packed his schedule, but he'd promised to spend his time in the evenings with me. It had been said jokingly at the time, with a wag of his eyebrows and insinuation in his tone.

I'd laughed but agreed.

A naughty glimmer had come into his eyes when I'd said yes, and then he'd kissed the crap out of me. A kiss that had been full of promises that had turned out to be empty.

Every night, he texted me with an excuse about why he couldn't see me. Meetings running late or late meetings that had turned into business dinners. I didn't buy any of it, but I couldn't say I minded that he hadn't gotten around to spending any more time with me.

That night after I'd walked out on him in the bar, I hadn't heard him next door with his ex. *Thank the Lord.*

I also hadn't seen either her or Landon around again. *I really should send the Lord a bouquet of flowers for that, but double thank you to the big man upstairs for that one.*

While I hadn't seen any of the three people who had become the bane of my existence, that didn't mean that they weren't there. Cyrus and Samantha lurked in my thoughts, and the more I imagined them together, the more I understood why they had been together and why they probably were again.

They were the ultimate power couple. She was the perfect partner for a man like him, polished, beautiful, and with that upper crust accent that spoke of money.

I wondered when she'd tell Landon that she was cheating on him just like he had on her. Maybe she already had, or maybe she was doing it just as I sat there on St. Mark's square, my hands full of pigeon feed and my soul full of sadness and regret.

The days passed in a blur, and eventually, my time in Italy came to an end. It was a bittersweet goodbye to a country I knew I wouldn't see again.

Our flight back to New York was uneventful and mostly silent, with only a few words exchanged between us. When we landed, I texted April to pick me up. I also received a text from my bank congratulating me on paying off my loans.

Holding out my hand to Cyrus when we stepped out of the terminal and into the wave of humidity that welcomed us home, I gave him a forced smile. "It was a pleasure doing business with you. I'll see you around, Cyrus."

"You don't want a ride?" he asked as he frowned at my hand but didn't shake it.

Eventually, it got awkward and I let it drop. "No, I'm fine. Thanks."

Thankfully, I'd let April know more or less when our plane would be landing and she pulled up as if she'd been sent by the gods themselves to save me. Honking her horn, she rolled down her window and grinned at me.

"Well, are you coming, my little Globetrotter?" she called out and slapped the side of her car. "I have margaritas and pizza ready and waiting at home."

"Coming." I turned back to Cyrus and gave him a little wave. "I guess this is, uh, goodbye. Thanks again for everything."

He opened his mouth, then closed it again and pressed it into a firm line. Returning my wave, he grabbed the handle of his bag and stalked off in the direction of the long-term parking lot.

April glanced between the two of us, an unhappy expression on her face as I climbed into the car after loading my suitcase into the trunk. "What happened?"

"You were right." I sat back against her seat with a thud and groaned as I fastened my seatbelt. "I never should have gotten involved in any of this."

"It was that bad, huh?" She reached out to pat my leg as she merged into the traffic. "I'm sorry. Do you want to talk about it?"

"I got deluded," I said. "I know you warned me, and I know I didn't listen, but I really thought it was going well."

"It did seem to be." Her brows pulled together. "So I ask again, what happened?"

"It was worse than bad. He didn't only want to use me to make his ex jealous. He wanted to make her jealous so he could get her back."

April's jaw dropped and she slammed her hand into her horn. "Move, asshole. We're in need of margaritas here. Stat."

When the driver in front of her didn't move, she swerved around him only to have to slam on her brakes as we hit our first traffic jam. She puffed out a heavy breath. "I'm sorry. I did try to get us to the alcohol faster. Keep talking. I'll do my best to make sure we get to it as soon as we can. Adi's staying with a friend from school for the night, so I'm all yours."

"How did you know I'd need you?" I asked, my voice quiet.

She shrugged and shook her head. "I didn't, but I thought there might be a chance. You don't go to a place like Venice with a man like that and not need a girlfriend to come home to."

"You're the best." I turned my head to face the window, took a

226

breath, and then broke open my heart to spill the contents all over her car. "I should have listened to you. I was such a knucklehead to believe I could keep things platonic with Cyrus. At first, it really was just attraction. He was also a nice person, or at least I thought he was. I've since learned differently."

"When did you end up realizing it was more than that?" Sympathy colored her tone, and I was grateful that at the very least, she hadn't said she'd told me so. Even if she had. *A true friend.*

I shook my head against the fabric of her seat. "I'm not sure the exact moment, but it was somewhere after realizing I was jealous that he cared enough about his ex to make her jealous and the moment I realized there was more to it for him than that."

She hesitated. "He really got back together with her in front of you?"

"He may as well have." Tears burned my eyes as I remembered that night. "In a wicked twist of fate, it turns out his ex is the same woman Landon is married to."

"What?" Her voice bounced around the inside of the car and I winced. "Are you serious?"

"Unfortunately." I breathed past the tears threatening to fall, but my voice still came out thick. "Cyrus encouraged me to tell her about Landon cheating on her when he found out. I did. They got in a huge fight. She ended up at the same bar as us and he couldn't take his eyes off her."

It got too hard to talk without crying and I dragged in another few breaths while April released a string of curses worthy of every single one I hadn't uttered. "That bastard. Are his balls still attached to his body? Because they shouldn't fucking be."

"I wouldn't know," I said flatly. "I wasn't the one doing anything with his balls for the rest of the trip."

"You really think he got back together with her?" she asked after a brief pause. "Did you see them together?"

"No, but I didn't see either of them separately either. They might have been together, but maybe not." I shrugged. "I don't know, but if you'd seen the way he looked at her, you'd know she was the one he's wanted all this time. God, he was watching her like a hawk circling its prey."

"Bastard," she repeated. "I can't believe he did that to you."

"We never made each other any promises he didn't honor. He took me to Italy, paid off my debts, and didn't fall in love with me. It all went exactly as he said it would."

Silence fell between us for several long minutes. Horns honking as we made our way through the traffic seemed to be the melancholy cacophony welcoming me back to my real life. The one where there were no super hot, super sweet billionaires popping in every other day, no invitations for exotic trips, and no passionate nights after disagreeing on plans for a wedding that wasn't even ours.

A choked sob escaped me and April squeezed my leg. "I'm so sorry, babe. You didn't deserve this."

"I did," I said. "You warned me. He warned me. I should have known, but I refused to listen. I thought I had it all under control and then I just had to go believing in some fucked-up fairy tale that wasn't even real."

This time the silence that fell between us was stunned. April was first to break it but only as we were nearing her apartment. "You fell for him hard enough to swear about it?"

I nodded, tears finally breaking free. They tracked down my cheeks and tasted salty on my lips. "I really did. He was everything I never thought I wanted, and now I don't know what I'm going to do. This isn't like Landon. It feels a million times worse, especially because this time, I really should have seen it coming."

"You never cursed over Landon, so I already knew it was worse" she said, demonstrating once again that she knew me better than I knew myself sometimes. "Just so you know, I was really hoping to be wrong on this one. In fact, I've never wanted to be wrong so badly. I was holding out hope that Cyrus was going to prove me wrong about all male kind."

"You and me both apparently." Bitterness tinged my tone and I hated it.

"For what it's worth," April said, honesty and regret making her voice sound course, "this guy really did seem different. I don't think you can blame yourself for falling for his act because if he got me to believe it just by hearing about him, he's really good at it."

"Yeah, he was good at it." Just like he was good at every flipping thing he did. "I don't think he meant for it to be an act, though. He really never said anything that didn't turn out to be true."

"He made you believe it, though," she said softly. "That's almost worse, as far as I'm concerned. This was the first time I hoped I was wrong about a guy after everything that happened with Adi's father. I'm sorry that I wasn't."

"So am I," I murmured before drifting into silence once more. "Do me a favor and just slap me next time, okay? None of this believing I'm right stuff. It only seems to get me burnt."

In a surprising reversal of roles, April shook her head firmly. "I'll never stop believing you're right, girl. I can't. One of us has to stay optimistic and it has to be you. One day, you'll find your Prince Charming and he really will prove to all of us that not all men are untrustworthy assholes."

I doubted that, but I nodded anyway.

If only because April had just admitted to needing to believe. I'd already faked being a wife. How much harder could it really be to fake being an optimist?

CHAPTER 36

CYRUS

One week after getting back from Italy, Peter was tired of me dodging his calls. He was waiting for me when I got home, sitting on my couch with a beer in his hand and an expectant expression on his face.

He stood up when I walked in and spread his arms wide. "Well, well, well, the prodigal brother returns. Where have you been, dude?"

"In Italy," I grunted as I kicked off my sneakers and dragged my sweaty shirt over my head, letting it fall to the floor.

My brother gave me a look, then handed over a beer he had waiting for me. "From the looks of things, I think you might have been to the gym after. Unless you just ran here all the way from Venice."

"Smart ass." It was the best I could come up with as I collapsed on the couch and kicked my feet up on the coffee table. "Why are you here?"

"What? Do I need a reason to visit my little brother when I know he's been back in the country for a week and I haven't heard a peep from him? I was worried, Cyrus. Jesus. What's wrong with you?"

"Nothing." I hoped he read the implied "fuck off" between the lines.

He didn't, but it really shouldn't have surprised me.

"I checked with all the wedding suppliers from that list you sent me before you left," he said, starting almost cautiously. "They've all assured me everything is on track."

"Yeah, well, the wedding is in two weeks. What did you expect?" I hooked one arm behind my neck and rested my head against it. "Your bachelor party is coming up and it's going to be tame, just like you requested. Everything else was on that list. So what's up?"

"Where have you been all week?"

"Working." I shot to my feet and glared at him as I began to pace. "Fuck, Peter. What's with all the questions? I've been busy with your fucking wedding for months, and everything is set to go as you've found out for yourself. Why are you up my ass about this?"

Peter, annoyingly, ignored my outburst. "What happened to Luna? You weren't like this when she was around, which tells me that she's not anymore."

"Nothing happened to her. I told you we were just friends. I've gotten back into my investments. You know, my actual job. Luna has gotten back to her actual work, too. You might remember that neither of us are fucking wedding planners in our real lives."

He held up his hand, palms turned out as he lifted a brow. "Don't bite my fucking head off, asshole. I know you're not a wedding planner and I've thanked you plenty of times for helping out. For the rest of my life, I'll be grateful to you for everything you've done and so will Jenny."

The words hit me like a blow to the chest, stomach, and jaw all at once, but he wasn't done. "Throughout your whole life, I've been proud of you. No matter what, I've always had your back. I listened to all your bullshit opinions, and I've never seriously argued with you, but I'm starting to see that might have been a mistake."

"Yeah?" I lifted my chin and my eyes narrowed to slits. "Why's that?"

"Because right now, you're acting like an entitled child who got his favorite toy taken away. I get that people lash out at those closest to them, but really? Like I said, I've been proud of you your whole life, but I'm really fucking disappointed in you right now."

Those were the words that finally knocked the wind out of my sails. With another grunt, I sank down on my haunches, dropped my head into my hands, and released a silent scream.

Peter's callused hand was rough on my shoulder, but it was comforting nonetheless. When I finally lifted my head again, he inclined his toward the couch. "Let's sit down and actually talk, okay?"

"Okay." I picked my beer up off the coffee table when I passed it and chugged at least half before sitting down. "Why are you disappointed in me?"

It burned all the way down to my soul to know how Peter felt about me. In all my life, he'd never said those words to me.

He'd always been my most staunch supporter, even back when our parents had still been alive. Other guys might not have gotten along with their older brothers, but Peter had always been something of an idol to me.

Sure, it wasn't like we'd never fought before, but it had never felt like this. All the other times, it had been over some superficial bullshit. This wasn't that.

It felt like this stretched down to the very fiber of our respective beings, and since most of what I'd believed about mine had recently proven to be wrong, I sucked it the fuck up and listened to what my brother had to say.

There was no judgment in his eyes when he turned to face me, but there was a ton of worry. "Firstly, throwing all the wedding planning you've done back in my face? Not cool, bro."

"I know," I admitted and scrubbed my hands over my jaw. "I never meant for it to sound like that was what I was doing, but I know it ended up coming out like that."

"That's not exactly an apology."

"I know that, too." I groaned and released a deep sigh, digging deep for words that would actually matter. "I really am sorry for saying what I did. Despite how much I've protested and all the shit I've talked, it means a lot to me that you trusted me as much as you did with something as important to you as your wedding."

He punched my shoulder but not hard enough for my torso to move. "See? Was that so hard?"

I breathed in through my nose and shook my head. "I guess not. I'm sorry for being a dick. Can we move on now?"

"No." Fuck. "What really happened with Luna?"

"I don't know, man," I said, partially honestly. "Everything was fine, going according to plan, and then it wasn't."

Peter studied me a long minute. "What happened right before it didn't?"

"Sam walked into the bar we were at after having a very public fight with Landon. Landon who—get this—also happens to be Luna's ex." I laughed dryly at the way Peter's eyes grew wide. "Yeah, I know. He cheated on her with Luna, or on Luna with her. I'm not really sure who came into his life first, but he cheated."

"Wow, that's..." Peter shook his head. "Fucked up. Beyond fucked up."

"You're telling me," I said. If there was one thing we saw eye to eye on, it was our stance on fidelity. "Anyway, so Luna asked me if she should tell Sam and I said yes."

He nodded slowly. "I agree. It was the right thing to do."

"Exactly." I screwed my eyes shut. "So Luna tells Sam, who comes out of the bathroom screaming at Landon. Luna and I get the hell out of Dodge, and we're drinking at the bar on the rooftop when Sam comes in and starts throwing back shots like it's—"

"Sam was drinking?" My brother's jaw went slack when I nodded.

"Yeah. A lot. At first, I thought maybe it was water, but I watched the bartender for a few minutes to be sure. She was definitely drinking. Whiskey, no less."

"No way," he breathed. "That's bad, but what does it have to do with Luna?"

"I don't know. That's where it all gets weird for me. She asked me if we were just friends, I said yes, and then she said 'do what you have to do' or some shit like that and stormed out." I put my arms out to my sides before rubbing my hand over the back of my head. "Before I could follow her to find out what the fuck was going on, Sam came up to me and begged me to talk to her."

"What did she want?"

"In a nutshell? Me." I watched as Peter's eyes grew almost comically wide again. Then he burst out laughing. It was so unexpected that I had to join in. "I heard her out because I thought it might keep her from drinking if I did. Then I told her to move on and went down to Luna's room."

"What did she say when you told her what happened?"

I hung my head as I shook it. "Nothing, because I never told her. She really just wanted to be friends, Peter. It wouldn't have been fair to dump everything I was feeling on her, so I left. I was caught up in meetings during all the days that followed and then I booked more for the nights. I didn't know if I could act like a friend to her. I still don't, so I haven't spoken to her since we've been back."

"Let me get this straight," he said slowly. "You finally admitted to yourself that you have feelings for this girl and then you didn't have the balls to tell her?"

"It wasn't that. She doesn't want the same things I do. It's not fair of me to change the rules now. I've been clear all along and she took me at my word. Until I can keep that word to her, I have to stay away."

"You're insane." He brought his hands to his hair and tugged at it. "Certifiably fucking insane."

"Why? Because I'm trying to keep my word to a girl I promised I'd always be honest with? Telling her anything now and not telling her how I feel about her would be lying. I can't do that, but I also can't tell her how I feel because then everything our relationship was built on would be a lie."

"Yeah, it's a real catch-22," he said, sarcasm dripping from his voice.

"It is," I protested.

"No, it's not." He lifted his gaze to mine, a gleam of determination in it I hadn't seen for a long time. "Listen to me and listen to me well, baby brother. That girl likes you as a hell of a lot more than a friend. I mean, fuck, have you even realized that your very names almost make it that you're meant to be? Cyrus means sun and Luna means moon. You literally cannot have one without the other, bro."

"Considering we didn't choose our own names, I'm pretty sure that doesn't mean anything." I hadn't actually noticed it before, though. "It doesn't matter anyway. She barely even looked at me on our flight back and called her friend for a ride. Whatever happened that night, she doesn't want me."

"So that's it?" He lifted both his eyebrows, disbelief clear as day in his eyes. "You're going to give her up just like that?"

"I haven't given her up because she isn't mine to give up." I slumped back on the couch and rested my head against the leather. "She never was, so let it be, bro. It's over. There's nothing either of us can do about it."

I could see he didn't agree, but it hardly mattered. I wished I was wrong, but I wasn't. I'd seen the way Luna had looked at me. He hadn't.

Whatever there might have been brewing between us, it was over. I was nothing to her now.

Despite my best efforts, or maybe in spite of them, I wasn't even her friend. Which was good because there was no way I'd ever really be able to be friendly with perhaps the only woman I'd ever really been in love with.

CHAPTER 37

LUNA

"What are you doing here?" My eyes nearly fell out of my head when I opened my front door and saw Peter freaking Coning standing on the other side of it. "You're getting married in—" I twisted around to check the clock on the wall behind me. "Six hours, Peter. You're getting married in six hours."

He rocked back and forth on his heels, then shrugged. "I know, but I had to talk to you."

"What? Why?" Terror wrapped its icy tendrils around my heart and squeezed. "Is everything okay? Cyrus? Jenny?"

I felt blood draining from my face and rushed out into the hall, though I wasn't really sure why. There was no one else there, no blood on the walls.

A low chuckle drew my attention back to my unexpected visitor, who arched his brow as he sent a pointed look my way. It was only then that I realized I was still in my pajamas, my hair was a mess, my feet were bare, and my cup of tea was clutched between my numb fingers.

Whatever was going on, I wasn't going to be much help to him in this state. It dawned on me then that he looked completely relaxed, which probably meant that both his brother and his fiancée were fine.

"Chill out, Luna. No one has any life-threatening physical injuries, and as far as I know, everything is progressing smoothly at the venue."

"Which brings me back to my original question, then. What are you doing here?" I peered at him curiously, motioning him into my apartment.

My cheeks flushed at the state of my apartment and myself, but there was no turning back now. Peter was already closing the door behind him.

He was dressed casually in faded blue jeans and a white T-shirt, sporting a five o'clock shadow and his hair slightly messy. Just like it had been the last time I saw him. I was starting to think there was just no taming it.

Letting out another chuckle, he shook his head at me. "I'm not running out on the wedding or anything. My suit is at the venue and I'm headed there as soon as we're done here. I only need an hour, max, to shower and get ready. Don't worry. I'm not here to ask you to deliver some message to my brother or my bride about how I just couldn't go through with it."

Relief rushed through me. I might not know Peter and Jenny all that well, but I'd have hated to have seen him running. After everything they'd been through—heck, after everything I'd been through just to get their wedding planned alongside the Grinch—it would have been a real darn pity if he called it all off.

I nodded and walked farther into the apartment, setting my tea down before folding my arms. As I opened my mouth to speak, he beat me to it.

"I heard about what happened in Italy."

I blinked, surprised that he wanted to talk about *that* on this of all days. "Okay. Do you want to sit down?"

"Thanks," he said, flashing me a smile that was so similar to Cyrus's that it made my heart weep in my chest.

Peter perched on the very edge of my couch and rubbed his hands on his thighs. "I can't stay very long. I have this thing to get to."

"By thing, you mean your wedding?" I frowned, so lost about what the point was he was trying to make.

He rolled his eyes at me, shaking his head as he sighed. "Neither of you have any sense of humor these days."

"Neither of us?" My frown deepened. "Wait, are you drunk? Do you see two of me right now?"

"I guess if I was, it would make more sense to you what a groom—who most certainly is not running away from his wedding, thank you very much—is doing with his brother's ex hours before his wedding."

"We were just friends." It was an automatic reply by this point.

Peter rolled his eyes again. "You guys are the damn worst. I swear. You're as bad as the other. I had hoped that you, at least, would have let all that friend bullshit go by now."

The intensity of the frustration in his tone chipped at something deep inside me, and all the walls I'd so carefully constructed before opening my door came crumbling down. My shoulders dropped and I let the muscles in my face relax, showing him exactly what a mess I really was.

"There she is." He gave me a sympathetic smile. "That looks more like a woman who went through what you did just three weeks ago and is actually feeling it."

"I lost a good friend that week," I said because that was a big part of the problem. "I'm allowed to look bad."

"You don't look bad, Luna. You look like shit. I mean it with love, though, so please don't be pissed at me."

"I won't be pissed at you. You're only telling the truth." I cocked my head and slumped back on the couch. "So what did he tell you?"

"I'll summarize it for you. Whatever you think was going on with him over there wasn't what was really going on."

"What are you talking about?" Even just thinking about what I thought had been going on there made my stomach twist and another wave of nausea rolled through me at the sharp pain in my heart.

"This is just a guess, but you think he did something with Samantha. Don't you?"

I nodded, swallowing the tears that threatened to rise. There was a time for crying but in front of the man's brother on his wedding day wasn't it.

"You should have seen the way he looked at her, Peter. If you had, you would understand why I'm so certain about it. His eyes didn't leave her, not for a second."

He sighed and shoved his hands through his hair multiple times. "For fuck's sake. I'm assuming you're talking about when he saw her in the bar?"

"Yeah," I said, my voice soft. It felt like if I even spoke too loudly about it, I would shatter all over again.

"It's not what you think." He leaned forward, elbows on his knees and his fingers looped together. "I know how that sounds, but it really isn't. Nothing happened between them. You have my word."

"How do you know?" I narrowed my eyes on his. "You weren't there, Peter. All you have to go on is Cyrus's word."

"Maybe, but you have mine. He didn't get together with her while you guys were in Italy. He hasn't hooked up with her since before she left him and he never will again. But none of this is mine to tell you."

"Why did you come here then?" I squeezed my eyes shut.

It had taken everything I had in me not to think about the wedding all morning. I could picture it all so clearly in my mind's eye, could practically see the venue coming together as each hour passed.

Of course, in every one of my mental pictures, Cyrus was there. He looked so damn handsome in his tux. And that was about where I had to shut down the thoughts because then the waterworks wanted to turn on.

I couldn't cry about him. Not anymore. Cyrus had never wanted me as more than a wedding planner and friend. I couldn't waste weeks pining over him.

Okay, so I had wasted weeks pining. But I wouldn't waste them pining *and* crying about it, for heaven's sake.

Peter's expression softened as his eyes swept across whatever pain was visible on my face. "I came here because every time I've seen my brother these last few weeks, he's looked exactly the same as you do right now. I can't take it anymore."

He drew in a deep breath and sat up straighter. "Here's the truth, Luna. He didn't fuck Sam. You'll have to speak to him to get the whole story because like I said, it's not mine to tell. But that's what it boils down to. He didn't fuck her and he doesn't want her. He loves you, Luna."

"He doesn't love me." I scoffed and pulled a face at Peter. "Firstly, he's made it pretty darn clear that he cannot and will not fall in love, least of all with me. Secondly, if he did love me, why isn't he the one who came here to talk to me?"

"He's not here because he's a stubborn asshole who is convinced he's lost you, that you don't want him that way, and that he doesn't deserve you anyway." Peter stood up and lifted his arm before glancing down at his watch. "I have to go. The venue coordinator wants to see me in thirty minutes to finalize some details about timing during the reception. Please come today, Luna."

"What?" My head felt all muddled and my heart was racing. I couldn't quite make sense of even seeing him here today, never mind everything he'd just told me. "Why would you want me there?"

"Because you worked harder than anyone else to make this day happen exactly the way we wanted it to and you deserve to see how it plays out. If you won't do it for Cyrus, do it for us. We want you there, Luna. Please come."

I sighed. It was the last thing I wanted to do. I was pretty sure that band-aid I'd slapped over the crack in my heart was slipping already and I hadn't even seen Cyrus yet. On the other hand, I really did like Jenny and Peter. If they wanted me there, I could suck it up and freaking be there.

It was their wedding day, which meant they should get everything they want from it. "Okay, I'll come. For you."

"Thank you." Peter's voice was gentle, understanding. "It will mean a lot to us both to have you there, Luna."

"Then there is where I'll be." I stood up as well, surprised when Peter enveloped me in a giant hug before loping out the door.

For the rest of the day, it seemed kind of unreal that I was about to go to the wedding. I played with the idea of not going, and knowing I was going to see Cyrus if I did made a pit of despair form in my stomach.

Even once I was dressed and ready to go, I still considered just staying home. But the look in Peter's eyes when he'd told me how much it would mean to them if I went haunted me, as did the pleading note in his voice.

As for all that stuff he said about Cyrus, I couldn't deny that I desperately wanted to know if it was true. I doubted it, but it felt like I owed it to myself to really find out.

Besides, at least if I saw him again and got to talk to him one last time, hopefully find out everything I hadn't wanted to know three weeks ago, I could finally get some closure. Maybe if I got closure, I'd be able to get some sleep tonight as well.

The dress I'd gotten for the wedding when I was still going to go as Cyrus's date hung a little looser on me now than it had when I'd bought it. I guessed that was what three weeks of hardly eating or sleeping did to a person.

Smoothing out nonexistent creases in the soft purple fabric, I grabbed my clutch and opened the darn door. I was going to this thing, if only so I'd be able to eat and sleep again.

All my indecision meant that I arrived at the venue just before the ceremony was due to start. Just as Cyrus and I had planned for it to, it was happening in the garden.

My eyes begged to sneak a peek at the corner he'd led me around to make out with me, but I refused to let them. *We're here to celebrate love and the start of a wonderful adventure. Not some kissing that should never have happened.*

Pep talk complete, I took a seat in the back and admired how it had all turned out. Once Cyrus and Peter walked in, the flowers, chair covers, and tie backs, all of it disappeared and he was all I could see.

The easy smile on his face when he looked at his brother, the scowl whenever he looked anywhere else. His piercing green eyes seemed empty, almost lifeless. They were still intense, but it was like there was absolutely no emotion in the body they belonged to.

It sent a shiver running through me to see him like that, so cold and looking as ruthless and callous as ever. His light brown hair was artfully mussed and my fingers itched to run through it, to see a

241

spark of the fun, playful guy I knew he had hidden inside there in his eyes.

But I ignored the urge. I would never get to do or see any of that again, and I had to accept it.

The ceremony passed in a beautiful blur as I tried to avoid staring at the best man. Peter's face when Jenny came down the aisle was priceless, though.

Tears ran unashamedly down his cheeks and the smile he wore was so bright it would be able to power several large cities for months. Crap, even Cyrus was smiling as Jenny floated toward them.

She looked like a princess and I felt tears stinging the backs of my eyes. I was so freaking happy for these two.

Once the vows were said and the rings were exchanged, they shared a kiss that bordered on inappropriate, then threw their hands into the air, and all their guests started clapping and hollering. I joined in, wiping tears away in between all the clapping.

Peter spotted me as they made their way through the guests, waving me over. Unfortunately, Cyrus saw at the exact same time.

Jenny got to me first and threw her arms around me. "Thank you so much for coming, Luna. Really, we can't tell you how much it means to us."

"It's my pleasure," I lied as I hugged her back. "I'm glad everything turned out so well."

"Almost everything," she murmured, pulling her head away. Her eyes met mine before they darted toward Cyrus. "Not *everything*, everything. You two should have been here together."

I gave her another squeeze. "Don't worry about it. Just enjoy your day."

"I'm planning on it." She winked, then was whipped away by more adoring guests.

Peter paused before following her. "Thanks for showing up. Remember what I said."

"Thanks again for the invitation," I said, giving him a quick cele-bratory hug before he went off after his bride, sliding his arms around her waist and laughing at whatever the conversation was he'd stepped into.

Cyrus was still fighting his way through the crowd with many people stopping him to talk. Which gave me the perfect opportunity to make my getaway.

I'd seen him. That would have to be enough closure for now.

My lungs felt like they couldn't expand enough to drag in any air and my heart seemed to be going through a washing machine stuck on the spin cycle. In a word, I was battered and I needed to get out of there.

I almost made it, too. As I reached the bottom of the stairs leading out of the hotel, my name rang out above the sounds of traffic and street vendors.

"Luna! Wait. I need to talk to you. Luna!"

When I turned around, it was to find Cyrus standing on the second stair from the top, one hand gripping the railing and the other in his hair. The look on his face was unlike anything I had ever seen from him before. His gorgeous features were twisted in what looked like excruciating pain and the same emotion was reflected in his eyes.

So I waited because if any of that was about me, maybe we really did need to talk.

CHAPTER 38

CYRUS

S he stopped.

I almost couldn't believe she'd actually stopped.

Standing at the bottom of the staircase with a gentle breeze ruffling her dress and those blue eyes wide, she looked up at me. Uncertainty flashed across her features, like she couldn't decide whether to stay or to run.

I jumped into action and rushed down the stairs before she could decide to run. Her shoulders pulled back and her chin came up. Despite her sweet nature, Luna knew what it was to stand up for herself and that was exactly what she was about to do.

She was no shrinking violet and I had no doubt that she wasn't just going to accept any apologies without making me tear open my soul and give her every bit of truth inside it.

I hadn't been prepared to do that today.

Peter hadn't told me she was coming, and when I first saw her, I thought I was hallucinating. It wouldn't have been the first time that I thought I saw her, only to blink and find the woman I was staring at wasn't her at all.

When I realized it really was her, the world stopped spinning around me. The ceremony, the bride, and groom—all of it fell away and all that remained was Luna. In that moment, I knew there was no way I could let her leave without at least trying to talk to her.

If she didn't want to listen, I would try again tomorrow, and the next day and the next. Because I couldn't give her up. I'd tried to let her go, tried to get myself to a place where I could be her friend again, but with every day that had passed without seeing her, I had only become more miserable.

It had gotten to the point where even I had to admit I had turned into a pathetic mess. Yesterday, when I'd been sitting on my couch with yet another pint of ice cream, a pair of sweats on that I'd put on about three days ago, and staring glumly at the dark television screen, it had dawned on me that I was acting like a heartbroken teenager.

From there, I'd had revelation after revelation, eventually ending up in the shower where I'd washed the pathetic off and swore to myself that I was going to get her back. Whether she wanted me or not, I was hers.

There was no more denying it and nothing I could do to fucking change it, but I didn't think I would have even if I could. I wanted to belong to Luna. I trusted her with everything I was and had, but if I wanted her to have even an iota of trust in me again, it was time to stop lying on the couch, feeling sorry for myself. It was time to take action.

I'd had a game plan, which would have started the day after Peter's wedding, but now, here she was. The plan had gone to shit, and I'd have to flay my heart open sooner than expected, but I was willing to improvise.

I needed Luna in my life any way I could get her. If that was as a friend, then so be it. I'd be that pathetic guy who was head over heels over his best friend until such time as I could make her see that we could be so much more. If that time never came, well, I'd respect whatever decisions she made, but I'd never stop fighting for her.

Reaching the bottom of the staircase, I stopped next to her and looked down into those blue eyes. They were stormy now in a way I'd never seen them, and I was about to step right into that storm and do my fucking best to ride it out.

"Thank you for stopping," I said, itching to take her hands or cup her face or even just to see her crack a smile, but none of those things happened. She stared back up at me stoically, not saying a word.

A small shrug of her shoulders seemed to be the best response she could manage. *But she's still here.*

That had to count for something. "Can we talk?"

"You're talking," she said, her tone flat as she crossed her arms over her chest.

I glanced at the busy sidewalk we were on, at the pedestrians frowning at two people in formal wear locked in some kind of stand-off. "Okay, we'll talk here then. Truth be told, Luna, I don't give a fuck who hears me, as long as you do."

Keeping my eyes on the infinite blue depths of hers, I took a deep breath, mentally grabbed my balls, and took the plunge.

"I love you, Luna. I love you like I've never loved anyone before. You're the only woman I've ever really loved and the only woman I ever want to love."

She sucked in a breath, and her eyes grew misty, but she pressed her lips together and shook her head with this profound kind of sadness on her features. "You don't love me, Cyrus. If you loved me, you never would have slept with your ex."

"Never would have what now?" My eyebrows mashed together. "You really think I slept with Sam?"

"I saw the way you were looking at her. You couldn't take your eyes off her. It's okay, Cy. We never—"

"I didn't fucking sleep with her," I burst out, shoving my hands deep into my pockets to keep from taking her into my arms and making her understand that she was the only woman I wanted. "I wasn't even looking at her. I was looking at the bartender. I wanted to be sure I wasn't jumping to conclusions just because she happened to be sitting there."

"You're expecting me to believe your eyes weren't riveted to your stunning ex, but to the bartender serving her?" Luna scoffed. "Nice try, Cyrus."

"I don't think she's stunning. She doesn't hold a candle to you, as far as I'm concerned."

Luna opened her mouth to protest, but I didn't let her. *Also, fuck it.*

Yanking my hands out of my pockets, I framed her face in them and let her see every fucking thing in my eyes.

"There's only one woman who has ever truly stunned me and that's you, Luna. Samantha's packaging may not be bad, but all I see is what she has on the inside. And trust me, that ain't pretty. Sure, there was a time I'd thought she was hot, but there has never been a time that I thought she was stunning. Like I said, the only woman I've ever applied that word to is you."

"But—"

"Just hear me out, baby, please. The furthest I went with her that night is to email her sponsor when I got back to my room. I was alone when I did it, by the way. We talked on the rooftop. Then I left. I went straight to your room, but when I got there, I couldn't bring myself to knock. I'd realized that we didn't want the same things anymore. I didn't want to be your friend anymore, but I also didn't want you to think I'd been dishonest with you all along. I was trying to respect your wishes."

Luna chewed on the inside of her lip as she searched my eyes. "Her sponsor?"

"Yeah." I sighed and rubbed the back of my head. "I guess we should get that part out of the way first. I got ahead of myself. God, I'm really bad at this."

The smallest of smiles played at the corners of her lips. "Just keep going."

"Okay, yeah. So her sponsor. Sam had a rough childhood. Both of her parents were full-blown, barely functioning alcoholics. Her mother drank herself to death when Sam was twelve and her father ended up in prison. I think he's still there."

She swallowed heavily, her eyes filled with sympathy. "Wow, that really sucks."

"What makes it even worse is that Sam herself developed an addiction to alcohol when she was something like fifteen. By the time I met her when we were in our early twenties, she'd been in rehab three times. I still have her sponsor's contact details because contacts just get transferred from one device to the next these days."

"And that's why you were watching her bartender?" she asked, her voice breathy. "To confirm whether or not she was drinking?"

"Yeah." I reached for Luna's hands and she let me take them. "I hate that woman, and her history doesn't justify what she's done, but I don't literally want her to die. Which very well could happen if she's drinking again."

Luna's fingers wrapped around mine and she gave them a gentle squeeze. "I'm sorry. I had no idea."

"You have no reason to be sorry, Luna. I should have told you what I was doing. I just didn't think about doing it. My mind was all fucked up about you and how I felt about you. Then I saw her drinking and everything happened so fast that I didn't realize what was going on until it was too late."

"I didn't see you for those next few days, either." Sadness tightened the skin around her eyes again. "I thought you were with her, but if you weren't, then where were you?"

"I really was in meetings." A sheepish grin formed on my lips. "They might just have been meetings that I scheduled so I wouldn't have to deal with the realization that I love you."

Contrary to what might have happened if life went exactly like we wanted it to, Luna didn't melt into my arms or throw her arms around me to kiss me stupid. She took a step away from me instead, released my hands, and tilted her head.

"How am I supposed to believe that, Cyrus? You've spent the entire time I've known you telling me you couldn't and wouldn't fall in love."

"Yeah, well, life is what happens when you're busy making other plans, isn't it?" Reaching out, I slid a finger under her chin and lifted it until her eyes were on mine. "Look, just come home with me. We can talk more there. I—"

"You can't leave Peter's wedding."

"Uh, yes, I think he can." Peter's voice suddenly piped up from somewhere on the staircase. Both of our heads swung in its direction,

248

and he was standing there with a far too smug grin on his face. "You guys have already organized this whole thing and you've attended the important part. Pretty sure we can forgive you for skipping the reception."

Gratitude toward my brother fueled my grin as I held my hand out to Luna. "You heard the man. What do you say?"

CHAPTER 39

LUNA

C yrus's eyes were burning into mine as he waited for my answer. So much of what he'd said was difficult to process, especially since I'd gotten so many things so very, very wrong.

What I hadn't gotten wrong was that belief I used to have that I could trust him, that he was a good guy. I still couldn't quite believe he'd said that he loved me. It was going to take me a while to fully comprehend that one, but I wanted to.

"Yeah, okay. Let's go." I took the hand he offered me and felt my lips curve into the smile at the feeling of having it there. His large palm was warm against mine, his fingers wrapped around mine so tightly that it was almost as if he was afraid I would run off if he didn't keep me with him. "I'm not going anywhere, Cy. I'm done running."

"You are?" he whispered, taking a step forward to close the distance between us until his chest was pressed right up against mine.

I nodded, tilting my head back so I'd be able to look into his eyes. "I don't want to just be your friend anymore, either. I haven't wanted that for a long time, but I was scared too. It took me too long to admit it even to myself, and by then, I was convinced it would be easier to stop seeing you at all if you didn't feel the same way."

"I would say that great minds think alike, but in our case, I think it's more of a 'fools never differ' situation."

I held his hands tighter at our sides and pressed myself up as close as I could get to him. It might have been a tad inappropriate for being in public, but I was finding that it didn't bother me so much anymore. I'd spent far too long without this man and I was done with it.

"At least we were foolish together." I pushed up on my toes and pressed the lightest of kisses to his jaw, my lips brushing against his stubble when I said, "Let's go, then. We've got a lot of catching up to do."

Cyrus grinned and simply looked into my eyes like he couldn't believe he was really seeing me. Keeping one of my hands in his, he propelled us into motion once he finally tore his gaze away from mine.

The walk back into the hotel and through the lobby to the parking lot was almost surreal. I kept sneaking glances at him to make sure it was really him and that this was really happening.

On the way to his place, he told me what he'd talked about with his ex that night and that he'd flat out refused her when she suggested getting back together. The more he talked, the more everything clicked into place.

"Why didn't you tell me any of this sooner?" I asked once we were in the elevator, heading up to his penthouse.

Our sides were pressed together and Cyrus was watching the glowing red numbers climb from floor to floor with an impatient tick in his jaw. He glanced down at me when I asked the question, though, then gave me one of his sexy smirks as he shook his head.

"Because I had my head too far up my ass to do anything about how I felt. I thought I'd lost you, even though I'd never had you, and didn't know how to deal."

The elevator doors slid open and he practically dragged me out, digging his keys out of his pocket as we made the short walk down the hallway. Once again, my mind was churning to process what he'd said.

"You're being surprisingly open about all this."

As he turned the key in the lock, he gave me a look over his shoulder. It was filled with regret, passion, and amusement, all at the same time, and I realized his emotions were on as much of a roller coaster as mine were.

"I promised you I'd always be honest with you, and trying to hide shit from you didn't go so well for me last time. So yeah, I'm an open book to you, baby. Ask me whatever you want. I'll never hide anything from you ever again."

Swinging his door open, he took my hand and led me inside. I barely heard the door shut behind us as I got a look at the state his previously immaculate penthouse was in. "What happened here?"

There were piles of clothing littering the floor, along with empty tubs of ice cream, fast food wrappers, and God only knew what else. On his coffee table were several half-drunk bottles of beer, empty whiskey bottles, and dirty glasses.

When I turned to face him, his cheeks were actually just a little flushed. He shrugged his broad shoulders and closed his eyes as he answered. "I told you. I didn't know how to deal. What you're looking at is the embarrassing evidence of the mess I turned into without you."

A soft chuckle escaped me as I walked back to where he'd stopped just inside the door. "My apartment looks the same. I was so embarrassed when Peter came by earlier. So I guess this means you really do love me, huh?"

When his eyes opened, they were filled with more emotion than I ever thought I'd see from him. Fierce determination mixed with what could only be described as absolute, unconditional love made his irises seem like they were glowing with warmth.

"Yes, Luna Willet. I really do love you. What I said earlier was true. I love you more than I ever thought it was possible to love someone. You're it for me, and I will spend the rest of my life trying to be it for you."

"You already are," I whispered, unable to tear my gaze away from his.

Before I could get the next words out, Cyrus's mouth was on mine and he was showing me just how much he loved me. He kissed me with unbridled passion until my lips were swollen and my chest was rising and falling in pants against his.

When he finally lifted his lips from mine, he kissed my jawline, my cheeks, my eyelids, and the tip of my nose. His hands ran along my sides and one settled on the nape of my neck as he moved his mouth back to mine.

There was so much passion in what he was doing, but he was also so tender that it made my heart clench and soar as if it was trying to reach him. I wrapped my arms around his neck and showed him as much devotion as he was showing me.

"Make love to me, Cy," I whispered against his ear when he bowed his head to press lavish kisses to the column of my throat.

"Yes, please." He groaned against my skin as if leaving it was the hardest thing he'd ever had to do. Then he picked me up with one arm under my knees and the other supporting my back.

"You know this is a bridal carry, right?" I teased breathlessly, my eyes on his and the smile on my lips soft.

"Yep, and one day, we're going to be doing this with you wearing a white dress. In the meantime, we'll call it practice."

I giggled, but my heart was racing at his words. More than anything else he'd said, the fact that he'd just alluded to us getting married at some point in the future proved to me that he was in this with me for real and for the long haul.

It was exactly what I needed to hear before I handed over the last piece of my heart to him. It wasn't about having a wedding or even needing him to commit to marrying me. It was because it meant that he'd really thought this through, and he still wanted me in his life in the future.

When he set me down in front of his bed, he took his time unzipping my dress, removing my underwear with excruciating slowness and the softest of brushes of his fingers against my heated skin. I returned the favor, starting with the formal black tie around his neck and never breaking eye contact with him until we were both naked.

He looked at me with such reverence that it brought tears to my eyes and then laid me down before following me onto the bed. There were no more words between us as our bodies connected, confirming all the things we'd said to each other and sealing all the promises we'd made with long, slow kisses.

When my orgasm finally washed over me, Cyrus swallowed my moans and followed me over the edge without ever lifting his mouth away from mine. It was like we'd been fused together, and I never wanted it to be any different.

It took a long time before we stopped kissing and our breathing returned to normal. His eyes were on mine, and he didn't seem to be ready to move yet, which was good because I wasn't ready for him to do it either.

"You know, you still haven't told me if you love me too," he said, his big body covering mine as he kept himself propped up on his elbows.

The longer hair on the top of his head fell across his forehead in that way I loved, and the planes of his face relaxed. I smiled up at him and batted my eyelashes innocently. "Oh, I haven't? Well, darn. Look at the time. I should go."

He used his hips to keep me pressed to the mattress, lowering just a little bit more of his weight onto me. I didn't complain, though, because I loved the feeling.

"You should go, huh?" His eyes darted from one of mine to the other, a playful smile appearing on his swollen lips. "Are you sure about that? Because I happen to know what your plans were for tonight and we've officially changed them."

"Have we?" I frowned, pretending to be confused. "I don't know about that. I—"

Moving faster than he should have been able to, Cyrus rolled to my side and his hands found my bare stomach. His fingers started moving, and before I even realized what he was doing, I was laughing so hard my cheeks hurt.

Cyrus Coning is tickling me. How crazy is that?

Swatting at his hands while I tried to get away from him, I let him pull me closer to his body when he wrapped his arms around me anyway. Landing with my palms on his chest, one of them right over his heart, my laughter subsided when I saw there was genuine uncertainty lurking in his gorgeous green depths.

I planted kisses on both corners of his mouth and kept the tips of our noses touching as I told him the last words I ever thought he'd want to hear from me. "I love you too, Cyrus. You're everything to me. I don't know when it happened, but you've become my heart and my soul, and I never want to be without you again."

"Then you don't have to be," he assured me right before wrapping me up in his arms and kissing me until I truly believed we would never be apart again.

EPILOGUE

LUNA

"I can't believe we're really here," April said, her eyes on mine in the reflection of the full-length mirror. She stood behind me, her hands on my hips as she blinked back tears. "You look beautiful, babe. The most beautiful bride I've ever seen."

Bride. Eeeep! But yes, that's me. The bride, and I had the most beautiful form-fitting, mermaid-style, sweetheart-neckline dress on to prove it. It was an ivory color instead of snow white and was covered in the most delicate lace I had ever seen.

The funniest part of all? I really didn't care. Sure, I loved the dress. It was gorgeous and perfect and comfortable, but I'd have married Cyrus at City Hall wearing a burlap sack, and I still wouldn't have cared.

Because as much as the perfect wedding used to be a dream of mine, it wasn't anything compared to the excitement I felt about my impending marriage. In fact, I'd gone so far as to suggest that we didn't even need to have a wedding.

The day after he proposed, Cyrus had said that the only thing he wasn't looking forward to was the wait between that day and the day I became his wife. I made a proposal of my own then, but he hadn't gone for it.

"Let's go down to City Hall when we get back. That way, we wouldn't have to wait," I'd said as I stared into his forest green eyes, his light brown hair glowing almost gold under the bright Italian sun.

Cyrus had chuckled, kissed me silly, and then shook his head. "I waited for our first anniversary and brought you all the way back to Venice to pop the question. I can wait a little longer. I would wait forever if it meant giving you exactly what you've always dreamed of."

"You're everything I've always dreamed of, Cy," I'd said, cupping the strong line of his jaw. The most gorgeous ring I'd ever seen winked at me as it caught the sunlight in this new position, and a happy sigh escaped. "I don't need some fairy-tale wedding when it's you I get to marry. You, us, our lives together. That's what's important."

Lifting his big hand to rest it over mine, he'd brought my palm to his lips and placed a soft kiss in the center. "That's too bad, princess, because a fairy-tale wedding is exactly what you're going to get. You deserve everything, and this, at least, is something I can give you."

I'd tried to change his mind, but he wouldn't budge. "Spring in New York City is what you've always wanted, and that's what you're getting."

So we'd waited another whole year for this day. It was our second anniversary and the day I'd finally, *finally* get to marry my best friend. Well, best friend of the male persuasion anyway.

April, as the best friend of the female kind, was wearing a soft lilac dress, and surprisingly, her massive smile hadn't dropped once since it had appeared when I'd told her the news. She looked gorgeous, and since it seemed like she'd started to come around to the whole idea of everlasting love recently after all, I was hoping she might find it today in one of Cyrus's business-associates-turned-friends.

Because as it turned out, Cyrus could actually be a pretty freaking nice guy when he wasn't being a dick twenty-four seven. I'd already known it, but as it had become known to others, he'd actually managed to acquire a handful of true friends in the years we'd been together.

A few of them were pretty hot. Not Cyrus hot, but then again, there was no one else like him, if you asked me. I was hopeful that one of them would catch April's eye.

"Thank you," I said, my voice soft as I met her eyes. "This all still feels like a dream in a way."

April smiled as she gave me a squeeze. "That's because that damn man of yours has made all of your dreams come true. I mean, talk about swoon-worthy."

"He really has," I agreed. "He's spoiled me, but I guess I can't complain about it."

Adi, who had recently turned nine, sighed as she collapsed into one of the armchairs in the bridal dressing room, her own lilac dress billowing out to the sides. "Do you think I'll ever find love, Luna?"

"I'm sure you will, angel face. Just not too soon." Alas, Todd hadn't turned out to be the love of her life. He was more like her bestie now, and as far as I knew, she hadn't had another crush since. Which was good. She was only nine, for crying out loud.

I dragged in a deep breath before I spun on the round pedestal the venue had placed in front of the gilded mirror in the dressing room and stepped down. "You'll remember to check in on the shop every so often while we're gone, right?"

April nodded. "I'll make random spot checks on Cyrus's hired hand. Don't you worry. Do you know where he's taking you yet?"

"No, but apparently, he's already bought my guidebooks, plural, and will give them to me once we're on the plane." A shiver of excitement ran through me. "But honestly, I don't care where that plane ends up carrying us to. As long as it's with him."

April fanned her face. "Jeez, woman. You've really got it bad. You reek of corny clichés right now."

I swatted her shoulder and laughed. "Whatever. You know you're just jealous."

"As if." She rolled her eyes, but then they went wide when there was a knock at our door. "Oh my God. It's time. Adi, baby, it's time. Come on. Come on."

They rushed through the penthouse suite of the hotel that had acted as the bridal suite for the day and flung the door open. Peter stood outside, looking dapper in a light gray suit as he held his arm out for me to take.

"You ready to do this, sis?"

"You know you can't technically call me that for at least another forty minutes, right?" I hid my smile behind the curtain of my loosely curled hair and heard him chuckling.

"That's just a technicality. It became true the minute you two saw each other at my wedding and decided to skip out together."

"You said we should go," I protested as I linked my arm with his.

He smirked. "Exactly, and from then on, you officially became my sister because there was no fucking way he was ever letting you go again."

Heat burned behind my eyes, but I refused to cry. If I started now, I was going to blubber my way all through the ceremony, and after all the effort Cyrus had gone through to make this day perfect, I absolutely refused to ruin it.

"I still can't believe he got a venue in the Flower District," April said over her shoulder. She and Adi were a few paces ahead of us, walking down the carpeted hallway.

Stained-glass windows offered views of the flower-drenched sidewalks below and my knees felt as weak at the sight of it as they had when he'd first brought me here. Contrary to what I might have believed when we'd gotten engaged that day on the bridge in Venice, Cyrus had taken it upon himself to organize this wedding.

Since he'd been helping me with the business end of the shop pretty much from the day after we'd gotten together officially, he'd actually become rather adept at all things wedding. He also visited the Flower District with me often and had forged some pretty decent bonds with our preferred vendors.

The shop was doing better than ever with both of us involved, and as we were pretty decent customers, he'd apparently gotten plenty of help with our wedding from the men and women who dominated the street below.

Their first order of business had been securing this hotel as our venue. I stepped out into the small garden where the ceremony was being held. The sweet, floral scent from all over that met my nostrils made me feel so much that my eyes welled up again.

A string quartet spotted Adi and April as they rounded the corner and started their song, both of them walking slowly down the petal-dotted aisle. Peter smiled at me as he watched them go. "Let me be the first to welcome you to our family, sis."

He leaned down and pressed a kiss against my temple. "I'm ready whenever you are."

"I've been ready for a year," I said as I tightened my grip on his arm. "Let's do it."

April and Adi's song morphed into the wedding march, and the next thing I knew, Cyrus came into view and everything else faded. I had eyes only for him and I nearly broke into a sprint to get to him faster.

It was only Peter's steady presence at my side that made me keep my composure. Cyrus was also wearing a light gray suit with a white button down but no tie. He hadn't styled his hair too much and that favorite lock of mine was hanging just so over his forehead.

Just like me, he couldn't seem to be able to look anywhere else than right into my eyes. His eyes were filled with so much love that my first tear for the day finally escaped because I never thought I'd be lucky enough to be looked at like that. But especially not by him.

Peter kissed my cheek when we reached the front, squeezed my hand when he removed it from his arm, and placed it in his brother's. Cyrus wasted no time in pulling me to his side and folding his arm around my back as we faced the officiant.

"My god, Luna. You're breathtaking. Fucking beautiful, my love. But I hope you haven't grown too attached to that dress because I'm ripping it off the first chance I get."

The officiant's eyes widened and he cleared his throat, though I wasn't sure if it was because he felt scandalized or whether it was just his way of getting people's attention.

After welcoming our family and friends, he looked at Cyrus. "Our couple has decided to write their own vows and I believe you're up first."

Cyrus nodded and turned to face me. He didn't pull out a sheet of paper to read from. He just looked right into my eyes and, without any further ado, jumped right in.

"When I met you, I didn't think I'd ever be able to love, but that was only because I hadn't yet met the one person who made me want to. The one person who had been made for me."

There was an "aww" from our small gathering of family and friends, but I was hardly aware of it. All I could focus on was Cyrus.

"From the very first day you walked into my life, you threw it upside down and challenged everything I thought I believed in. More than that, you made me want to believe that I was wrong, even if I never would have admitted it."

Scattered chuckles made him crack a grin and take a pause to wait for them to die down. "You made me want to do better, Luna, to be better, and in doing so, you made *me* better. A better businessman, a better brother, a better man."

He smiled. "You showed me it was okay not to be a dick to everyone all the time, taught me to expect the unexpected, and that there is happiness to be found all around us if we only stop to look for it. You show me the beauty in the world and force me to slow down and notice it. It's an incredible thing to see the world through your eyes, baby, and I'll never be able to tell you how grateful I am that you let me."

His throat moved as he swallowed, his voice growing tighter. "Most of all, you made me fall so fucking hard for you and I've never been as happy as I have been since. Thank you for being you and for letting me be me with you."

He paused to take a breath and held my hands tighter, his eyes never leaving mine even as they teared up.

"So here goes nothing, I guess. The vows. I promise to make your tea just the way you like it every morning and solemnly swear to stop shopping at Bachelors-are-us. I promise to print every photograph of us you like and to put them all up on our walls."

A heavily pregnant Jenny jumped up and began cheering. Cyrus rolled his eyes at her, but he couldn't hide his grin. "I thought Jenny would be happy I decided to include that one."

His gaze came back to mine. "I promise not to be a Grinch whenever the romantic in you comes out to play, and I promise to keep trying to make your dreams come true each and every single day. The thing is, baby, you've already made all of mine come true just by being who and how you are. Every morning that I get to wake up next to you, every day and night that I get to spend by your side, it's more than I ever could have dreamed of having. So if I'm being honest, you've more than made my dreams come true. You've exceeded dreams I didn't even know I could be dreaming."

Tears were pouring down my cheeks by now, but I didn't mind. I wasn't going to let go of Cyrus's hands for anything in the world. Even if I did end up having panda eyes in most of the photos of our ceremony.

"I don't quite know how I'm supposed to follow that," I said, my voice shaky when the officiant motioned to me. "But I'm going to try."

I took in several deep gulps of air and allowed my focus to narrow completely on Cyrus. "You are the most incredible man I've ever met. You forget to give yourself credit sometimes, love. All of those things I do for you, you do for me too.

"From the very first time I met you, you have been my champion, my protector, my partner in chaos and crazy. You have opened up my eyes and showed me that it is possible to protect without patronizing or being condescending to someone and that it's okay to let myself be protected in that way."

I had to stop to breathe for a second. "You let me be vulnerable with you so we can be strong together. You are and always have been my safe haven and my shoulder to cry on, but you are also my happy place."

There was so much emotion in Cyrus's eyes that I nearly cracked, but I also really wanted to say everything I needed to say. "You're my spring in the middle of winter and my stars on a cloudy night. I love how much we laugh together and how much fun we have together. I love our playfulness and teasing, but I also love knowing that we can be serious together when we have to be."

"I love that you keep me grounded while letting me soar, that I can come home to you every night and see you smile when I walk in the door."

Four months after we'd officially started dating, I'd moved in with him. He'd asked every day for two months, and eventually, I had to agree it made sense. At that point, I hadn't seen the inside of my own apartment for a month and keeping it had become more of a headache and an unnecessary expense than a necessity. Even with the business doing well and dating a billionaire who had offered to buy the place for me, I still refused to waste money.

"I love that you can be silly one minute and serious the next. I promise not to secretly get rid of all your stuff from Bachelors-are-us. I promise to remind you to use the hot tub and to have at least one cup of coffee a week from your fancy machine."

I squeezed his hands. "I promise to love you unconditionally and that I will still be there even if you lost everything you have tomorrow. I promise not to jump to conclusions when I see you staring at something and promise to always hear you out. I can't wait to start this new adventure with you, my love. I love you, from now until forever."

Cyrus had tears tracking down his cheeks, but he didn't seem to care enough to wipe them away either. Ring boxes appeared, and the officiant asked us to give each other our right hands and repeat after him.

One by one, we took our turn to slide the other's ring into its new permanent place, and when that was done, Cyrus barely waited for us to be pronounced husband and wife before sweeping me off my feet and dipping me almost all the way to the ground as he kissed me.

Whoops and cheers broke out, but it was all just white noise to me. It was only once Cyrus broke off our kiss when it was becoming somewhat inappropriate that I realized where we were again.

I couldn't stop crying, smiling, or looking at my new husband. He brought my left hand to his mouth and planted a kiss on the ring.

Then he thrust our joined hands into the air victoriously. "Fuck yeah. I'm a happily married man, baby!"

"Ladies and gentlemen," the officiant said into the microphone to be heard above the din resulting from Cyrus's exclamation. "May I present to you, for the very first time, Mr. and Mrs. Coning."

That was the beginning of our happily ever after. Cyrus took me to Greece for our honeymoon after all, just like he'd promised that he would, and ten years, four kids, and a house in the suburbs later, we were very much still living the dream.

The End.

ABOUT THE AUTHOR

Hey there. I'm Weston.

I'm a former firefighter/EMS guy who's picked up the proverbial pen and started writing bad boy romance stories. I co-write with my sister, Ali Parker as we travel the United States for the next two years.

You're going to find Billionaires, Bad Boys, Mafia and loads of sexiness. Something for everyone, hopefully. I'd love to connect with you. Check out the links below and come find me.

OTHER BOOKS BY WESTON PARKER

Maybe It's Fate

Say You Do

She's Mine Now

One Shot At Love

Caught Up In Love

Let Freedom Ring

Maine Squeeze

Between The Sheets

Follow You Anywhere

Take It All Off

Backing You Up

Give Me The Weekend

Come Down Under

Going After Whats Mine

Fake It For Me

My Favorite Mistake

Heartbreaker

My Holiday Reunion

Spring It On Me

Airforce Hero

Brand New Man

Pretending To Be Rich

Good Luck Charm

Light Up The Night

Set the Night On Fire

Turn Up The Heat

Ignite The Spark Between Us

Captain Hotness

All About The Treats

Show Me What You Got

Come Work For Me

Trying To Be Good

Have Your Way With Me

Love Me Last

My Last Chance

My First Love

My Last First Kiss

Made For Me

Hotstuff

Take It Down A Notch

My One and Only

Desperate For You

Take A Chance On Me

Fair Trade For Love

We Belong Together

Dropping The Ball

Standing Toe to Toe

Pay Up Hot Stuff

Love Your Moves

The Billioanire's Second Chance

Printed in Great Britain
by Amazon

43761088R00158